ECHOES OF UNSAID WORDS !!

DEVANSHI KANANI

"Dedicated to my husband,

MR. RAJ VAGHASIYA,

the silent guardian of my submerged emotions and

the echo of every unvoiced longing."

Contents

Foreword

Greetings to the readers,

It is with immense pleasure and pride that I introduce *Echoes of Unsaid Words*, a novel that beautifully explores the complexities of human emotions, relationships, and the power of words—both spoken and unspoken. The author of this book is not only a talented writer but also a student whose growth I have had the privilege to witness firsthand.

She is no stranger to struggle. Having faced and continues to face challenges in her early life, the idea for this novel evolved through a journey of perseverance and self-discovery. Every chapter reflects her resilience, her sensitivity to the nuances of human connections, and her ability to transform personal experiences into a compelling narrative.

This book follows her previous success with *Failure: It Never Ends Unless...*, a non-fiction work that resonated deeply with readers, inspiring many who had faced their own setbacks. The success of that book marked a significant milestone in her writing journey, and with *Echoes of Unsaid Words*, she steps boldly into the realm of fiction, demonstrating a profound understanding of the human condition.

I congratulate her on this wonderful achievement and wish for this book to attract the success it undoubtedly deserves. May it resonate with all who read it, and may her continued path be filled with happy and healthy learnings.

MR. SHANKAR CHOUHAN

Preface

The idea for this novel came to me during the stillness of the COVID-19 pandemic—a time when the world seemed suspended in a fragile state of uncertainty. Initially, writing was simply a way to escape, to develop a new skill while the walls of isolation closed in around us. We were all locked away in our own little cubicles, far from the warmth of loved ones, while the air grew heavy with longing and the silence became deafening. Life felt like it had paused, teetering on the edge of despair.

When I began writing *Echoes of Unsaid Words*, it wasn't with a grand plan or intricate plot. I had only one character in mind—Dev. He emerged as a solitary figure, a spark in the dark, and from him, a world began to unfold. Slowly, other characters joined him, their stories intertwining and expanding until they formed a vivid tapestry of relationships, emotions, and unsaid truths.

I've always been struck by the sentiment that "every fiction is, in some way, non-fiction." Stories, even those imagined, are rooted in realities we've seen, felt, or feared. They are born from moments that have happened, are happening, or may yet come to pass. In that spirit, this novel draws deeply from the world around me, weaving fragments of reality into a narrative that is as much about what we say as what we leave unspoken.

Before writing this novel, I underestimated the power of fiction. I believed it was a whimsical indulgence, a flight of fancy with no grounding in real effort or meaning. But as I shaped *Echoes of Unsaid Words*, I realized how profoundly wrong I had been. These characters are not merely creations; they are reflections of life's essence. I lived with them, breathed with them, and felt their struggles and joys as my own. They became my companions, my confidants, and, at times, my teachers.

When I wrote the final chapter, it felt like bidding farewell to a part of myself. The act of writing had been a journey—a catharsis—that left me changed. The title *Echoes of Unsaid Words* was born out of this experience. It represents the emotions too profound to articulate, the connections that linger beyond words, and the reverberations of silence that shape our lives in ways we often fail to notice.

At its core, this story delves into the complexities of friendship, trust, mental health, and the power of understanding. It follows "Ninja 9," a group of nine college friends who receive a cryptic email summoning them back to their alma mater in Bangalore. The identity of the sender remains a mystery, but the reunion becomes a catalyst for uncovering hidden truths, healing old wounds, and piecing together the fragments of their shared past. Through this journey, their unsaid words find voice, weaving a story of resilience and connection.

This novel is my labor of love, and sharing it with you fills me with both excitement and vulnerability. It is not just a story but a piece of my heart, a collection of whispers that demanded to be heard. I hope it resonates with you, makes you pause, and perhaps even echoes within your own life.

I welcome your thoughts, your critiques, and your shared experiences. For every story evolves, not just in its writing but in the way it is received.

Thank you for embarking on this journey with me.

AUTHOR
DEVANSHI KANANI

Prologue

The rain tapped gently against the windowpane, filling the room with its soft, rhythmic melody. Aksha sat by the window, her knees drawn to her chest, eyes fixed on the droplets tracing uneven paths down the glass. Outside, the world was blurred, wrapped in a misty gray veil, but Aksha's thoughts were far from the present.

Aahana.

The name echoed in her mind, stirring a bittersweet ache she couldn't ignore. Memories of their time together came rushing back, vivid and relentless, like the rain that refused to let up. Aahana's laughter rang in her ears—bold, warm, and boundless, a sound that could brighten even the darkest of days. Once, they had been inseparable, two souls who communicated in glances, laughter, and silences, without the need for elaborate explanations.

Aksha closed her eyes, letting the past pull her in. Aahana's face came to life in her mind—her eyes sparkling with mischief, her lips curled in a grin that always promised trouble.

"Come on, Akshu! It's a crime to sleep when there's biryani calling your name!" Aahana's voice was as vivid in her memory as it had been that night.

"It's also a crime to sneak out of the hostel at midnight!" Aksha had hissed, glancing nervously over her shoulder as they crept past the warden's quarters. "If we get caught, I'm blaming you."

Aahana stifled a laugh, pulling Aksha by the wrist. "Caught? Please. I'm a professional escape artist. Stick with me, and you'll be fine."

Despite her protests, Aksha had found herself following Aahana through the narrow, bustling streets of the city. The air was thick with the aroma of sizzling spices, the chatter of vendors, and the hum of excitement.

"I can't believe you dragged me out here for food," Aksha muttered, though her eyes betrayed her curiosity as they landed on a stall laden with colorful sweets.

"Food?" Aahana stopped in her tracks, spinning dramatically to face her. "Not just food. This, my dear Akshu, is an experience. The kind that makes life worth living!"

Before Aksha could respond, Aahana darted toward a vendor distracted by a group of customers. In one swift motion, she snatched a plate of gulab jamun and rushed back to Aksha, her grin wide with triumph.

"What are you doing?!" Aksha gasped, eyes wide in horror as she glanced between the stolen dessert and the oblivious vendor. "Aahana, this is theft!"

"It's borrowing," Aahana corrected, popping a syrupy ball into her mouth. "We'll pay him next time."

"There won't be a next time if we get arrested!"

"Relax, Akshu. Here, have one." Aahana held out a gulab jamun, her eyes twinkling with laughter.

Reluctantly, Aksha took a piece, her lips pressing into a tight line as she bit into it. The sweetness exploded in her mouth, and despite herself, she couldn't suppress a small smile.

"See? Totally worth it," Aahana declared, nudging her.

"You're impossible," Aksha muttered, shaking her head. But the tension melted away as they both dissolved into laughter, their voices blending with the lively chaos around them.

That night, they had roamed the streets until their feet ached, sharing stories, teasing each other, and making memories Aksha thought would last forever.

ᛞᛞᛞ

Another memory surfaced—a quieter one. It was during their final year of college when Aksha had been overwhelmed by the crushing weight of academic pressure. With deadlines looming, lectures piling up, and the relentless fear of failure gnawing at her, she'd locked herself in her room, shutting out the world. Her mind spiraled into anxiety, each passing minute feeling like an eternity.

A sudden knock on the door broke her out of her spiral. Before she could even respond, the door swung open, and Aahana stormed in, a box of cupcakes in one hand and her phone in the other.

"Okay, okay, you're not getting away with this," Aahana declared with a grin, kicking the door shut behind her.

Aksha, slumped over her desk, barely looked up. "Aahana, please. I need to focus."

"Focus?!" Aahana shot back, setting the cupcakes down with a flourish. "You're sitting here, drowning in papers, and you're telling me to leave you alone? Nope. Not happening." She flopped onto the bed next to Aksha, ignoring the mountain of textbooks scattered across the floor. "You're gonna take a break, and we're gonna eat cupcakes, and we're gonna listen to our playlist, okay? And you're going to stop pretending like you're not human."

Aksha tried to protest, but Aahana had already hit play on their favorite song, the familiar beats filling the room. Aahana opened the box, offering Aksha a cupcake with a mischievous grin.

"Come on, Aksha, I know you're secretly craving this."

Reluctantly, Aksha took the cupcake, still not entirely convinced. "Aahana, I can't. There's too much to do."

But before she could finish her sentence, Aahana smooshed a bite of cupcake into her face.

"Hey!" Aksha exclaimed, half-laughing, half-shocked.

"That's the spirit!" Aahana said, her voice laced with triumph. "Now, you have no excuse. You're already covered in frosting. Might as well go all in."

Within seconds, the room turned into a battlefield, both laughing and dodging frosting attacks. The stress, the fear of failure, everything seemed to melt away in the chaos. Their giggles echoed off the walls, drowning out the nagging thoughts in Aksha's mind.

Eventually, they collapsed together on the bed, both covered in frosting, their faces flushed with laughter.

"You know," Aahana said, her voice softer now, "I need you to promise me something."

Aksha wiped a smear of frosting from her cheek and looked at her, eyebrows raised. "What?"

"Promise me you won't bottle up your feelings. Ever again," Aahana said seriously. "You're allowed to be overwhelmed, but don't shut me out. Don't shut everyone out. We're in this together, okay?"

Aksha paused, the weight of the promise settling in. "Okay," she whispered, the words slipping out more easily than she expected. "I promise."

Aahana smiled, brushing frosting off her own face. "Good. Because no one should ever have to go through this alone. Not you, not me. Not anyone."

The promise lingered between them, unspoken but understood. As they sat there, the world outside seemed far away—just two friends, surrounded by crumbs and frosting, holding onto each other through the chaos of life.

But the memory that hurt the most was from Aksha's wedding day. It was supposed to be the happiest day of her life, yet Aahana's absence loomed like a dark cloud over the celebration. She had waited for her, scanning the crowd for a glimpse of her best friend, but Aahana never showed. No explanation, no calls—just silence. It was a betrayal that had left a scar, one that still throbbed with every beat of her heart.

Her gaze shifted to the laptop on her desk, where an email sat open. The subject line read: *"Reunion—Bangalore. Be there."* It was from an anonymous sender, but the message was unmistakable. Ninja 9, their once tightly-knit group of friends, was being summoned back together after years of silence.

Aksha's fingers hovered over the keyboard, hesitation gripping her. Her heart surged at the thought of seeing Aahana again, the best friend who had once been her anchor. She imagined the familiar warmth of Aahana's laugh, the way her eyes sparkled with mischief. The ache of longing grew sharper, pulling her toward the possibility of reunion.

But her mind interjected, sharp and unyielding. It reminded her of the pain Aahana's departure had caused—the unanswered questions, the deafening silence, the feeling of abandonment that had lingered like an open wound. Could she face Aahana after all this time? Could she confront the fractures in their friendship without breaking further?

The rain outside mirrored her turmoil, its steady rhythm underscoring her internal conflict. She leaned back in her chair, the soft tap of droplets against the glass filling the silence. Her heart and mind wrestled, each pulling her in a different direction.

I want to see her, but what if it hurts too much? What if it's too late? she thought, the questions swirling in an endless loop. The email's words blurred on the screen as her vision misted, her emotions threatening to overwhelm her.

Aksha sat there, staring at the now-blank screen, her mind racing. The reunion wasn't just a gathering of friends—it was a confrontation with everything she had avoided for years. The past felt so close, yet the future remained uncertain.

"Maybe it's time to hear the echoes," she whispered, the words fragile yet resolute.

Closing the laptop, she leaned back in her chair. The rain continued its gentle percussion, a rhythmic reminder that the past could never be erased, but perhaps, it could be rewritten. The world outside seemed to hold its breath, as if waiting to see whether Aksha would take the first step toward the memories that still haunted her—the ones tied irrevocably to Aahana.

1

Mystery Mail and Mischief

Bip… Bipppppp… Bipppp… Bipppppppp…

Dev's phone kept buzzing, ringing again and again. He sighed as he looked at it. There was a big project he had to finish, and the deadline was very close. If he didn't finish, he wouldn't get his summer break. His boss had made that clear: no work done, no break.

Dev wasn't like most people in the busy office world. He was super smart, good-looking, and always made others laugh, even when things got tough. He was relaxed and had a big smile on his face all the time. Everyone liked him because he made work feel less stressful.

In meetings, where people usually felt worried about deadlines, Dev would crack jokes that made everyone laugh and feel better. Some coworkers got a little jealous of him, but even they couldn't stay mad when he was around.

But Dev had one big habit: he was always late. He loved sleeping in, so he often came to the office long after others started working. Still, he'd walk in with a funny excuse and a cheerful smile that made people forget they were annoyed. Being late might have been a problem for others, but Dev made it seem okay.

His team even joked about "Dev Time," planning things knowing he'd show up late. Instead of getting upset, they adjusted because his cheerful attitude made up for it.

Dev's desk was like him—fun and full of life. He had little plants and toys that made people smile when they saw them. For Dev, work wasn't just about finishing tasks; it was about making everyone around him happy.

Even after work, Dev kept spreading good vibes. He'd plan surprise hangouts or fun team outings that helped everyone relax and bond.

Even though he wasn't always on time, people loved him for showing them that work didn't always have to be serious. He proved that laughter and kindness could help everyone do better. Dev wasn't just a coworker—he was the heart of the team, reminding them that happiness makes all the difference.

Ignoring Anu's calls had become a habit, but this time, Dev picked up. "Hey…"

Anu didn't waste a second. "Are you crazy? Did you forget about me? Why aren't you answering?"

Dev, always quick with a joke, grinned. "Ignoring you? That'd be a disaster! I'd like to keep my breakup record clean, thanks." He chuckled. "My phone was on silent, and work had me swamped. So, what's the deal? Did your makeup go wrong, did you invent another weird recipe, or… wait, don't tell me—you quit your job again?"

Anu rolled her eyes but couldn't help smiling. She was used to Dev's teasing.

Anu wasn't just another person chasing perfection. In a world where everyone wanted to look flawless, she embraced imperfections. To her, being real was much better than trying to be perfect.

As a fashion designer, Anu poured her heart into her work. Every dress or outfit she made told a story about being unique. She didn't follow the usual rules of beauty—instead, she celebrated what made people different.

Her designs weren't just clothes; they were works of art. Each stitch showed her belief that true beauty comes from being yourself. Through her creations, she gave people the confidence to stand out and feel amazing just the way they were.

In a world full of trends and rules, Anu's work was a breath of fresh air. She didn't just design clothes; she inspired people to be proud of their true selves. Her passion left a mark, proving that the most beautiful thing you can be is authentically you.

Anu frowned on the video call. "Enough with the jokes, Dev! This is serious."

Dev leaned closer to his laptop screen, raising an eyebrow. "Alright, alright. Don't blow a fuse. What's this about? Did you get an email? I haven't checked mine yet."

Anu sighed, her expression a mix of exasperation and anticipation. "Not me—it's about you. Check your inbox already!"

Dev tilted his head. "About me? Okay, give me a second." He turned his attention to his laptop, his fingers flying over the keyboard.

As he scanned his inbox, his eyes suddenly widened, and his jaw dropped. "Hey! What's this email? Who sent it? This is unbelievable!" he shouted, his excitement bursting through the screen.

"What does it say? Tell me!" Anu said, leaning toward her camera, trying to get a glimpse of his laptop.

Dev looked back at the screen, his face glowing with joy. "It's an invitation! The reunion's happening! I can't believe it! They're inviting us all back for a celebration!"

Anu gasped, covering her mouth in surprise. "The reunion? Oh my God, this is huge! This is exactly what we needed!"

"I know, right?" Dev said, practically bouncing in his chair. "I feel like singing, dancing—doing everything at once!"

Anu laughed, her smile filling the screen. "Well, Mr. Superstar, you better start planning. This is a big deal. And no backing out this time!"

Dev chuckled, holding up his phone. "For this, I'll set an alarm on every device I own. No 'Dev Time' this time, I promise!"

Anu smirked, crossing her arms. "Good, because if you mess this up, I'll personally drag you there myself."

They both laughed, the excitement buzzing through their screens as they shared the moment together.

ppp

Subject: *Echoes of Unsaid Words - Reunion Invitation*

Dear Ninjas,

*It's time to reconnect and revisit the memories we've all shared. We're excited to invite you to the **Echoes of Unsaid Words Reunion**, where old friends, forgotten moments, and cherished memories will come together once again.*

This reunion is more than just a gathering; it's an opportunity to relive the past and celebrate the bonds that have lasted over time. Get ready for a week of fun, laughter, and memories we've kept in our hearts.

We can't wait to see everyone and create new memories while reminiscing about the old ones.

Warm regards,

Shadowheart,

Echoes of Unsaid Words Reunion Coordinator

ppp

"Heey, buddy! Hold on, calm down. If we got it, others might have too. Let us ask them," Anu suggested.

"You're right. Let us chat on WhatsApp. It is easier to connect with everyone," Dev agreed.

Dev: Hey ninjas! Just got a mysterious email about a reunion. Anyone else?

Anu typing...

Rishi typing...

Manan typing...

Anu: Same here! What's the deal? Did you all get it too?

Rishi: Got it! The email's cryptic. Reckon it's from one of us?

Manan typing...

Manan: Got the same. Whoever's behind this sure knows how to build suspense.

Roy typing...

Roy: Count me in. Let's solve this mystery together!

Maher typing...

Maher: Received it too. Do we have any clues?

Dev: Guess we're all on the same page. Let's unveil this mystery at the reunion!

Anu: Agreed! Can't wait to see what's in store for us. ??

Manan: Alright, confess—who's the mastermind behind this reunion email?

Roy typing...

Roy: Not me! I'm innocent this time.

Anu typing...

Anu: Seriously, guys? I thought one of you would fess up by now.

Maher typing...

Maher: My money's on Dev. He's been suspiciously quiet.

Dev typing...

Dev: Hey, don't point fingers at me! I'm as clueless as the rest of you.

Aksha typing...

Aksha: You guys are terrible detectives. Maybe it's none of us, and we're just part of someone else's grand plan.

Aarush typing...

Aarush: Or maybe it's a secret admirer trying to get us all back together. ?

Anu: Secret admirer? Aarush, are you watching too many rom-coms again? ?

Aarush: Hey, you never know! Could be someone's way of rekindling old sparks.

Manan typing...

Manan: Plot twist: the email is from a long-lost ninja society trying to recruit us.

Roy typing...

Roy: Or it's the ghosts of our college days haunting us.

Anu typing...

Anu: This is getting weirder by the minute. Let's just hope it's a fun surprise and not some elaborate prank. ??♂??

Aarush typing...

Aarush: Either way, I'm in. But seriously, who's behind this?

Manan typing...

Manan: Could it be Aksha planning a surprise for us?

Roy typing...

Roy: Nah, Aksha's not into surprises. She's probably busy ignoring the mail.

Dev typing...

Dev: Seriously, who could it be? Maher, any ideas?

Maher typing...

Maher: Nope, but if it's a surprise, I hope it's a good one!

Aksha is reading the messages but not responding.

Manan: Maybe Rishi's planning a grand celebration. What do you think, Rishi?

Rishi typing...

Rishi: ? I plead the Fifth.

Roy: Come on, spill the beans, Dev. Did you set this up?

Dev: (laughing) I wish! This time, I'm as clueless as the rest of you.

Anu: Let's make a bet—five bucks on Aksha being the secret planner!

Aksha: (finally responding) You guys and your bets. I have no time for surprises.

Manan: Aksha, don't ruin the fun! Embrace the mystery!

Dev typing...

Dev: Mystery or not, I hope it involves good food.

Anu typing...

Anu: Always thinking about food, Dev. Classic!

Maher typing...

Maher: Can we focus on finding out who planned this instead of food?

Aksha typing...

Aksha: (sending a ? emoji) I second that.

Aarush typing...

Aarush: Maybe we'll find out at the reunion. Till then, let's just enjoy the suspense.

Dev: So, everyone's in for the reunion, right?

Anu: Absolutely! Wouldn't miss it for the world.

Manan: Count me in! This sounds too good to pass up.

Rishi: I'll be there for sure. Let's solve this mystery together.

Maher: Same here. This is going to be fun!

Roy: Of course, I'm in. Let's see what surprises await.

Aksha: (silent, still reading the messages but not responding)

Aarush: Looks like it's unanimous—well, almost. Aksha, you're coming too, right?

Aksha typing... then stops.

Manan: Typical Aksha. Always keeping us guessing. ?

Dev: Well, Aksha or not, this reunion's happening. Let's make it epic!

ᗧᗧᗧ

2

Between Love and Loneliness

"Why is she always a topic of discussion between us? Why is she always the reason for fights between us? Why are misunderstandings between us always created by her?" Aarush's voice was firm but tinged with frustration as he bombarded Aksha with a barrage of questions.

Aarush Kapoor, the charismatic CEO of a leading multinational company, commanded attention with every word. At 38, his sharp features, piercing hazel eyes, and impeccably styled hair reflected his position as a man at the pinnacle of success. Tailored suits and effortless elegance were his armor, but it was his charm and eloquence that truly captivated those around him.

Despite his towering professional persona, Aarush's philosophy set him apart. For him, success was never about the numbers—it was about impact. "In the end, it's not about the profits we make, but the lives we touch," was a mantra he lived by. This guiding belief wove compassion into his leadership, earning him both respect and admiration in the corporate world.

Yet, behind the poised exterior was a man deeply rooted in personal values. Aarush found balance in his love for Eastern philosophy, which taught him the art of harmonizing ambition with inner peace. But no philosophy guided his heart more than his love for Aksha, his wife and the anchor of his life. Her unwavering support was his sanctuary, her smile his triumph. Aarush often credited her as his greatest source of inspiration, weaving small, thoughtful gestures into their busy lives to keep their bond alive.

Now, in their shared space, that bond felt strained. Aksha's hands moved methodically as she organized clothes in their wardrobe, her back turned to him. Her movements, though precise, lacked the usual grace. Aarush could sense the turmoil in her silence, and though her face was unreadable from his angle, he knew her too well to miss the signs.

When she finally turned, her expression revealed a mixture of anger and pain—not the fleeting kind, but the kind that lingered, cutting deeper with each passing second. Her disappointment weighed heavily in the air between them, magnifying the unspoken emotions that neither seemed ready to confront.

"Aksha..." Aarush began softly, his frustration ebbing into regret as he took a step closer.

Her eyes flickered with something unsaid, something unresolved. She turned back to the cupboard, adjusting the rows of neatly folded clothes, but her hands trembled ever so slightly. What should have been a simple chore now felt like a metaphor for their relationship—attempting to bring order to chaos, to fold away the creases of misunderstanding.

Aarush reached out, his voice quieter now. "I didn't mean to hurt you."

Still, Aksha remained silent, her profile stoic yet vulnerable. The pain in her expression wasn't loud—it didn't need to be. It was in the slight downturn of her lips, the heaviness in her gaze, the way her shoulders seemed to carry the weight of everything left unsaid.

In that moment, amidst the silence and the orderly rows of clothes, Aarush saw more than just his wife's disappointment. He saw the fragility of emotions and the strength it took to carry them alone. The wardrobe wasn't just a task; it was a mirror, reflecting their shared struggles and unspoken fears.

Aarush realized that some battles couldn't be won with logic or eloquence but with patience and understanding. Standing there, watching Aksha fight back the tears she refused to shed, he knew this was one of those moments where words would only be noise.

So, he didn't speak. Instead, he stepped closer, letting his presence convey what his words couldn't—that he was there, ready to fold away the misunderstandings and make space for healing.

And in that quiet, poignant moment, their unspoken emotions echoed louder than any argument ever could.

"I've told you several times, and I'll say it again. If she is joining, forget about me. I won't come. I won't hold you back. I can manage on my own," Aksha said, her voice calm but resolute.

Aksha Kapoor, Aarush's wife and a talented abstract painter, is a woman of quiet strength and deep emotions. She runs her own art studio, a space that feels as alive as her colorful, expressive paintings. Her art is her voice, a way to share emotions she rarely puts into words.

On the outside, Aksha appears confident and self-assured, handling challenges with poise. But beneath this strong front lies a deeply sensitive person, someone who feels things intensely. In her studio, away from the world, she allows her emotions to flow freely onto the canvas. Each brushstroke reflects her thoughts, her joys, and sometimes her pain.

Her relationship with Aarush is the cornerstone of her life. Despite their differences and the demands of their individual careers, they share a bond built on love, respect, and understanding. Aksha often channels her feelings for Aarush into her paintings, exploring themes of love, connection, and the complexities of human relationships.

But love isn't always easy. Moments like these, when hurt feelings and misunderstandings arise, test their connection. Aksha believes that understanding each other is the key to a strong relationship. For her, it's about being patient, listening, and creating a safe space where they can both be their true selves.

Aksha's art reflects who she is—strong but vulnerable, bold yet thoughtful. It's her way of finding balance in her life, of expressing the parts of herself that words can't always capture. And through her paintings, she not only connects with herself but also with

Aarush, strengthening their bond in ways that go beyond words.

"Aashu, my sweetheart! Try to understand, dear. I can't go without you. I can't leave you alone. You know that, right? I love you, na baba," Aarush pleaded, his voice soft yet insistent, hoping to bridge the growing gap between them.

But despite his efforts, Aksha remained silent, lost in her own thoughts. Her hands moved methodically, preparing coffee, her focus unwavering. She didn't respond, her quiet demeanor creating an invisible wall between them.

The silence in the room felt heavy, almost tangible. Aarush knew this silence well—it wasn't just an absence of words. It was Aksha's way of expressing her deeper feelings, a language of quiet pain that he had learned to read over time.

As the coffee brewed, its warm aroma filling the room, Aarush couldn't ignore the unspoken emotions hanging between them. Her silence carried the weight of her hurt and hesitation, and it resonated louder than any argument ever could.

"Baby," Aarush began again, his tone gentle but resolute. "I can't go alone. And on the other side, I also want to hang out with my buddies. Did you realize it's been five years since our marriage? And five years since the last gathering with 'Ninja 9'?"

He paused, searching for her eyes, hoping for a glimmer of understanding. "It's not just a reunion for me. It's a chance to relive those memories, to reconnect with a part of me I've missed. But none of it will feel right if you're not there with me."

Aksha continued her preparations, her silence unbroken, but Aarush wasn't ready to give up. He knew the path to her heart wasn't through grand gestures but through patience and understanding. He stood there, waiting, hoping his words would eventually reach her.

In the quiet tension of that moment, over the brewing coffee and unsaid words, the couple found themselves on a delicate edge—a mix of love, longing, and the hope that they could bridge the gap between their worlds once again.

ϷϷϷ

Ninja 9, a legendary group of friends, began their story at KES College of Science in Bangalore, India. What started as a group of strangers quickly turned into a bond stronger than family during three unforgettable years.

Made up of nine unique individuals, each with their quirks and strengths, Ninja 9 wasn't just a group of friends; they were a family. Together, they faced the ups and downs of college life—supporting each other through challenges, celebrating victories, and sharing countless moments of joy.

Within the walls of KES College, they learned more than academics. They discovered life lessons, navigated relationships, and created memories that would stay with them forever. From late-night chai sessions to shared laughter and tears, Ninja 9 found strength in unity, learning to appreciate their differences and support one another.

When they graduated, Ninja 9 left college with more than just degrees. They carried a treasure trove of memories and an unshakable understanding that true friendships are timeless. But amidst the camaraderie, a love story quietly blossomed between two members—Aksha and Aarush, affectionately called #Aakrush.

Their love story began in the second year of college, adding a new layer to Ninja 9's bond. As their relationship grew, Aksha and Aarush became a symbol of the deep connections formed within the group. Shortly after graduation, they married, their wedding becoming a joyous celebration for the entire group.

#Aakrush's union added a touch of romance to Ninja 9's story, but it also marked their final reunion. As the celebrations ended, an unspoken distance began to creep into the group. No plans for future reunions were made, and over time, Ninja 9 found themselves drifting apart. Though they stayed connected online, the vibrant bond they once shared seemed to fade.

For Aksha, the transition after marriage was particularly challenging. The lively, spirited Aksha that everyone knew seemed to retreat into herself. She began to distance herself from aspects of her past, leaving her friends puzzled and concerned. Her struggles post-marriage cast a shadow over the group, and no one dared to suggest another reunion, fearing it might bring her pain.

Aksha felt like she had lost a part of herself. The once inseparable Ninja 9 now felt fractured, and it took her months to find her footing again. The group, too, grappled with this change, unsure of how to move forward without hurting her.

And so, Ninja 9 remained suspended in a bittersweet limbo—connected by memories yet held back by unspoken fears. Their story, once full of laughter and togetherness, now lingered in a space of quiet understanding, each member carrying the weight of their shared past and uncertain future.

ᗡᗡᗡ

"Excuse me!!!" Aksha yelled, her voice sharp with frustration. "I never made any rules about you keeping distance from your friends. They're also my friends! Stop blaming me for this, Aarush. I'm so tired of hearing this same thing over and over for the last five years," she continued, her anger boiling over.

Aarush, sensing the storm in her words, knew there was no point in arguing anymore. She was beyond reasoning in that moment. He decided to walk away to avoid saying something that might make things worse.

"Alright. F.I.N.E.," he mumbled, grabbing his keys and heading for the door.

"Wait, Aarush!" Aksha called out, her voice now tinged with regret. "I'm sorry. I shouldn't have snapped like that." But by the time she spoke, Aarush had already left.

She stood there, her emotions a swirl of regret, murmuring to herself, "I never thought you'd think I was trying to push you away from your friends. I hurt you... I hurt you deeply."

ᗡᗡᗡ

As the clock struck nine times, Aksha stood by the balcony, her gaze fixed on the entrance. The quiet of the night wrapped around her, but it did nothing to ease the heaviness in her chest. She was waiting, hoping for Aarush to come home. The minutes stretched on endlessly, and two hours without him felt like an eternity.

She remembered the request she had made earlier, asking Aarush for space, wanting a week alone to clear her thoughts. But now, standing there on the balcony, she couldn't shake the emptiness that surrounded her. What used to be a peaceful spot for reflection now felt like a reminder of her loneliness.

Finally, unable to bear the silence any longer, Aksha turned away from the balcony and walked back inside. She picked up her phone, her fingers trembling slightly. She needed to talk to Aarush, to apologize for how she had acted. She dialed his number, her heart pounding in her chest, hoping he would answer.

"Someone is missing me," a playful voice teased from behind. Aarush had managed to sneak up quietly, trying to surprise her. As Aksha focused on dialing his number, she felt his warm breath close to her ear, the soft whisper pulling her from her thoughts. His presence, gentle and familiar, brought a rush of comfort, and in that moment, the distance they had felt earlier seemed to dissolve.

The balance between being alone and together settled between them, the brief separation fading into the background as they stood side by side. The stillness of the night around them was now filled with quiet conversations, soft laughter, and the occasional brush of hands, their closeness speaking volumes.

The balcony, once a place of solitude, became their sanctuary—a space where they could just be, together. The rustling of leaves and the distant hum of the city blended into a calming lullaby, setting the tone for the peaceful moment they shared.

Aarush's fingers gently traced circles on Aksha's palm, a small gesture that conveyed more than words ever could. It was a silent promise, a reminder that even in the quietest moments, their bond was strong.

"You scared me," Aksha began, her voice filled with a mix of playful reproach and lingering worry. She let out a soft sigh as she thought back to the moment of fear.

"I'm sorry," Aksha replied, her voice filled with regret. "It was my mistake. I shouldn't have raised my voice. I shouldn't have acted that way. Please don't leave me again. I've realized I can't stand being without you, not even for a minute." Her words were simple, but the weight of them was clear, her vulnerability shining through.

Aarush looked up at her, his eyes softening as he took in her apology. "Come on," he replied with a smile, his voice teasing yet affectionate. "I didn't go anywhere. I just stepped out to grab us some food. But then one of my colleagues stopped me, and I got a little delayed."

"You'll never change, will you?" Aksha teased, her tone a playful mix of scolding and affection. "You don't even think to let me know where you're going. I was so worried about you."

Aarush chuckled, his expression light. "And you," he said, lifting an eyebrow in mock seriousness, "you'll never change either, will you?"

Their laughter filled the air, wrapping around them like a warm embrace. In that moment, all the worries and tension seemed to fade away, replaced by the simple joy of being with each other. The night, the balcony, and the quiet city were now witnesses to their love, a love that, despite the occasional bumps, had only grown stronger with time.

The laughter they shared turned into a more heartfelt conversation. As they talked about their day, dreams, and hopes, the balcony became a place for them to open up. Their words flowed easily, with glances and gentle touches that spoke louder than anything they could say.

> **"***Marriage is a mix of chaos and harmony. Like an orchestra, there are moments of disagreement where voices rise, but through it all, there's a strong connection of love between them.***"**

When they argue, the tension feels like a storm—loud and intense—but after the storm, there's always peace. The quick switch from fighting to holding each other shows how deeply they care for each other.

In disagreements, there's beauty too—a beauty born from the balance of passion and tenderness. It's knowing that after the conflict, calm and understanding will return.

In marriage, not every moment is perfect. But what matters is how they get through it together, growing stronger with every challenges. Sure! Here's the exact copy as you provided:

Their love is shown not by avoiding conflict, but by facing it and coming out even more united.

Frustration and love can happen together in marriage. It's the ability to express emotions openly—whether in anger or affection—that makes their bond strong and real.

"I love you," Aksha whispered softly, her words carrying the weight of deep emotion in the quiet of the night.

"I love you too, Ashu," Aarush replied, his gaze locking with hers, expressing more than just words could.

> "*In relationships, confrontations often come up, but they also help couples grow closer and understand each other better. These tough moments open the door for honest conversations, strengthening trust and bringing them even closer. They remind them of the true strength of their connection, rooted in love and vulnerability.*"

Their conversation wasn't about big gestures but small, intimate moments where they could truly be themselves. The night air, filled with the soft rustling of leaves and the sounds of the city below, became the perfect setting for their bond to deepen. Aksha's hair danced in the breeze, and Aarush looked at her with admiration, thankful for the love they shared.

"I love you," Aksha repeated, her voice holding all the meaning of their shared history and the future they were building together.

"I love you too, Ashu," Aarush answered, pulling her closer, as if to capture the moment and never let it go.

Time seemed to slow as they sat together, the world outside their little bubble fading away. The twinkling city lights mirrored the stars above, creating a serene atmosphere around them.

"Shall we go?" Aksha asked after a while, her eyes sparkling with excitement for what was to come.

"No, I want to stay like this, with you," Aarush replied, his gaze full of affection, wanting to hold on to the quiet intimacy they were sharing.

Aksha playfully teased him. "Come on, I'm asking about our summer holidays."

A mischievous grin spread across Aarush's face as he leaned in, a hint of excitement in his voice. "Well, I've already planned a surprise. A getaway, just the two of us, to a place where we can forget everything else and just enjoy each other."

Aksha's curiosity piqued, and Aarush couldn't help but smile. "What's the surprise?" she asked, eager for more details.

Aarush leaned in closer, his lips almost brushing her ear. "It's a secret for now, but trust me, it'll be perfect. Sun, sand, and a lot of us."

Aksha's eyes sparkled with interest, and Aarush's grin deepened as they both shared a playful moment. Their love story, filled with teasing and laughter, was a reminder of the joy they found in each other's company.

"I meant the email invitation for Ninja 9," Aksha clarified, the light-heartedness in her voice punctuating their bond, bringing them even closer.

Aarush chuckled softly, his eyes twinkling with a knowing smile. "Ah, now I get it," he said, leaning back slightly but keeping his arm around her. "You know, if you really want to go, then I think it's a green flag from me. I'll support whatever makes you happy, Ashu."

Aksha raised an eyebrow, surprised by his response. "So, you're okay with it?" she asked, a hint of disbelief in her voice.

Aarush nodded, his expression softening. "Of course. You've been saying you miss them, and I can tell it's important to you. If that means you need to reconnect with them, I'm with you, 100%.

Besides, we both know that Ninja 9 is a big part of who we are, right?"

Aksha smiled, her heart warmed by his understanding. "Thank you, Aarush. You always know how to make me feel better."

Aarush kissed her forehead gently. "Anything for you, Ashu. Now, let's figure out how we'll surprise them. It's time for Ninja 9 to come together again."

ϷϷϷ

3

Welcome to Ninja's World

"Get up, Dev! It's already 10 o'clock, man. We can't afford to be late today," Anu said, her voice filled with excitement as she tugged at his blanket.

Dev, lost in the depths of his dreams, barely registered her presence. He mumbled something incoherent and rolled over, pulling the blanket tighter around him.

"Seriously, Dev? What's wrong with you? Why are you like this?" Anu huffed, standing over him with her arms crossed. "Don't make me drag you out of bed!"

"What's with all the shouting, Anu? You're ruining my sleep," Dev grumbled, peeking at her with half-closed eyes. "And... wait, when did you even get here? I didn't hear you come in."

Anu smirked. "I came in when you were too busy romancing your pillow. Now, get up before I lose my patience."

"Okay, fine. Welcome. You're here. Now let me sleep," Dev replied nonchalantly, turning his back to her.

That was the final straw for Anu. "You lazy idiot! One day, your sleep and laziness will be your downfall. Mark my words!" she yelled, delivering a swift kick to the mattress for emphasis.

Realizing Anu was on the verge of full-blown irritation, Dev decided it was better not to push his luck. "Alright, alright. I'm up!" he said, sitting up with exaggerated reluctance.

"Good. Now, get ready. I'm making pancakes and your favorite coffee," Anu called out from the kitchen as she busied herself with breakfast.

Dev rubbed his eyes and stretched before dragging himself to the kitchen doorway. The aroma of coffee and pancakes was already filling the air. "Wait, pancakes? Coffee? What's going on? Did I forget something important? Is it your birthday? Or mine? Or... something else?" he asked, a mischievous grin forming on his face.

Anu glanced at him over her shoulder, rolling her eyes. "Don't flatter yourself. I just thought I'd make sure you eat before you run off."

As he leaned against the doorframe, Dev's teasing smile softened. Watching Anu bustle around the kitchen, pouring coffee and flipping pancakes, he felt a wave of quiet gratitude wash over him.

In the stillness of that moment, he thought, *How lucky am I to have her in my life?* Anu wasn't his girlfriend—at least not officially. But the way she cared for him, the little efforts she made, the warmth she brought into his day, all of it spoke volumes.

"Thanks, Anu," he said suddenly, his tone unusually sincere.

"For what?" she asked, turning to him with a curious expression.

"For being you," Dev replied, his smile genuine now.

Anu paused for a moment, then shrugged playfully. "Well, somebody has to keep you alive, lazybones."

Their laughter filled the room, the kind of laughter that spoke of a bond stronger than words.

"These pancakes smell amazing," Dev said, walking into the kitchen and leaning on the counter. "Are you trying to bribe me into being productive today?"

Anu smirked as she poured syrup over the stack of golden pancakes. "If bribing you gets you out of your zombie mode, then yes. You should be grateful I'm even making this effort."

Dev grabbed a piece of pancake from the plate before she could stop him. "Mmm, you're spoiling me. Keep this up, and I might start expecting breakfast in bed every morning."

Anu swatted his hand playfully. "Keep dreaming. This is a one-time offer because today is special."

He leaned against the counter, coffee in hand, and asked with mock seriousness, "Special? Did I forget something? Is it your birthday? Or mine? Wait—did we miss Pancake Day?"

Anu rolled her eyes dramatically. "Dev, don't tell me you've already forgotten about the reunion!"

Dev froze mid-bite, his face a mix of realization and guilt. "Oh... right. The reunion. Ninja 9, the epic squad reunion. How could I forget?"

"You clearly did," Anu replied, crossing her arms. "You're lucky I woke you up. Otherwise, you'd still be hibernating while everyone else is catching up on three years' worth of memories."

Dev scratched the back of his head sheepishly. "Okay, okay, I admit it. I may have underestimated how important today is. Thanks for not letting me screw it up."

"Don't thank me yet," Anu said, placing the plate of pancakes in front of him. "You still need to get ready, and I'm not going to wait for you all day."

"Are you excited?" Dev asked between bites.

"Of course," Anu said, her voice softening. "I haven't seen everyone in years. It'll be nice to catch up, laugh about old times, and... you know, see how much we've all changed."

"Yeah," Dev said, his tone contemplative. "It'll be good to see the gang again. Though I wonder how awkward it'll be. You know, considering all the changes since college."

Anu shot him a reassuring smile. "Change doesn't mean we've lost the bond, Dev. We'll pick up right where we left off. That's the magic of friendships like ours."

Dev grinned, lifting his coffee mug in a toast. "To Ninja 9—chaotic, dramatic, and completely irreplaceable."

Anu laughed, clinking her mug against his. "To Ninja 9."

As they finished their breakfast, the kitchen filled with an air of anticipation and nostalgia, both of them silently looking forward to rekindling the connections that had shaped some of the best years of their lives.

Dev pushed the empty plate aside and sipped his coffee, leaning back in his chair. "By the way, do you think Aahana got the reunion invitation?"

Anu paused mid-sip, a shadow of uncertainty crossing her face. "She should have. Everyone in Ninja 9 was on the email list, right? But... whether she'll come or not is another question entirely."

"Yeah," Dev said, a pensive look taking over his usually carefree expression. "Things have been... complicated with her since everything happened."

Anu nodded, her voice softer now. "You mean since Rajeev..."

Dev exhaled heavily, setting his coffee cup down with a soft clink. "Yeah. After she got engaged to Rajeev, it's like she just... pulled away. From all of us."

"I don't blame her," Anu said, her tone empathetic. "She must have her reasons. Maybe it's hard for her to revisit those memories. But still, it hurts. She was such an important part of Ninja 9. It's strange to even think about a reunion without her."

Dev ran a hand through his hair, his brows furrowed. "If she does come, it's going to be... tense. Aksha, Aarush, and Aahana in the same room after everything? That's a lot of unresolved feelings to bring under one roof."

Anu tilted her head thoughtfully. "True. But maybe this is exactly what we all need—a chance to talk, to clear the air. It's been years, Dev. Maybe time has softened some of the edges."

He snorted, but his smile was wistful. "You're always the optimist. But you might be right. If anyone can break through Aahana's walls, it's us."

"Especially Aksha," Anu added with a pointed look.

Dev raised an eyebrow. "You think Aksha will even try? Things between her and Aahana weren't exactly smooth the last time they spoke."

"Aksha might surprise us," Anu said, shrugging. "She's grown a lot, you know? And deep down, I think she misses Aahana just as much as the rest of us. Maybe more."

Dev sighed, his gaze drifting to the window. "I hope you're right. It would be nice to see everyone together again, laughing like we used to. Even if it's just for one night."

Anu reached out and placed a reassuring hand on his. "We'll take it as it comes, Dev. Whatever happens, we'll face it together. That's what Ninja 9 is all about, right?"

He smiled at her, his usual playful glint returning to his eyes. "Right. And worst case, we'll just distract everyone with pancakes. You really outdid yourself this morning."

Anu laughed, swatting him lightly. "If only life's problems could be solved with pancakes. Come on, sleepyhead, we need to get ready."

As they cleared the kitchen and began preparing for the day, both couldn't shake the mixture of excitement and apprehension brewing in their hearts. The reunion wasn't just about catching up—it was about confronting the past, rekindling old bonds, and maybe, just maybe, finding a way to move forward together.

As Anu rinsed the dishes, Dev leaned against the kitchen counter, absentmindedly tracing the rim of his coffee mug with his thumb. His thoughts began to drift, spiraling inward toward a place he rarely allowed himself to go.

ᑭᑭᑭ

Aahana......................,

Her name alone was enough to stir something deep within him—a blend of longing and regret. She had always been an enigma to him, a storm he had willingly walked into without ever understanding its depth. Their connection had always been... complicated.

He remembered the way her laughter used to light up the dullest moments, the sharp wit she wielded like a weapon during their banter, and the quiet vulnerability she tried so hard to hide. Aahana had a way of making people feel seen, yet she always seemed to hold a part of herself back, as if afraid of being truly known.

And he? He had never found the courage to confront what she meant to him.

In the quiet of his own heart, Dev had known for years that his feelings for Aahana went far beyond friendship. But he had buried them, convinced that she would never see him that way—or worse, that admitting his feelings would shatter the delicate balance of their group.

The last few years had only deepened the chasm between them. Her engagement to Rajeev had felt like a final nail in the coffin of his unspoken love, yet he couldn't bring himself to resent her for it. How could he? Aahana deserved happiness, even if it wasn't with him.

But the thought of seeing her again, after all this time, made his chest tighten. Would she still be the same Aahana he had fallen for, or had time and distance changed her in ways he couldn't predict? Would she even want to come to the reunion, to face the ghosts of their shared past?

ᐊᐊᐊ

"Dev?" Anu's voice pulled him from his reverie. She was standing beside him now, her expression a mix of curiosity and concern. "You okay? You looked like you were a million miles away."

He forced a smile, masking the whirlwind of emotions inside. "Yeah, just thinking about the reunion. Wondering how it's all going to play out."

Anu studied him for a moment, her brow furrowing slightly. "You're thinking about Aahana, aren't you?"

Dev's smile faltered, but he didn't deny it. "Maybe. It's hard not to."

Anu placed a comforting hand on his arm. "You should talk to her, Dev. If she comes to the reunion, maybe it's your chance to finally say what you've been holding back all these years."

He let out a dry laugh, shaking his head. "And say what? 'Hey, Aahana, remember me? The guy who never had the guts to tell you how he felt?' Yeah, that'll go over well."

Anu's grip on his arm tightened, her gaze steady. "You'll never know unless you try. What's the worst that could happen? She's already distanced herself from us. At least this way, you'll get some closure."

Dev didn't respond, but Anu's words lingered in his mind. Could he really face Aahana after all this time? Could he finally put into words the feelings he had carried for so long?

He wasn't sure, but as he followed Anu out of the kitchen to get ready, one thing was clear—if Aahana did show up at the reunion, it would be a moment of reckoning he could no longer avoid.

"Anu, wait... you know what I'm thinking?" Dev suddenly defied her, his eyes twinkling with mischief.

"No, I don't want to hear any more of your *bakwass*. Go freshen up," Anu replied, not missing a beat, though there was a hint of a smile playing at the corners of her lips.

Dev raised an eyebrow, leaning in with a teasing grin. "What if my wife turns out to be just like you? Don't you think you and I would make the perfect match?" he flirted, the words rolling off his tongue with ease.

Anu burst out laughing, shaking her head in mock disbelief. "Hahaha... you're too late for that, man. Try another option," she said, still chuckling. "Why? What's the problem with you?" Dev prodded, genuinely curious.

"I'm already taken," Anu stated matter-of-factly.

"Taken? By whom?" Dev asked, raising an eyebrow, surprised by her sudden declaration.

"By me," Anu answered, her voice laced with a hint of pride, her independence radiating from her like a force field.

Dev laughed, shaking his head. "Typical philosopher," he teased, the playful banter rolling between them like a familiar rhythm.

"Yes, I am," Anu affirmed.

As he sat there, trying to shake off the lingering thoughts about Aahana, his playful side kicked in. He grinned, his eyes lighting up with mischief. "By the way, Anu," he said, his tone suddenly shifting to something more teasing, "do you remember that classmate of yours from school? The one who had a huge crush on you? I bet he's still after you, and probably showing up at the reunion, huh?"

Anu shot him a glare but couldn't hide the smile that tugged at the corners of her mouth. "You are such a troublemaker," she said, rolling her eyes but laughing all the same.

Dev leaned back, a smirk on his face. "Oh, come on! It's been years, but I bet he's still got that soft spot for you. Or maybe you're too independent for him now?" he teased, knowing full well that Anu always prided herself on doing things on her own terms.

"Why don't you ask him yourself when you see him?" she shot back, crossing her arms playfully. "Besides, I'm not interested in some old crush."

Dev chuckled, enjoying the playful banter. "Well, maybe if he sees how much you've changed, he'll finally give up on his 'dream girl' status," he joked, his voice dripping with exaggeration. "Or maybe he'll realize it's me who's the real match for you. You know, I've always been your biggest fan."

Anu snorted, pushing him lightly. "Dream on, Dev. You know we're too different for that," she teased, knowing full well that their friendship was rooted in a deep understanding of each other's quirks and strengths.

Dev's smile softened for a moment, his thoughts drifting back to the reunion. "Maybe. But no matter who shows up, Anu, you'll always be the one who can light up the room," he said sincerely, his teasing tone giving way to genuine admiration. "And that's what I love about you."

"Enough!!!" Anu says with a playful push that sent him stumbling toward the bathroom. "Now, go on. Freshen up, and stop distracting me."

Dev grinned as he shuffled toward the bathroom, muttering, "How irritating is this friend of mine? Never misses a chance to tease me." But there was a warmth in his heart—Anu had always been like this: witty, independent, and fiercely confident in her own right.

Anu stood there for a moment, watching him go. A small smile tugged at her lips as she thought, *How did I end up with a friend like him? He never stops flirting, but I wouldn't have it any other way.*

She turned to look around the room, her mind briefly drifting to her own journey—one of independence, strength, and determination. She had always been her own architect, forging a path that reflected her values and aspirations. Anu had built her life with resilience, turning challenges into stepping stones. Her confidence was the quiet power that fueled everything she did, a reminder that she was the master of her own story.

In her own way, she had learned to embrace life fully—shaping it to fit her desires, without apology, and never backing down. As much as she loved her friends, Anu found joy in the freedom that came from making her own decisions. She was the kind of person who wore her independence like armor, making choices that were aligned with who she truly was.

That was Anu—a woman of strength and self-reliance, carving out her own place in the world, empowered by the knowledge that no one could define her except herself. And with that realization, her smile grew, knowing that no matter what the future held—whether it was the reunion or something else—she was ready to take it on with the same fearless attitude she always had.

Anu paused for a second, the banter fading into something more meaningful. She could see the sincerity in his eyes and smiled, feeling grateful for the friendship they shared. With that, they both knew that the reunion—no matter what awkwardness or surprises it might bring—would be another chapter in their journey, one that they would face together.

ᗧᗧᗧ

4

Stirring Coffee, Stirring Memories

As Dev and Anu arrived in Bangalore, the charm of the city was unmistakable, and they couldn't help but be in awe of the perfect balance between tradition and modernity. The air was filled with the sweet scent of fresh coffee, and the lush greenery of the city's parks, like Cubbon Park and Lalbagh Botanical Garden, provided a serene escape from the usual city hustle.

The architecture, a blend of regal old-world charm and sleek modern designs, stood as a testament to the city's rich history and rapid progress. Bangalore Palace, with its grandeur, stood tall alongside the towering skyscrapers. As the sun dipped behind the cityscape, the streets came alive with twinkling lights and the buzzing energy of Commercial Street's markets. The aroma of street food, rich with spices and tempting flavors, mingled with the evening breeze, contributing to the city's vibrant atmosphere.

Nights in Bangalore were equally captivating, with its many pubs and rooftop lounges offering the perfect view of the twinkling city lights. The warmth of the city's people added to its welcoming vibe, making every moment here feel special. Anu, having heard so much about Bangalore, was eager to experience its charm firsthand, and Dev, ever the easygoing companion, was ready to explore.

As they stepped out of the cab, Dev was taken aback to see a man holding a sign with their names written on it. "Good afternoon! I hope you had a safe journey," the man greeted them, handing over bouquets of fresh flowers that carried the sweet fragrance of the city's gardens.

Dev and Anu exchanged a surprised glance, their curiosity piqued. They took the flowers and followed the man, marveling at the perfectly orchestrated arrangements that greeted them at every turn. It felt like a scene straight out of a movie. Neither of them had any idea who had planned it all, but they couldn't deny the excitement building within them.

When Dev opened the car door for Anu, he noticed a small card tucked beneath her seat. "Welcome to Ninja's World," it read in bold letters. They exchanged another puzzled look, intrigued by the mysterious message.

Dev, with his usual teasing grin, broke the silence. "Looks like we've stepped into some grand adventure. Wonder what this 'Ninja's World' is all about," he mused, his voice full of playful curiosity.

Anu laughed softly. "Maybe it's just an elaborate prank," she joked, though her eyes sparkled with intrigue.

Despite the teasing banter, Anu appreciated Dev's nature—the way he could turn even the most ordinary situations into light-hearted moments. It wasn't just his jokes that made him fun to be around; it was the way he respected others. His humor never crossed any lines, and he knew exactly how to make people laugh without ever causing discomfort. Whether he was poking fun at her or anyone else, there was a gentleness to his teasing, and Anu found that comforting.

Dev, always the joker, had a unique way of making the people around him feel at ease. His humor was playful and inclusive, never at anyone's expense. Anu admired this about him—the balance between fun and respect. It was rare to find someone who could be so effortlessly charming, so light-hearted, yet so thoughtful and considerate.

In Dev's lighthearted jokes and his thoughtful gestures, Anu saw the depth of their bond. He could make her laugh on the toughest days, and that's something she valued deeply. And as they ventured deeper into this mysterious "Ninja's World," they both knew one thing for sure: whatever surprises lay ahead, their friendship would carry them through with laughter, respect, and an undeniable sense of adventure.

"Sometimes words are not required to express your feelings; your actions are enough to speak on your behalf."

Anu stepped inside, her eyes wide with astonishment. "Dev, seriously, are we like VIPs now? Who on earth could pull off these grand arrangements? Whose brilliant mind is behind all this? Who's the mastermind orchestrating our very own mini-celebration?"

Dev, with a mischievous twinkle in his eye, feigned deep contemplation. "Ah, Anu, my dear Watson, the game is afoot! We've stumbled upon a mystery of epic proportions. Elementary, my dear Anu, elementary. I suspect it's the work of the Secret Society of Surprise Planners, dedicated to making ordinary moments extraordinary."

Anu couldn't help but burst into laughter at Dev's theatrical deduction. "Secret Society of Surprise Planners? Really, Dev? You've been watching too many detective shows."

Dev, adopting a mock-serious demeanor, replied, "Anu, my investigative process is unparalleled. We shall unmask the genius behind our lavish surprise, and mark my words, it'll be someone with a cape and a flair for dramatic entrances!"

As they continued to banter about who might have planned their unexpected celebration, the room filled with laughter. The mystery of the surprise became a playful whodunit, with Anu and Dev acting as the detectives in this light-hearted puzzle.

"I don't know about you, Anu, but speaking for myself, I totally get what I deserve," Dev earnestly tried to preach to her.

Anu, adopting a sarcastic tone, replied, "Oh, absolutely! You and respect are like oil and water—worst match ever. But hey, at least you're consistent."

Dev, feigning offense, placed a hand on his heart. "Anu, my dear, you wound me! I'll have you know that respect is my middle name... well, almost. But seriously, who needs respect when you have charm and a killer sense of humor?"

Anu rolled her eyes, unable to suppress a chuckle. "Charm and humor, Dev? You're basically a walking contradiction. But fine, let's hope this reunion works its magic. Maybe it'll sprinkle some 'respect dust' on you, and the crises between the Ninjas will magically vanish."

Dev, playing along, crossed his fingers dramatically. "Respect dust, Anu? That sounds like a superhero's secret weapon. Watch out, world, for I shall be transformed into Captain Respect in no time!"

As they kept joking around, their excitement for the reunion grew. Their playful talk made them look forward to the Ninja gathering even more, imagining how they would solve problems together and have lots of fun.

As Dev and Anu strolled through the vibrant streets of Bangalore, the city seemed to awaken with the echoes of their laughter, reminiscent of the old college days. The very pavement beneath their feet resonated with the cadence of youthful memories, and the air carried the whispers of shared adventures.

Commercial Street, once just a bustling marketplace, transformed into a living museum of their collegiate escapades. The storefronts, witnesses to their impromptu shopping sprees and hasty decisions, seemed to nod in acknowledgment.

Passing by Mekhri Circle, the heart of their late-night conversations and spontaneous plans, the traffic lights flickered like playful memories, urging them to relive those golden moments. The cityscape around them took on the hues of nostalgia, every corner telling a story, every intersection a crossroad of shared journeys.

Cubbon Park, bathed in the soft glow of streetlights, became a haven of recollections. The familiar benches, once witnesses to whispered secrets and silent confessions, beckoned them to sit and bask in the nostalgia.

As they meandered past UB City, the skyline glittering with urban elegance, the towering structures seemed to applaud their journey from students navigating life to the professionals they had become. The flyovers overhead mirrored the soaring ambitions they once harbored.

Lal Bagh, with its lush greenery, stood as a testament to the endurance of their friendships, each tree and flower a silent witness to the evolution of their bonds.

Through the kaleidoscope of memories, Dev and Anu found themselves transported to a time when every street corner held the promise of discovery and every alleyway whispered secrets. Bangalore, the city that had woven itself into the fabric of their youth, now stood before them, a living, breathing testament to the beauty of shared experiences and the enduring charm of their college days.

In this vivid tapestry of memories, Bangalore emerged not just as a city but as a mosaic of experiences. Each landmark, from the modern marvels to the historic palaces, contributed to the unique symphony that was Bangalore—a city that breathed life into the memories etched in the minds of those who had the privilege of calling it home.

ԷԷԷ

"If my memory serves me right, this path leads straight to Momo's farmhouse. Am I correct?" Anu questioned, breaking the nostalgic silence in the car.

"Yep, I was thinking the same," Dev chimed in, supporting Anu's speculation.

Manan, or as he's affectionately known to the Ninjas, "Momo," was the heart and soul of their group. The funniest guy they knew, Momo earned his nickname because of his never-ending ability to surprise everyone. He had a round face that looked almost cartoonish, with a nose that stuck out proudly, adding to his charm and making him the cutest member of the Ninja squad.

Momo came from a typical Gujarati family, where the pressure to succeed in traditional careers was high. His father, a big businessman, had dreams of his son following in his footsteps. Even though Momo didn't have any plans of becoming a doctor, as was the family's expectation, he found himself managing a new land project in Bangalore—a project that turned out to be the perfect outlet for his surprising talents.

In the group, Momo stood out like a character from a funny comic book. Cute, yes, but when the situation called for it, he could be as serious as anyone. His ability to turn the mundane into something extraordinary was legendary. Whether it was suddenly dancing to a Bollywood song in the middle of a dull gathering or spontaneously organizing treasure hunts across Bangalore, Momo was always ready to infuse energy into any situation.

The Ninjas loved Momo not only for his sense of humor but also for his thoughtful nature. His nickname wasn't just a casual label—it was a testament to how he could make the ordinary feel magical. Despite his less-than-stellar 42% in his 10th-grade exams, his family pushed him toward the science stream, hoping he would eventually become a doctor. But Momo had other plans. He dreamed of studying business, and after much persuasion, he managed to convince his father to let him pursue his passion.

After moving to Bangalore for college, Momo, far from the familiar streets of Ahmedabad, initially missed home. But he quickly adapted to the new city and found his own rhythm. Outside of his studies, he discovered a passion for cooking, which made him an even more beloved member of the Ninja house. He became the official chef, turning even bitter gourd into something delicious.

In addition to being the culinary genius of the group, Momo had a knack for being the Ninja group's personal alarm clock and reminder. He adhered to family traditions, such as not using oil or shaving on Saturdays, and always made sure that shoes were left outside their cottage.

Momo, or Manan, was a special part of the Ninja group, a living contradiction of surprises. From average exam scores to managing big projects, and from cooking great meals to surprising everyone with his spontaneous spirit, he proved time and again that he could turn any situation into something extraordinary.

ၣၣၣ

"Wait a moment," Anu interrupted, her voice filled with doubt. "Do you think Momo organized this reunion?"

"No, uhhh, I don't think so," she hesitated.

"Yeah, I agree," Dev chimed in, shaking his head. "Momo can't pull off something like this. He can't even plan his way out of a paper bag."

"True, maybe you're right. But then who?" Anu wondered aloud, her brow furrowing as the mystery deepened.

As Anu and Dev mulled over the mastermind behind the heartwarming reunion, a surprising suspect emerged—Momo. Their deep friendship had always meant knowing each other's every quirk, their likes, dislikes, and all the nuances that defined them. Yet, this confusion was unsettling. Momo, the prankster and troublemaker, was suddenly at the center of a mystery they couldn't quite solve. The very idea of him orchestrating something so meaningful was both puzzling and intriguing.

Anu exchanged a puzzled look with Dev. Their usual certainty about their friends had given way to uncertainty. Could Momo—always the joker, always the one who made them laugh—be the one behind such a thoughtful and heartfelt gesture?

"A person is the best revised version of his friend," Dev philosophized, his voice carrying a hint of nostalgia and introspection, as he sank into his usual deep thoughts.

"I still think it's Momo," they both said simultaneously, their laughter spilling out in the most natural way, filling the air with warmth and amusement.

"Hahaha, what timing!" Dev laughed, his eyes twinkling. "Still, I admit, you and I are the best match ever," he teased Anu, his mischievous grin softening with a deeper affection.

"Shut up," Anu shot back with a mock glare, giving him a playful whack on the shoulder. Her expression held a mixture of affection and camaraderie, a silent acknowledgment of the bond they shared.

Dev gasped dramatically, clutching his heart. "Oh, the brutality! Attacked by my supposed best match! This is worse than any war I've faced!"

Anu burst out laughing at his over-the-top theatrics. "War? Really? You're such a drama queen!" she teased.

Dev grinned, adopting a mock-serious expression. "Well, the battle for the title of 'Best Match' is fierce, my friend. Not everyone can handle it."

Anu rolled her eyes, still chuckling. "You're ridiculous, Dev. But I guess that's why you're my partner in crime."

"And don't you forget it!" Dev declared proudly, striking an exaggerated superhero pose that earned another round of laughter from Anu.

Their banter, as always, was a constant reminder of how effortlessly they could slip into these familiar roles—partners in crime, laughter, and life.

In their teasing, the laughter wasn't just background noise; it showed the years of funny moments and the special bond that made their friendship one for the books.

In that moment, beneath the jokes and laughter, emotions flowed, weaving together their shared history and experiences. The bonds of friendship, marked by secrets, inside jokes, and unspoken understanding, created a rich backdrop to their playful exchange. The emotions lingered in the air, making the laughter feel even more real and the connection between Dev and Anu deeper and more meaningful.

ৡৡৡ

The car turned onto a road flanked by trees, their branches forming a lush green canopy that gradually enveloped the vehicle, leaving the hustle and bustle of the city behind. As the urban landscape faded away, nature's embrace unfolded, and the air became fresher, carrying with it the scent of earth and freedom.

As they neared Momo's farmhouse, the surroundings transformed into a beautiful, dreamlike landscape. Sunlight filtered through the leaves, casting soft, dancing patterns on the road. On one side, a winding stream sparkled in the sunlight like a liquid mirror, adding a touch of magic to the scene.

The car moved slowly, allowing them to soak in the peaceful countryside. The air was fresh, filled with the sweet scent of flowers, while birds sang cheerful songs. The gentle rustling of leaves created a soothing backdrop. Rolling green fields stretched out on either side, dotted with colorful wildflowers that swayed gently in the breeze.

Tall, ancient trees lined the road, their branches forming a natural canopy overhead. Light and shadow played a delightful game, making the whole area feel like a fairy tale. The sky was a vibrant blue, with fluffy white clouds drifting lazily, adding to the serene atmosphere.

As they got closer to the farmhouse, the charm of the countryside became even more apparent. Wooden fences bordered neat gardens bursting with color, and occasionally, they spotted friendly farm animals grazing in the fields. A red barn with weathered charm stood as a picturesque landmark, adding to the idyllic setting.

The peacefulness of the place felt like a warm embrace, inviting them to relax and leave all worries behind. Surrounded by nature's simple beauty, it felt like the perfect escape from the chaos of everyday life—a place to unwind and enjoy the serene countryside together.

Inside the car, the atmosphere shifted to one of shared nostalgia. Anu and Dev exchanged glances, their faces lighting up with smiles as they neared the place that held so many college memories. Their laughter and banter flowed freely, a symphony of familiarity echoing through the vehicle.

Suddenly, an unexpected jolt disrupted the tranquility, causing them to grip the edges of their seats. The car swerved slightly, and an audible gasp escaped from Anu. The sudden interruption snapped them back to the present moment, the dreamlike ambiance giving way to a heightened sense of alertness.

"What was that?" Anu exclaimed, her eyes wide as the car steadied itself.

Dev, who was at the wheel, glanced in the rearview mirror. "Just a bump in the road, nothing to worry about. We're almost there."

As the car continued on, they exchanged relieved glances, the jolt serving as a gentle reminder that even in the midst of nature's tranquility, unexpected surprises could still find their way. The anticipation of reaching Momo's farmhouse lingered, a mix of excitement and curiosity building as they neared their destination, ready to rekindle old memories and create new ones in the idyllic countryside.

5

Laughter, Love, and Lingering Mysteries

Manan greeted Roy with a warmth that contrasted with the coolness of Roy's appearance, making it clear that their connection ran deeper than mere acquaintanceship. As Dev stepped out of the car, Anu and he exchanged a glance, taking in Momo's transformed persona with a mixture of disbelief and curiosity.

"Look at Momo," Dev remarked, his voice tinged with astonishment. "He's changed so much. I wouldn't have expected this from him. Now, are you sure it's him?"

"Hmm, I think it's just an illusion," Anu replied, her words laced with amusement. "It's hard to believe he's the same person."

Both of them chuckled, brushing off the doubts that lingered, yet something about Momo's presence seemed different—more polished, less mischievous, as though the years had altered him in ways they hadn't anticipated.

Meanwhile, Roy stood across the way, greeted warmly by Manan. Roy Christian had always been the center of attention, his magnetic presence drawing every gaze effortlessly. With his undeniable charm, he captivated those around him, but his allure was more than skin deep. Roy's charisma was a double-edged sword, concealing a mystery that lay just beneath the surface. It was an enigma that intrigued everyone who met him, but few truly understood the depths of his true self.

Roy's bright blue eyes, like windows to his soul, held a flicker of sadness behind their sparkling allure, betraying the complexity of his emotions. His perfect features—sharp jawline, Roman-like nose, and jet-black hair—seemed almost too flawless, as though he had been sculpted by some higher force. Yet, his outward appearance of strength and perfection only served to deepen the mystery surrounding him.

Raised by a caretaker rather than his parents, Roy had long lived in the shadow of their wealth and influence. His parents were prominent business leaders, their names revered in high society. But the gilded image of their life was shattered by a silent, unspoken truth—their marriage had crumbled. The separation, a quiet scandal, was rarely spoken about, a shadow over the luxury they paraded to the world. The collapse of their relationship, though hidden from public view, had left its mark on Roy, deeply affecting his own sense of belonging in that same high society he was meant to inherit.

Roy had always felt like an outsider. While his parents thrived in their respective empires, their marriage—a union once celebrated—had slowly deteriorated under the weight of their individual successes. The glamorous dinners and public events were only distractions from the silent tension in their home, a place filled with unspoken frustrations and broken dreams.

This complex backdrop had shaped Roy into the person he was today: charming, yet rebellious, never fully fitting the mold that society tried to impose on him. His desire to stay young and defy expectations was reflected in his wardrobe—a collection of clothes that made him seem like a teenager trying to escape the weight of adulthood. The contrast between his youthful appearance and the sophistication of his family's name created an almost surreal image, leaving everyone who encountered him with the impression of a man who, despite his success and allure, was struggling to reconcile his identity.

Roy's bright blue eyes were always a reminder of the internal conflict that simmered beneath the surface—eyes that hinted at both the pain of personal battles and the weight of inherited prosperity. He was a paradox, someone who seemed to have it all, but was constantly seeking a way to break free from the expectations tied to his family's name. His timeless allure was captivating, but it was his quiet rebellion and the mysteries of his past that truly made him unforgettable.

ϷϷϷ

"Welcome, man! Welcome to our world. What a fantastic arrangement, dude!" Mann exclaimed enthusiastically as he saw Dev and Anu, rushing to greet them with open arms.

Anu stood, momentarily speechless, as her gaze swept across the farmhouse. She was captivated by its beauty—lush greenery stretched across the landscape, while vibrant flowers painted the surroundings in bursts of color. The air was rich with the sweet fragrance of blooming blossoms, creating a sensory experience that felt both grounding and uplifting.

The farmhouse, with nature's tapestry woven into every corner, felt like a serene oasis, a world apart from the noise and chaos of the city. Majestic trees stood tall and silent, their leaves rustling with the wind, whispering secrets only the earth could understand. The golden light of the setting sun bathed the grounds in a warm glow, casting long shadows and creating a peaceful, almost magical atmosphere.

As Anu continued to take it all in, memories from their college days began to flood her mind. The decorations, so carefully planned in those carefree years, now seemed to whisper the laughter and joy of those simpler times. The shared dreams, the camaraderie, the late-night talks—all those moments stood etched in her mind as a living testament to the enduring strength of their friendship. The farmhouse, with its blend of nature and nostalgia, felt like the perfect stage for the reunion that would bring their stories back to life.

An unexpected surge of emotions welled up within Anu. Bangalore, the city that had cradled their friendship and love, was more than just a backdrop to their youth. It was the place where they'd stumbled and soared, where memories had been born and preserved. The reunion at the farmhouse was like a pilgrimage—a return to the origins of their most cherished moments, a journey into the heart of the bonds they had built.

Memory, Anu thought, was the architect of their lives. It had shaped them into who they were, each moment like a brushstroke in the painting of their shared existence. It was both a gift and a trap, freeing them with cherished revisits while holding them captive in nostalgic mazes, constantly urging them to reflect on what had truly endured through time.

Her eyes landed on a large framed photo near the front yard. It was an image frozen in time from #Akrush's wedding, a day that had held immense sentimental value for all of them. The photo captured the smiles, the poses, and the pure joy of that day—a reminder of the unbreakable bond that had only grown stronger with the passing years.

"I fall for you again, dude," Mann continued, his eyes fixed on Dev, who was clearly relishing the attention. Dev, standing there in awe of his friends' reactions, didn't seem to notice the playful affection directed at him.

Anu, pulled back into the present by Mann's comment, couldn't help but laugh. She marveled at Dev's uncanny ability to be the center of attention, even when he was just soaking in the astonishment of his friends.

"Wait, what did I do?" Dev asked, his eyebrows raised in genuine confusion, his innocent expression adding to the charm of the moment.

"Don't tell me you didn't plan this whole reunion," Manan asked, a teasing suspicion in his voice. His eyebrows were arched, challenging Dev with a playful accusation.

"No, man! He didn't. In fact, we thought it was your clandestine operation," Anu interjected, her voice light with a mischievous tone, a sparkle in her eye as she joined the teasing.

"No, I didn't," Manan protested, raising his hands in mock surrender as though fending off the accusations. "Whatever it may be, let's leave it. We're here now; let's enjoy it."

The conversation hung in the air, charged with a mixture of playful mystery and excitement. As they all tried to figure out who orchestrated the surprise reunion, the mystery became part of the fun. No one seemed to mind the unanswered question; the joy of being together again and the laughter that filled the air were enough to make the unknown feel like an extra gift.

"Dev, darling," Manan teased, a mischievous grin spreading across his face. He leaned toward Dev, his smile practically radiating with the potential for mischief.

"You rascal, forget it! Don't come near me. You're still the same," Dev responded with mock exasperation, his hands raised as if defending himself from an impending prank.

Roy, watching the exchange, couldn't help but add his own lighthearted comment. "You two are like a comedy duo, seriously," he chuckled, shaking his head. "You never fail to entertain."

Anu, unable to resist the playful energy between them, turned to Manan, her eyes sparkling with amusement. "Just for once, okay? It's been so long."

Manan, seizing the moment, turned to Anu as if asking for permission, his face lighting up with mock sincerity. "You heard her. I have official consent!"

Dev's eyes widened in exaggerated horror, and he immediately recoiled. "No, dude. I'll never allow you to kiss me. I don't want my face covered in your saliva... uhhhhh..." He made a dramatic gesture, raising his hands to ward off the impending kiss, adding another layer of humor to the unfolding scene.

Anu chuckled, watching their antics. "You two are impossible."

Manan just winked, pulling back with a laugh. "Next time, my friend. Next time." The air was thick with the easy camaraderie of old friends, the kind that only time and shared memories can create.

Laughter echoed around the farmhouse as the trio continued their playful exchange, their banter creating a light-hearted atmosphere that felt like a scene straight out of a sitcom. The playful dance of teasing and jokes spread through the air, and soon everyone was caught up in the infectious joy of the moment. Manan's failed attempt at a kiss became the highlight, drawing laughter from all corners, adding a layer of warmth to the reunion.

Anu, still standing at the entrance, holding her handbag, watched with a fond smile. The sight of her friends laughing and enjoying each other's company stirred something deep within her. A mix of excitement and nervousness fluttered in her chest, like butterflies in a garden of anticipation, as if this moment meant more than she was willing to admit.

"Well, it seems like everything will be alright," she whispered softly to herself, offering a silent pep talk, her eyes scanning the scene before her. The laughter, the camaraderie, the unmistakable energy of friendship rekindled—it was all around her, filling her with a warmth that made her heart swell.

As Manan continued to tease Dev, Anu's smile deepened. There was a profound sense of gratitude bubbling up inside her for the friends who had become family. She marveled at how their shared history had weathered the test of time and how, despite everything, this moment felt like a beautiful continuation of what they had always shared.

"Come on, Anu, it's just a reunion," she chuckled softly to herself, trying to downplay the significance of the gathering as a casual get-together. But in truth, deep down, she couldn't shake the desire for this to be something more—something memorable, something that would stay with them forever.

Her inner dialogue continued quietly, like a comforting mantra: *Remember, it's about the joy of reconnecting, the laughter shared, and the memories made anew.* She reminded herself to stay grounded in the present, to savor the moment, and to let go of any unnecessary expectations.

With a final nod to herself, Anu took a deep breath and stepped forward. Her heart was open, ready to embrace the warmth of old friendships and the promise of new memories. The playful banter between her friends played in the background, a soundtrack to her hopes, as she moved into the heart of the reunion. No matter what, this day would mark a new chapter in their lives—a chapter she hoped they'd fondly revisit for years to come.

Finally, after a series of comical attempts, Mann managed to catch Dev, his arms wrapping around him in a playful but determined hold. With a flourish, he planted a quick, theatrical kiss on Dev's cheek, drawing a loud gasp from the group.

"You bastard! How can you enjoy without me?" Roy exclaimed, his voice dripping with exaggerated melodrama. He threw his hand over his heart, as if wounded by the betrayal, and joined in the theatrics, adding to the hilarity of the moment.

"Yep, me too," Anu chimed in, striking a dramatic pose of mock disappointment, her hand on her hip. "How dare you leave me out of this!

The group erupted into laughter as Mann feigned innocence, holding his hands up in mock defense. "What can I say? Dev's got that irresistible charm," he teased, clearly enjoying the playful chaos he'd stirred up.

The trio, now united in their antics, along with the reluctant but amused Dev, found themselves caught in a hilarious standoff—each one trying to outdo the other in their exaggerated gestures and witty remarks. The playful drama continued, the laughter only growing louder with every line.

Dev, who had been caught in the middle of it all, shook his head with mock frustration, but the mischievous twinkle in his eyes betrayed his enjoyment. "You guys are ridiculous," he muttered, though a smile tugged at the corners of his lips.

As the laughter finally settled down, the air around them seemed lighter, filled with the warmth of old jokes and shared moments. The playful rivalry was a reminder of the bond they had—one that could withstand time, distance, and, of course, the occasional theatrical kiss.

In the maze of life's challenges, friends serve as the comforting lights that illuminate the dark corners of our hearts. Their presence brings peace, their advice steers us through confusion, and their laughter makes every moment feel lighter. Through shared smiles, tears, and experiences, they prove that together, any storm can be weathered, and every obstacle can be overcome.

The four friends, caught in a moment of unexpected hilarity, erupted into laughter, their joy ringing through the air like music. Playful teasing and genuine smiles followed each of them as they hugged, celebrating the miracle of this reunion. The surprise kiss—though unwelcome to Dev—became the evening's comedic highlight, reminding them all how easily they could fall back into their easy camaraderie. It was a moment of pure laughter and unspoken understanding that had only strengthened their bond.

"So, let's get in and freshen up. Meanwhile, I'll arrange some snacks for you," Manan suggested, his voice casual, yet brimming with the warmth of a true host. His hospitality was contagious, drawing everyone into the rhythm of the evening with an effortless charm.

As they moved indoors, Roy, ever observant, noticed Anu's distracted demeanor and couldn't help but ask, "Anu, is everything alright? Where did you disappear to?" His question cut through the fog of her thoughts, pulling her back into the present.

"Oh, yeah, all good," Anu replied, her voice quick, her words synchronized with Roy's as though his curiosity had hit the pause button on her internal monologue. She gave him a quick smile, grateful for the distraction that grounded her back to reality.

The group continued to head inside, leaving Anu's momentary lapse of attention behind. Little did she know, in the heart of their reunion, surprises and distractions were waiting, just around the corner.

"Don't worry; everyone will join us. Have patience," Dev murmured in a hushed tone, his concern for Anu's well-being evident in his eyes. He placed a reassuring hand on her shoulder, grounding her with his steady presence.

"I hope so," Anu responded, offering a smile that was more out of appreciation than conviction. The warmth in Dev's voice soothed her nerves, easing the subtle unease that had quietly lingered within her. In that brief exchange, the unspoken comfort between them spoke volumes, reaffirming the deep, quiet understanding they shared. As the reunion continued, Anu felt herself settle into the familiar rhythm of her friends' company, ready to embrace whatever this evening would bring.

ppp

A soft, melodic voice drifted into the room, its smooth cadence wrapping around their hearts like a familiar blanket. The voice echoed through the air, setting the perfect mood for a reunion, evoking both nostalgia and mystery.

"I guess it's Rishi," Roy said, narrowing his eyes, an amused smirk tugging at his lips. "Who else could make an entrance like that?"

Anu's eyes lit up instantly, a burst of recognition making her heart race with anticipation. "Yep, that's him," she responded, her voice teasing yet warm, laced with the excitement of their long-awaited reunion. "Only Rishi could make a cryptic, poetic entrance like that."

The familiar voice sent a ripple of energy through the group, igniting curiosity and excitement as everyone turned their attention toward the door. The playful air thickened with anticipation, like waiting for the curtain to rise on a grand performance.

Manan wasted no time. "He's here!" he yelled, his voice almost breaking with excitement as he ran toward the door. His movements were dramatic, as if the arrival of Rishi was nothing short of a grand event. His energy was contagious, making everyone feel the rush of nostalgia and joy at the same time.

The door swung open with a flourish, and there he was—Rishi, standing with an almost smug smile, his presence commanding the room as if he'd just walked off a stage. "Ah, the long-awaited reunion," he announced theatrically, his voice dripping with charm. "You've all missed me, haven't you?"

Manan practically tackled him into a bear hug. "Of course we have, you drama king!" he laughed, pulling Rishi into the fold of the group.

Anu couldn't help but grin, but there was a subtle shift in her expression—an almost imperceptible flicker of something else. As the group welcomed Rishi with the usual warm banter, she stood back for a moment, watching the exchange. There was a flood of emotions swirling inside her, a cocktail of excitement and a touch of anxiety. Everything seemed to be falling into place, yet there was a sense of something left unspoken in the air—an unspoken tension that hung there just beneath the surface.

As laughter echoed around her, Rishi slipped into the group with his usual flair. "It's good to be back, but can we get to the fun part?" he quipped, flashing his signature mischievous grin.

Everyone's laughter filled the room, yet Anu couldn't shake the feeling that there was more to this reunion than the laughter and lighthearted moments. Maybe it was the familiarity of it all, or maybe it was just the anticipation of the night ahead, but there was a strange energy she couldn't quite place.

Manan, ever the life of the party, noticed Anu's distracted look. "Hey, you alright?" he asked, his tone softer than usual, his gaze filled with concern as he gave her a nudge.

Anu blinked, snapping back into the moment. "Oh, yeah. Just a bit lost in thought," she smiled quickly, brushing off the undercurrent of unease that had crept up on her. "It's just... so much happening all at once."

Roy, watching her closely, leaned in and whispered, "You sure? It's been a while, and I know you better than that. Something's on your mind."

She turned to him, her gaze meeting his with a flicker of vulnerability. There was something in Roy's eyes—an understanding that no one else seemed to notice. "I'm fine. Really," she said, her smile a little too tight. "I'm just... trying to catch up with everything."

Rishi, overhearing the conversation, turned towards them with his signature cheeky grin. "What, are we getting too serious here? Come on, it's a reunion, not a therapy session." His attempt to lighten the mood worked, but Anu's mind remained clouded for just a moment longer.

Manan, ever the source of energy, clapped his hands loudly. "Alright, alright. Enough with the brooding. We're here to have fun, people! Let's get to the food, the drinks, and the good times."

As the group moved toward the living room, ready to continue the evening, the playful banter and teasing quickly filled the air again. The tension from before began to dissolve, replaced by the familiar rhythm of their camaraderie. The night was far from over, and even though Anu couldn't shake the tiny spark of unease inside her, she knew that the friends around her would make it worth it.

The sound of laughter grew louder, and as the night stretched on, Anu couldn't help but feel that, despite everything, this reunion would be one to remember—not just for the joy, but for the way it pulled them all together, like magnets drawn to the center of something bigger than themselves.

ppp

Rishi Mehra, the enigmatic poet of the group, was more than just a figure who stood tall at six feet with broad shoulders—he was a walking enigma. His presence alone commanded attention, but it was his deep, dark brown eyes that truly captured the essence of his soul. Those eyes, dark and profound, spoke of untold stories, of silent musings and emotions that went beyond words. There was a depth in them that seemed to understand what others couldn't articulate, offering silent comfort to those who caught their gaze.

His brown hair, a shade that matched the intensity of his eyes, fell in gentle waves and was usually tied back into a loose ponytail. It wasn't just for convenience—his hairstyle had a quiet elegance, almost as if it had been crafted to mirror the flow of his thoughts. His hair, like his eyes, seemed to hide secrets—whispered tales of poetry and moments of solitude. It gave him an air of mystery, one that was both inviting and elusive at once.

Rishi's attire often consisted of long kurtas with intricate patterns that seemed timeless yet effortlessly stylish. Each thread in the embroidery, each stitch, seemed to carry the weight of his contemplative nature. It wasn't just clothing; it was a reflection of his soul—a delicate balance of modernity and heritage, much like the man himself. His attire felt like an extension of his thoughts, flowing with ease and grace, never too loud but always noticed by those who understood the subtleties.

But what truly set Rishi apart was his dual life—a scientist by day, poet by night. To some, it might have seemed like an odd juxtaposition, but for Rishi, it was the perfect balance. As a researcher, he navigated the world of logic, facts, and formulas. But when the day's work was done, he dove into the realm of poetry, where logic and creativity merged. His words flowed effortlessly, reflecting his ability to explore both the tangible and the abstract with equal ease. He was a man of intellect, but his heart and soul danced to the rhythm of words.

The group's laughter would often fill the room, but in the quiet moments, when the noise softened, it was Rishi's voice that brought a different kind of depth. His shayaris—those beautifully crafted verses—became windows into his soul, showing a side of him that few could understand but many felt deeply. Each line, each metaphor, was carefully thought out, like an artist painting emotions with words. He didn't just speak; he gave voice to the unsaid, to the unspoken truths that lingered in the silence.

As Rishi entered the reunion with his signature charm, there was a palpable sense of anticipation in the air. The group couldn't help but wonder: what emotions would he unveil this time? What mystery would he unravel through his verses? Rishi was not just a poet to them—he was the silent observer, the one who could read between the lines of their conversations and bring hidden emotions to the surface.

Even as laughter echoed around the room, there was an undercurrent of intrigue, a quiet curiosity about what he might say next. What would Rishi's presence bring to this reunion? His very existence seemed to add an element of suspense to the gathering. With every word, every gesture, he was not just a friend; he was a key to unlocking the unexplored depths of their hearts and minds, leaving them wondering what truths were yet to be uncovered.

In the midst of the chaos and joy of the reunion, Rishi stood as a reminder that sometimes, the most powerful moments weren't in the laughter but in the spaces between, where silence and words collided in perfect harmony.

ϼϼϼ

As Anu sliced vegetables with practiced ease, her mind couldn't shake the growing curiosity that had been simmering since the reunion began. She stole a glance at Manan, who was stirring a pot with a casual rhythm, seemingly at ease in his own space. The question she had been holding back finally bubbled to the surface.

"Manan," she began, her tone light but with an undercurrent of suspicion, "I've been thinking... If you're not the one who planned this reunion, then why are we here at your farmhouse? I mean, of all places, why this one?"

Manan glanced at her, eyebrows raised in mock offense. "Whoa, are you interrogating me now? First, Dev, and now me? What's next—an investigation committee?"

Anu rolled her eyes, not letting him off so easily. "Come on, Manan. Seriously, think about it. If it wasn't you, who else would pick your farmhouse? It's just too convenient. And knowing you, this seems like something you'd do—pulling off a grand gesture and then acting all innocent about it."

Manan chuckled, shaking his head as he turned his attention back to the pot. "I swear on my precious farmhouse, Anu, it wasn't me. I didn't plan this. Honestly, I thought it was Dev's doing until he started denying it too."

"But why your farmhouse then?" Anu pressed, her eyes narrowing. "It doesn't add up. You're the only one with a place like this—spacious, private, perfect for a reunion. It's like the stars aligned too perfectly. Admit it, Manan. You're hiding something."

Manan sighed dramatically, placing the spoon down with exaggerated defeat. "Okay, fine, Sherlock. You've caught me—except, you haven't. I'll tell you the truth." He leaned against the counter, crossing his arms. "I got an email about two weeks ago. It was from none other than the Director of our college."

Anu blinked, caught off guard. "The Director? What did it say?"

Manan nodded, a small smirk playing on his lips at her reaction. "It was a polite, formal request. Apparently, someone reached out to him, suggesting my farmhouse as the ideal location for the reunion. He said it would be a meaningful way to reconnect and relive our college memories. Honestly, I couldn't say no to that."

Anu tilted her head, her brow furrowed. "But why would the Director get involved? And who would suggest your farmhouse?"

"That," Manan replied, his voice carrying a hint of intrigue, "is the million-dollar question. I have no clue who planted the idea, but the email was legit. It even had the college's official seal and everything. So, I figured, why not? It sounded like a good idea, and I didn't want to disappoint anyone."

Anu's eyes narrowed further, suspicion still lingering. "You expect me to believe that? It's just a coincidence that someone thought of your farmhouse? No strings attached?"

"Believe what you want," Manan said with a shrug, picking up the spoon again. "But if you ask me, whoever planned this did a fantastic job. Look around, Anu. Everyone's here, laughing, reconnecting, having a great time. Does it really matter who the mastermind is?"

Anu sighed, a reluctant smile tugging at her lips. "You're annoyingly good at dodging questions, you know that?"

Manan grinned, his signature mischievous glint returning to his eyes. "It's a talent, I admit. But seriously, Anu, let it go. Whoever planned this reunion wanted it to be special for all of us. Let's just enjoy it."

Anu shook her head, still not entirely convinced but willing to let the matter rest—for now. "Fine. But if I find out you're lying, Manan, I'm coming for you."

"Noted," Manan replied, holding up his hands in mock surrender. "Now, can we focus on finishing these snacks before everyone starts a hunger strike?"

With a playful roll of her eyes, Anu returned to her task, the playful banter lightening the atmosphere. Yet, deep down, she couldn't help but wonder about the mysterious planner. If not Manan, then who?

🍃🍃🍃

As the conversation shifted between fun and serious moments, Anu decided to change the topic. "Snacks are ready," she said, walking into the hall with Manan following behind her, carrying a tray of samosas.

This small change in focus brought a sense of comfort, reminding everyone to enjoy the present. Anu's announcement wasn't just about snacks; it was a way to let go of worries, even if just for a little while.

At the dining table, the smell of fresh samosas filled the air as everyone grabbed their plates. The mood lightened as they started chatting and teasing each other like old times.

"So, who's still single here?" Roy teased, throwing a playful look at Anu. "Any new crushes we should know about?"

Anu rolled her eyes. "Maybe we're all too busy being married to our work, Roy. Ever think of that?"

Rishi, ever the poet, added with a smile, "Married to dreams, tied to schemes, living the bachelor's dream—or so it seems." His playful rhyme earned a round of laughter.

Manan, grinning mischievously, pointed his samosa at Dev. "What about you, Dev? Any updates on your love life?"

Dev smirked and leaned back in his chair. "Love is like Wi-Fi—you can't see it, but you sure know when it's not working." His quick wit made everyone burst into laughter.

As the laughter settled, Roy asked, "What about Aakrush? When are they getting here?"

"Maybe tonight," Dev replied, sounding unsure. He quickly tried to steer the conversation away.

Rishi, not one to miss a chance, asked, "And Aahana?"

Dev stood up suddenly, clearly trying to escape the questioning. "Excuse me, I've got an important call to make," he said, walking out of the room.

Roy raised an eyebrow, amused. "Well, that was smooth," he said, chuckling as Dev disappeared. Turning to the rest, he continued, "But don't think I'm letting you all off the hook so easily!"

Anu sighed, shaking her head. "Roy, why are you like this?"

"Because someone has to keep things interesting," Roy shot back with a wink. Then, with mock seriousness, he leaned toward Rishi. "Tell me, Rishi, is there a muse behind all that poetry? Some secret love story we don't know about?"

Rishi chuckled, shaking his head. "A poet's muse isn't always a person, my friend. Sometimes it's the silence, the stars, or even a plate of samosas."

Manan, chewing on yet another samosa, raised his hand. "I'll take the title of your muse for these samosas. They deserve all the credit!"

"Manan," Anu began, leaning toward him with a sly grin, "if samosas are your true love, does that mean we should expect a wedding invite soon? I'll bring chutney as a gift."

Manan chuckled, shaking his head. "Don't be ridiculous. I could never settle for just one flavor. I need variety in my life."

"Ah, so you're a flirt even with your food," Rishi teased, taking a sip of his coffee. His poetic tone made even his jabs sound lyrical. "The man who cannot commit to a samosa—is there hope for him in love?"

"Why do I feel like I'm under trial here?" Manan retorted, holding up his samosa defensively. "Can't a guy just enjoy his snack in peace?"

Anu smirked, taking another bite of her plate of snacks. "Fine, we'll let you off the hook—for now."

The group settled into a moment of comfortable silence, savoring the food and the company. But Anu wasn't one to let sleeping dogs lie. She glanced sideways at Manan, her tone casual but her intent sharp.

"Alright, alright," Anu relented, laughing along with him. "But don't think you're off the hook entirely."

As the conversation shifted back to lighter topics, the atmosphere around the table remained charged with a mix of curiosity and camaraderie. Despite Manan's denial, the mystery of the reunion's mastermind lingered, casting an intriguing shadow over their otherwise joyous gathering.

"Fair enough," Roy said, laughing. Then he turned back to Anu. "And you, madam? What's the deal? Any workplace romances we should know about?"

Anu narrowed her eyes at him, her tone playful but firm. "Roy, if I ever date anyone, you'll be the last to know. You'd turn it into an episode of a reality show."

The table erupted in laughter, the camaraderie flowing freely now. Despite Dev's escape, the group continued their lighthearted banter, their bonds evident in the ease with which they teased each other.

For now, the mood was cheerful, with the playful banter keeping everyone entertained. But Anu still couldn't shake the feeling that under all the laughter, there were stories yet to be told.

At 8 o'clock, Rishi sat alone in his room, the warm glow of his desk lamp creating a quiet, cozy atmosphere. By the window, he seemed almost like a silhouette against the night, lost in his thoughts.

His pen hovered near his lips as he toyed with it, a habit he'd picked up during long writing sessions. An open diary lay before him, its blank pages waiting to hold his emotions. A steaming cup of coffee rested nearby, its comforting aroma filling the still air.

As Rishi scribbled a few lines, his pen came to an abrupt halt. His gaze shifted out the window, his expression frozen in surprise. His jaw slackened as he caught sight of a figure stepping out of a car parked below.

It was Maher.

The sight of her sent a jolt through him, his heart pounding with a mix of astonishment and curiosity. For a moment, time seemed to pause, the pen in his hand poised midair as if the moment itself demanded to be absorbed.

Maher stepped into view like a vision, her presence under the soft glow of the streetlights carrying an almost magical quality. She wore a canary yellow kurti that flowed gracefully, paired with rich maroon pants. The vibrant colors seemed to dance in harmony with her movements, capturing the beauty of the night around her.

Her nude lipstick highlighted the soft curves of her lips, a perfect touch of elegance. The fine lines of her eyeliner framed her almond-shaped eyes, making them impossible to ignore. They sparkled with an enigmatic depth, as though they held stories only she could tell.

To Rishi, Maher wasn't just stunning—she was mesmerizing, her every step radiating confidence and charm. The yellow of her kurti seemed to mirror her lively spirit, while the maroon pants added a quiet sophistication to her look.

Rishi watched, captivated. In that moment, she was more than a person—she was a vision of grace, a blend of poetry and reality that left him spellbound.

The quiet of the room was replaced by the quiet storm within him, emotions he couldn't yet name stirring in his chest. Maher's arrival wasn't just unexpected; it felt like the beginning of a story that had been waiting to unfold.

ԲԲԲ

6

The Weight of Words, the Light of Presence

Aarush had just arrived, stepping out of the car with the weight of the world on his shoulders. The others watched in silence, unsure of what to say, unsure if they should even approach him. He didn't look around, didn't acknowledge anyone. Without a word, he made a beeline for his room, the door closing behind him with a quiet finality.

The rest of the group stood in the living room, exchanging glances but not daring to speak. There was an unspoken understanding between them, a collective hesitation in the air. Aksha was not with him, and no one had the courage to ask why. Not now, not when the tension was so thick, and the situation so fragile.

"Should we...?" Roy began, but the words trailed off, swallowed by the silence that enveloped them.

Manan, who was usually quick with a joke or a retort, remained quiet. He stole a glance at Anu, who seemed just as lost in thought. The absence of Aksha hung over them, a shadow no one could ignore, yet no one dared to address.

"Let him be," Anu finally said, her voice soft but firm. "He's not ready to talk about it, not yet."

They all knew the weight Aarush was carrying, even if they didn't fully understand the depth of it. But the absence of Aksha, the unspoken hurt, was something too personal to discuss, something that only time and patience would unravel.

With a deep sigh, the group quietly moved away from the door to Aarush's room, each of them lost in their own thoughts, the evening's atmosphere shifting to one of muted understanding. They didn't have answers, but they all shared the same silent hope—that Aarush would find his way out of this pain, in his own time, in his own way.

���

Aarush's voice, thick with frustration, echoed through the room as he paced, unable to hold back. "What the hell? I'm on freaking leave. Don't you get that? Handle it yourself!" He ran a hand through his hair, his agitation turning the air in the room heavy.

"This is ridiculous! Gupta's in charge of this department. Why do they keep dragging me into this mess?" His words were sharp, each one more forceful than the last, as if yelling at the phone could somehow solve his problems.

The voice on the other end was offering excuses, but Aarush wasn't having any of it. "No, I won't tolerate this anymore. I need my space. I need a break. Just handle it without me for once!" The intensity of his frustration cracked through the tension, and when he slammed the phone down, it felt like the room itself took a deep breath.

The weight of his words hung in the air as Aarush continued to pace, his steps fast and restless, each one a sign of the storm inside him. At the door, Dev watched, his face a mix of concern and helplessness. He turned to Anu, his voice low, "My friend is in pain, and I can't do a damn thing to help him. I feel so useless."

Anu, leaning against the doorframe, shared his worry but tried to offer some perspective. "Don't worry, Dev. Yeah, he's struggling, but more than anything, he's missing her—Aksha. Can't you see? He can't live without her."

Dev sighed, helplessness creeping into his tone. "I wish I could fix this for him."

Anu's hand found his shoulder, a silent gesture of reassurance. "Sometimes, just being there for someone is enough. We're his friends. Our support means more than we realize."

They stood there together, watching Aarush in the throes of his frustration, both of them hoping their silent presence could bring him the comfort he needed.

The tension in the room was palpable, thick enough that it almost felt like a physical presence. Aarush's anger seemed to hang in the air, unanswered questions swirling around him. But in the quiet exchange between Dev and Anu, there was an understanding—one that transcended words.

Anu whispered, her voice soft but certain, "This is what makes us different, Dev. What we have, it's not just friendship. It's a bond that can bear the weight of our struggles."

Dev nodded, his gaze fixed on Aarush. "You're right. We might not have the answers, but just being here for each other—that's enough. It makes all the difference."

Aarush's room reflected the storm he was living through. His things were scattered everywhere, a chaotic mess that looked like the aftermath of a battle—a physical manifestation of the inner turmoil tearing at him. His open bag on the bed lay like an offering to the chaos, a symbol of everything he was trying to sort through.

Standing in the middle of it all, Aarush stared at the disarray, his eyes unfocused, as if searching for something in the clutter. One hand rested on his waist, the other on his head, mirroring the confusion that churned inside him. His sanctuary, once a place of comfort, now seemed to reflect the turmoil in his mind.

Every item strewn across the room was a part of the struggle, a reminder of the loneliness that threatened to consume him. Surrounded by the remnants of his life, Aarush felt the weight of separation, the sting of distance, and the loneliness that crept in like a shadow. Each misplaced belonging seemed to echo the emotional chaos that raged in his heart.

Amid the mess, Aarush's room mirrored the storm raging inside him. His belongings were scattered everywhere, making the place look like the aftermath of a whirlwind—just like his emotions. His open bag on the bed seemed like a silent testament to everything that had just fallen apart.

Standing in the middle of the chaos, Aarush couldn't tear his eyes away from the mess on the bed. It felt like his life had been strewn across the room. One hand was resting on his waist, the other rubbing his forehead, as if trying to clear the confusion clouding his mind. What was once his personal space—his sanctuary—now seemed to reflect the emotional turmoil he couldn't escape.

Every single item scattered around told a story of struggle. His fight against the crushing loneliness that felt like it was swallowing him whole. The remnants of his life were all around him, but they only seemed to amplify the pain of separation. Each object seemed to echo the emptiness he felt inside.

"Why, Ashu?" Aarush's voice broke through the silence, thick with frustration and a deep sense of betrayal. "I told you, we could've planned something else if the reunion wasn't what you wanted. Hell, I even booked the tickets." He paused, his breath catching. "You were the one who brought up the idea last night. How do you just change your mind like that? Why leave me stuck in this mess with no way out? You shouldn't have done this to me."

The room was still after his outburst, like everything had frozen in place. The weight of unmet expectations hung heavy in the air, as Aarush stood amidst the wreckage of plans he'd carefully put together, feeling the sting of a moment slipping through his fingers.

ᗡᗡᗡ

Same day in the afternoon.....

"Hey, babs!!! How long will you take? We've got a flight at 4 PM, remember?" Aarush asked, fresh out of a meeting, dialing Aksha's number directly.

"Yes, darling! Just a few more minutes," Aksha replied. Aarush gestured to his colleagues, signaling them to hand over her files to Mr. Shah. "How's your conference going?" she asked.

"Too good, babe! Just heading to the airport now," he said, clearly in a hurry.

"I'll be at your place in fifteen minutes. Be ready," she told him.

"No, listen! I might not be free. Don't worry about me. You go ahead; I'll catch up with you there," she insisted.

"No, I can wait for you," he responded, determined.

"Mr. Perfect, thanks for your concern, but I can drive safely. Don't worry about me," she reassured him.

"Mrs. Perfect, I think our trip to the airport will be better if we go together," he teased.

"It's my order," she said, her tone playful.

"I give up!!! Okay, see you at the airport," he laughed, giving in.

"You better be there!" she responded, pulling his leg.

"I love you," he said softly, his voice filled with warmth.

"I love you too," she reciprocated, her words echoing the deep affection they shared.

On the way to the airport, Aarush dialed Aksha's number multiple times, his anxiety rising with each unanswered call. Finally, she picked up, and before she could speak, he burst out, "Come on, babes! Where are you? Why aren't you answering? Did you leave for the airport? When will you get here? We need to check in, dear."

"Take a breath, man," Aksha's voice was calm and steady. "There's a note in the front pocket of your bag. Read it, and you'll have all the answers."

Confused and still on edge, Aarush replied, "I don't get what you mean. I'm here waiting—please just come."

"First, read the note," she said, a hint of patience in her voice.

"Stop beating around the bush, Aksha. Just tell me straight, what's going on?" Aarush asked, frustration creeping into his voice.

"I can't explain it right now. So I wrote a note for you. Have a safe journey. Call me when you get there. I love you. I'll miss you." With that, she disconnected the call.

Aarush stood frozen, staring at his phone, the screen blank except for his unanswered calls. The worry that had already been gnawing at him intensified. His forehead creased with concern, his heart heavy with confusion. With every attempt to reach her, the emptiness inside him deepened. He missed her more than words could capture, and the silence that followed each call seemed to magnify the distance between them.

"Where are you? What's happening? I miss you," he thought, his emotions tangled in a knot of longing and disbelief.

"*My Dearest Aarush,*

I hope this note reaches you in the midst of the excitement of your journey to the reunion. There's something on my heart that I need to share with you, and it's not easy for me to put into words.

First and foremost, I want you to know that my love for you is as strong and unwavering as ever. This decision isn't about any lack of love or commitment to us; it's about something deeper, something I didn't expect when we first planned to go to the reunion together.

As much as I wish I could be there with you and celebrate with the Ninjas, a wave of doubt and hesitation has settled in me. It's not that I don't want to be with you, it's just that I've found myself grappling with emotions I didn't anticipate. I realize now that my presence at the reunion might stir feelings that could disrupt the balance of our close-knit group, something I never wanted.

The Ninjas are so important to us, and I hold each one of them dear. For the sake of preserving the harmony we all share, I've made the difficult decision to step back and not attend the reunion. This was not an easy choice, and my heart aches knowing that I won't be there with you, or with all our friends.

I understand how much this gathering means to you and to everyone. Please know that my absence doesn't reflect a lack of love or affection. It's simply me trying to work through the emotions that have surfaced unexpectedly.

I believe in the strength of our love, Aarush. We've overcome so much, and I know we will continue to. I hope you'll understand why I've made this decision and will continue to cherish the bond we share. I'll miss you more than words can express, and even though I'm not there, my heart and thoughts will be with you and the Ninja 9.

Enjoy the reunion. Make beautiful memories, and remember that no distance will change my love for you.

Forever Yours,

Aksha **"**

The note held him captive, every word pulling him deeper into a whirlpool of emotions. As he read Aksha's message, he could feel her pain, her love, and the weight of her decision pressing against his chest. The repetition of her apologies—"Sorry... sorry... sorry..."—echoed in his mind like a haunting melody, each repetition heavier than the last, marking the depth of her regret.

Her words, though filled with sorrow, also carried a sweetness, a love that shone through the sadness. Aksha's raw honesty was evident in every line. She admitted to her initial selfishness and, in doing so, showed the courage it took to confront her own heart and mind. She wasn't just apologizing for not being there; she was sharing a vulnerable part of herself, a side of her he had never seen so openly before.

Her struggle was palpable—caught between her feelings and the responsibility she felt toward their friendship and the group. She didn't want to disrupt the balance, didn't want to be the source of any strain among them. Aarush could feel the weight of that decision, the internal battle she'd fought before choosing this path, and it touched him more deeply than he could have imagined.

With a quiet sigh, he carefully folded the note, slipping it back into his bag, her words still echoing in his heart. He silently accepted her decision, his own emotions tangled and complex. As he went through the motions of checking in for the flight, her absence settled over him like a thick fog. The journey ahead, though exciting, felt strangely empty now, and he could only hope that time would ease the ache in his chest. The words she left behind, however, would stay with him, a bittersweet reminder of love, loss, and the strength it takes to make difficult choices.

ϷϷϷ

At present

Aarush rummaged through his things, his frustration mounting as he searched for something he couldn't seem to find. He was visibly tense, his thoughts entirely consumed by Aksha. Although he was physically present, his mind was elsewhere. His belongings were scattered across the room, a reflection of his disarray. He let himself collapse onto the bed, covering his face with his palms, the weight of everything pressing down on him.

"What's going on, man? Can I help you with something?" Dev entered the room, his eyes scanning the scene. Anu stood by the door, quietly observing, sensing the tension in the air.

"I'm fine," Aarush lied, though his voice lacked conviction.

"You're such a bad liar, man. Your face is giving everything away," Dev teased lightly, trying to break through the heaviness.

Aarush chuckled, but it was forced, a hollow sound. "Yeah, I'm just looking for some papers, but I can't remember where I put them," he said, still trying to avoid the truth of what he was really searching for—his passport, as he thought about leaving.

"You're searching for something important, aren't you?" Dev asked, his tone softening as he sat beside him.

Aarush sighed deeply, his shoulders slumping. "Yeah, I guess... I don't know." He let out a shaky breath, the words he'd been holding in for so long about to spill over.

Dev put a reassuring hand on his shoulder and gently tilted his chin up, forcing Aarush to meet his gaze. "Look, man, we're miles apart right now, but our hearts are still connected. You can tell me anything. Whatever's going on, I'm here for you. What's really bothering you? Talk to me."

Aarush felt a lump in his throat, and for the first time in a while, he couldn't hold back. His emotions came pouring out, desperate for someone to understand, someone to help carry this weight he'd been carrying alone for so long. He had always shared everything with Aksha—good times, bad times, joy and sorrow—but now, he needed his friends. He wanted to cry, to let it all out.

Gripping Dev's shoulder tightly, Aarush finally confessed, his voice breaking, "I lost her, man. I lost Aksha."

Dev blinked in surprise. "What? Come on, man, don't say that. Just because she didn't join us doesn't mean she's gone. She hasn't left you."

"No, it's more than that. I feel like I'm losing her. She's changed, Dev," Aarush said, his voice barely above a whisper. He paused, running his hand through his hair, trying to collect his thoughts. "She's not the same as she was before. She's... different."

Dev's brow furrowed in concern. "How? What do you mean?"

Aarush's words hung in the air, heavy with the truth he had been too afraid to voice. He couldn't hold it in anymore. "Aksha is... not the woman I fell in love with. Aahana is always on her mind. Her thoughts, her life—it all revolves around Aahana now. And I don't know where I fit into all of that anymore."

Dev was quiet for a moment, processing what Aarush had just said. He glanced at Anu, who had silently moved closer, offering Aarush a glass of water. She didn't say anything, but her presence was a silent support.

Aarush continued, his eyes glossed over with pain. "I know she loves me. She always will. But I can't deny it anymore, Dev. She doesn't look at me the way she used to. She doesn't care the same way. I'm not her everything anymore. Aahana is."

Dev took a deep breath, his voice calm and steady as he spoke. "Aarush, listen to me. Aksha is going through something. She's not just trying to push you away. You have to understand that her bond with Aahana is deep. Aahana isn't just a friend—she's her family. Losing her, especially the way she did, that's a pain Aksha needs to process on her own. You can't be the one to fix it."

Aarush shook his head, his chest tightening. "But what if she's never the same again? What if I've already lost her?"

Dev placed a hand on his back, giving him a moment to gather himself. "You haven't lost her, Aarush. Not yet. And not if you keep being there for her. I know it's tough, man, but sometimes the best thing you can do is give her space to figure things out. Love isn't about holding on so tight that you suffocate the other person. It's about letting them breathe, even if it hurts."

Aarush took a shaky breath, the words sinking in, but doubt still clouded his mind. "I just... I don't know how long I can wait, Dev. I'm scared that one day, I'll wake up and she won't be there. And I'll have nothing left."

Dev looked him in the eye, his voice firm and reassuring. "You won't lose her. Not if you keep being patient. Let her find her way back to you, and when she does, you'll both be stronger for it. Don't give up on her, Aarush. You're still her home, even if it doesn't feel that way right now."

Aarush nodded, his breath steadier now. He wasn't sure what the future held, but for the first time in days, he felt a flicker of hope. Maybe, just maybe, things could work out. All he had to do was trust that love wasn't a race—it was a journey.

"I'm trying, Dev. I really am," he whispered.

Dev gave him a small, encouraging smile. "And that's all you can do, man. I'm here for you. Always."

As Aarush sat back, the weight on his chest felt a little lighter. His journey wasn't over, but with his friends by his side, he could face whatever came next.

"Relax, man, everything will be alright," Anu reassured, her voice soft yet steady.

Dev gave a subtle nod, appreciating her words, though he knew just how tough it was to console a friend in such a situation.

"A true friend is the one who knows exactly when and where to step in, making their entrance at the perfect time," he murmured, acknowledging Anu's timing.

Aarush, his emotions raw, let out a heavy sigh. "She pretends to hate her, even though deep inside, she still loves her. She still waits for her to come back," he shared, his voice thick with pain.

Anu placed a gentle hand on his shoulder, trying to offer comfort. "Don't worry, Aarush. I won't say it won't hurt, but I know everything will be alright. It might take time, but it will settle."

Dev, ever the optimist, added, "Yes! Someone had the courage to bring all the Ninjas together. We'll gather more, and we'll bring our Aksha back."

Anu raised an eyebrow, a playful smirk forming. "Correction, *Aarush's* Aksha," she teased, lightening the mood.

Aarush gave a small, rueful smile. "Aksha will only come back if Aahana does," he nodded, acknowledging the bond that connected all of them.

Before they could continue, a voice chimed in from the doorway. "What's cooking here without me?"

They turned to see Manan, standing with his signature cheeky grin.

"Cooking up plans without the master chef himself," Dev quipped.

"Plans? Count me in! What are we plotting?" Manan's enthusiasm was infectious, and the air lightened immediately.

"We're trying to figure out how to bring Aksha back," Dev explained, his tone serious but hopeful.

"And Aahana," Aarush added, his voice tinged with sadness.

Manan, never one to shy away from humor, grinned widely. "Ah, the Ninja drama at its finest! I'm in for this rescue mission. Let's summon the Ninja Council!"

Dev laughed. "Rescue mission or a comedy show? Your involvement is always a bit... confusing."

Manan shrugged, unfazed. "Why not both? A little drama with a touch of comedy makes everything more interesting."

Anu couldn't help but smile at Manan's playful attitude, despite the heavy mood. Even in the darkest times, the Ninjas found comfort in each other's company. Their bond, full of wit, humor, and unwavering support, was something that could weather even the toughest storms.

ᗏᗏᗏ

Aarush, lost in his thoughts, felt a tap on his shoulder. Startled, he turned around to find Aksha standing there, her eyes reflecting concern. She crossed her arms over his chest, embracing him from behind, a silent gesture that spoke volumes.

"Ashu, you are like a hangover to me; I can't stop thinking about you. Can't you stop haunting me with illusions?" he muttered, his frustration evident.

Aksha, undeterred, gently tapped his shoulder again. "I am an illusion to you? I am irritating you?" she responded, her voice carrying a playful tone.

"Don't test my passion," he scowled, but this time, there was a softness in his eyes that revealed the underlying emotions.

Aarush, caught in the whirlwind of disbelief, implored Dev to pinch him, to confirm that this wasn't just another illusion concocted by his mind.

"OMG," he marveled when he realized she was real, standing right there. Without wasting a moment, he enveloped Aksha in his arms, pulling her into his lap with a tight hug. She responded, feeling the safety and warmth in his embrace.

"You'll crush me!" she giggled.

"I don't care," he declared, holding her even tighter around the waist.

"What a pleasant surprise! I never thought of that. I lost all hope when I read your letter," Aarush admitted, overwhelmed by the unexpected joy.

"Calm down, dear. I am here. Be happy. Don't count the seeds; just enjoy the fruit," she teased, playfully pinching his nose.

In that moment, the room echoed with laughter, breaking the tension that had gripped Aarush. Aksha's surprise visit became a beacon of light, dispelling the shadows of doubt and sadness that had clouded his mind.

"Anyways, let me give you the extended version of the story! Thanks to Dev, the unsung hero of the night. It was a call that turned my plans upside down. I was all set to pack my bags and head to my uncle's home for some solace, but there was no escaping Dev's relentless persuasion.

He dropped this wisdom bomb on me: *'Everyone faces a painfully transformative moment in their life. It's like a storm, but let it make you stronger, smarter, and kinder. Just don't let it change you into someone you're not. Feel free to cry, scream if you must. Then straighten out that crown, and keep moving forward.'"*

Aksha looked at Dev with gratitude and continued, "He believes, and I do too now, that you can't let the one who's with you suffer for the one who left you."

And there you have it, the tale of how Dev, armed with wisdom and persuasive skills, convinced Aksha to stay and face the storm with the Ninja 9.

"I can't express how delighted I am," Aarush replied, sealing his joy with a kiss on her forehead.

"Are we welcomed to spoil your romantic moment?" Anu teased as she entered the conversation and greeted Aksha.

"We are also here," Maher announced on behalf of Rishi,and Roy, as they joined the gathering.

"Oh, sorry, no! Please. We will not allow anyone," Aarush said playfully.

"Look at you, man! A crying baby turned into a roaring lion now," Roy remarked.

"Yes, I am a lion when my lioness is with me," Aarush responded.

"For your condition, I have something to share," said Rishi.

"Oh, come on, man, waiting for that," Maher urged.

"Ah, Rishi, my poetic friend, looks like I need to enroll in your shayari class. Your words always touch the heart, but mine are still figuring out the way," Maher chuckled, injecting a shayrana touch to his comment. Everyone laughed, appreciating the camaraderie and wit among the friends.

Maher's comments on his words send a sweet current through his body. Everyone appreciated him for sharing, but Maher's remarks stood out more than any other words. He decided to add his touch by expressing his thoughts in the form of a shayari.

Rishi, with a twinkle in his eyes, responded to Maher's playful challenge. "Ah, Maher, my friend, the art of shayari is like a river that flows through the soul. Let me guide you through its meandering paths."

As the evening continued, the friends gathered around, creating an impromptu poetry circle. Under the soft glow of the hanging lanterns, Rishi began to weave his words into a delicate tapestry of emotions. His shayaris touched upon the essence of friendship, the beauty of life, and the magic hidden in everyday moments.

ᐯᐯᐯ

As the moon bathed the night in its silver glow, Maher felt a sense of fulfillment settle over him. The poetry class had blossomed into something more than he had hoped for—a moment of shared emotions, of vulnerability, and of creative connection. The words they spoke lingered in the air, each one a brushstroke of their inner worlds. They had come together, not as poets, but as souls seeking to express the unsaid, finding solace in the beauty of language.

Rishi, standing quietly in the shadows, watched Maher with a soft, almost wistful smile. There was something about the way Maher spoke, something that touched a part of him that he rarely acknowledged. As the verses flowed, Rishi's heart stirred, a silent conversation playing out within him, one only he could hear. The moonlight cast a tender glow on Maher's face, and in that moment, Rishi felt an unspoken connection that went beyond words, a feeling that had always been there, quietly growing in the background of their friendship.

Rishi stood there, his heart full of unsaid words, a quiet ache nestled in his chest. His eyes lingered on Maher as he spoke, the shayari flowing effortlessly from his lips, each word carrying weight, beauty, and an undeniable truth that seemed to resonate with the very core of Rishi's being.

Maher, my dear Maher, Rishi thought, the words echoing in his mind. *You are like a beautiful song of emotions, and your words are the notes that flow straight from your soul. When you create shayari, it feels like you're writing poetry directly from your heart. Each verse reveals a piece of who you are, a piece I can't help but get lost in, like I'm caught in the music of your words.*

His gaze softened as he watched Maher, his heart swelling with admiration and a yearning he could barely put into words. *Your inner beauty is like a hidden treasure, shining through in the small moments, in your kindness, in the way your laughter brightens everything around you. It's not just the words you say, but the warmth in your eyes, the gentleness in your spirit, that makes the world seem softer, more beautiful.*

Rishi's thoughts grew tender, his chest tightening with emotion. *I love how you find beauty in the simplest things, and turn them into verses that touch our hearts. Maher, you are a canvas of feelings, and I want to explore the masterpiece that is your soul. Your honesty, the way you share your thoughts, your vulnerability, they captivate me in ways I can't explain.*

He closed his eyes for a moment, savoring the memory of Maher's shayari, the way it wove itself into the fabric of their lives, binding them all together. *When you recite shayari, I see a reflection of your true self, a reflection that moves me deeply. Your choice of words, the way you understand the human experience—it's a gift, Maher. I treasure those moments when you share a piece of your heart, when your laughter mixes with the verses, creating a melody that lingers long after.*

Rishi's breath caught as he watched Maher, his presence calming yet stirring something in him he wasn't quite ready to confront. *It's more than just poetry—it's a connection, an unspoken bond that brings us closer, drawing me in even when words fail me.*

As the lanterns flickered softly around them, casting gentle light over their group of friends, Rishi felt a sense of quiet admiration, a silent longing that he wasn't ready to share. *Maher, you are a mosaic of emotions, and I'm drawn to each piece of you, wanting to uncover the layers that make you who you are—unique and beautiful in every way.*

He looked up, his gaze meeting Maher's, his heart racing. *Maybe one day, in one of those quiet moments between verses and laughter, I'll find the courage to share the silent song in my heart. Until then, I'll keep admiring you from afar, enjoying the magic of your shayaris and the charm of your presence.*

Roy reached Aarush with a grin, only to have a pillow launched in his direction. The playful exchange was quick to escalate, and before long, a full-blown pillow fight was underway between the two. Laughter filled the air as they dodged and swiped at each other, their voices echoing through the room in cheerful chaos.

"Alright, let's capture this in a frame! Time for a romantic couple moment," Roy said with a teasing tone. He quickly adjusted his cellphone, ready to snap a picture—a snapshot of joy, one that marked the first photograph of their reunion after the #Akrush wedding.

As the camera clicked, the moment froze in time, a celebration of friendship and new beginnings. But as the group gathered for the shot, a quiet void lingered in the background. Aahana's absence was palpable, a silent ache that no one spoke aloud. Her presence was missed, her laughter, her warmth—but for this moment, no one wanted to let sadness in.

The smiles, although a little wistful, remained genuine. They were determined to hold onto the joy of their reunion, not allowing the absence of one to overshadow the happiness of the many. Each friend cherished the unity they had, the bond that tied them together, and the silent hope that one day, Aahana would be part of this picture too.

ΡΡΡ

7

Echoes of the Heart

As Aksha strolled leisurely in the backyard, her attention absorbed by her phone and earphones, the group of friends seated nearby engaged in a lively, teasing conversation.

Manan, wearing his signature mischievous grin, started the banter. "So, Aksha, how's Aarush holding up?"

Roy immediately seized the opportunity, chuckling, "Oh, come on! Who are you even asking? Hahaha. Aarush isn't the same anymore. He's *married* now."

Aarush, ever quick on his feet, shot back, "Oh, I see! And what about you, Roy? Where are *you* at in your tally?"

Feigning thoughtfulness, Roy responded confidently, "Hmm… 163. No, wait—164."

Rishi, his eyes wide with mock disbelief, exclaimed, "Seriously, man? Are you keeping count?"

Anu, who had just grabbed an apple from the basket and taken a seat next to Maher, added dryly, "Ask him again. He's probably still counting."

"Hahaha! You stole my thunder," Roy said, laughing at her quip. The air buzzed with laughter, the kind that made even the smallest moments feel electric, reinforcing their bond.

The banter took a sudden turn when Manan, always one to stir the pot, leaned forward with a sly grin. "Alright, but on a serious note… don't you think it's time to settle down, Roy? Maybe think about being 'fixed' for once?"

"Manan, don't!" Maher interjected softly, almost pleading.

Rishi turned toward her, confused. "What's wrong?"

Maher hesitated, her gaze flickering nervously between her friends. Her heart wrestled with the urge to shield her vulnerabilities and the comforting presence of those who genuinely cared. She finally settled on a middle ground, sighing deeply.

"It's just... the usual ups and downs," she said, her voice carefully measured. "Every marriage has its challenges. But we're working through them, and everything is fine."

The words felt rehearsed, but no one pressed further. The group allowed the moment to pass, silently vowing to be there for her, should she ever need them. The laughter and light-heartedness resumed eventually, but the lingering weight of unspoken truths hung in the air, a reminder of the complexities woven into even the closest friendships.

Hiding stuff from friends is like making a tricky puzzle. It's hard because it messes with the trust between you and your pals. Keeping a secret feels like carrying a heavy load, and it changes how you all get along. The more you hide, the more you have to pretend, and that's tiring. It's like wearing a mask instead of being yourself. True friendship is about being open and honest. Trying to keep things under wraps messes with the simple goodness of just being real with each other. It's like building a wall that can get in the way of what makes friendships strong.

Rishi, though not entirely convinced, chose to honor Maher's decision not to delve deeper. The conversation among the group shifted, buoyed by laughter and lighthearted jokes, but an undercurrent of concern lingered, unspoken yet palpable.

As the night wore on, Rishi found himself stealing glances at Maher. Her laughter seemed a touch too loud, her smiles lingering just a fraction too long—enough to betray the effort she put into maintaining her cheerful facade. The unease within him grew, refusing to be silenced.

Eventually, he found a quiet moment to pull Maher aside. The backyard was dimly lit, the distant hum of their friends' chatter providing a faint backdrop. "Maher," Rishi began gently, his voice low and sincere, "I know you said everything's fine, but I can sense there's more to it. If you ever need to talk—about anything—I'm here for you. No judgment, just friendship."

Maher paused, her expression softening as she met his gaze. For a brief moment, her carefully constructed walls seemed to waver. The vulnerability in her eyes spoke volumes, but she quickly masked it with a grateful smile. "Thanks, Rishi. That means a lot. I really appreciate it. But... everything is okay. Honestly. Let's not worry about it, okay?"

Rishi nodded, his lips curving into an understanding smile. He didn't push further, knowing the boundaries of trust and patience. "Alright," he said softly. "But the offer stands. Always."

As Maher walked back to rejoin the group, her shoulders straightened, and her laughter blended seamlessly with the others. But Rishi couldn't shake the feeling that beneath her reassuring words and radiant smile lay a story untold.

He watched her retreating figure, his thoughts swirling. The bond they shared, forged through years of friendship and countless memories, told him that sometimes, the heaviest battles were fought in silence, in the spaces between spoken words. And for those battles, he silently vowed to be there, whenever Maher was ready to let him in.

ᠹᠹᠹ

"Heey, Ashu!! Come and join us, darling," Aarush called out, his voice carrying across the gentle murmur of conversation.

"I'm fine here," Aksha replied, her tone calm but distant, her gaze fixed on the far horizon.

Maher leaned toward Aarush, her voice low but firm. "Give her some space; she'll come around in her own time."

"Yeah, Maher's right. Let her breathe, man," Dev chimed in, giving Aarush a reassuring pat on the back.

Aarush hesitated but eventually nodded. "Okay, okay! But I don't like seeing her like this."

"I'll go keep her company," Anu offered, her eyes following Aksha's lone figure. Her suggestion was met with approving nods.

"Great idea, Anu," Dev encouraged.

"Alright, you guys carry on!" Anu announced as she headed toward Aksha, determination in her stride.

ᗡᗡᗡ

The farmhouse backyard stretched out like a sanctuary beneath the starry sky. Aksha walked slowly, her hands tucked into her sweater pockets, earphones dangling around her neck. Anu caught up to her, matching her pace.

"Hey," Anu started softly, falling into step beside her. "Beautiful night, isn't it?"

Aksha glanced sideways, a faint smile brushing her lips. "It is. Peaceful."

They walked in silence for a moment, the crunch of gravel underfoot and the distant hum of crickets filling the air. A soft breeze rustled the leaves, carrying the scent of jasmine. Fireflies flitted around them, their tiny lights flickering like stars brought to earth.

"You seemed a little... off earlier," Anu ventured carefully. "Want to tell me what's on your mind?"

Aksha exhaled, her shoulders sagging slightly. "It's nothing, really. Just... life, I guess." Her voice wavered, betraying the emotions she was trying to suppress.

"Life?" Anu repeated gently. "That's a pretty broad topic. Care to narrow it down?"

Aksha chuckled softly, a bittersweet sound. "It's hard to put into words. There's this... weight, you know? Like I'm carrying something I can't quite figure out how to let go of."

Anu stopped and turned to face her. "Aksha, we've been friends long enough for me to know when you're trying to downplay things. If you're not ready to talk, that's okay. But don't carry it alone.

You've got us—you've got me."

Aksha looked at her, the moonlight catching the unshed tears glistening in her eyes. "It's just... everything feels different now. After Aahana... after all the changes. I thought I'd adjusted, but sometimes it's like I'm standing still while the world rushes past me."

Anu placed a comforting hand on Aksha's shoulder. "I can't imagine how hard it's been for you. But you're not standing still. You're figuring things out at your own pace, and that's okay. You don't have to rush."

"I know," Aksha whispered. "But sometimes, it feels like I'm letting Aarush down, or even myself. He's so patient, but I know he worries."

Anu gave her a warm smile. "That's because he loves you. And we all do, Aksha. Take the time you need. And whenever you're ready, we're here to listen, no matter how messy or complicated it gets."

Aksha smiled back, a genuine one this time, albeit small. "Thank you, Anu. That means a lot."

As they resumed walking, Anu continued, her tone lighter now, "By the way, Aarush was totally sulking when you didn't join us. You should've seen his face—like a kid who lost his candy."

Aksha laughed softly, the sound mingling with the rustling leaves. "That does sound like him."

"Well, he loves his 'candy,'" Anu teased, nudging her playfully. "But seriously, don't shut him out too much, okay? He's as much in this with you as you are."

"I'll try," Aksha promised. And for the first time that night, the weight on her chest felt just a little bit lighter.

As Aksha and Anu lingered under the canopy of the stars, their conversation gradually gave way to a comforting silence. The moonlight bathed them in its silver glow, and for the first time that night, Aksha felt a sense of peace she hadn't experienced in a while.

Anu broke the silence gently, her voice barely above a whisper. "You know, Aksha, sometimes I think the hardest part of missing someone is feeling like the world keeps moving, but you're still standing in the same place, holding on to their memory."

Aksha nodded, her fingers absentmindedly tracing patterns on the bench. "It's exactly that, Anu. Everyone expects you to heal, to move on, but how do you move on from someone who was such a big part of you?"

Anu placed a reassuring hand on Aksha's shoulder. "You don't have to move on, not entirely. I think it's about learning to carry them with you in a way that brings comfort, not pain. Aahana wouldn't want you to feel stuck, Aksha. She'd want you to live fully, with her spirit lighting your way."

Aksha's lips curved into a bittersweet smile. "You're right. She would have scolded me by now for wallowing, then dragged me off to do something ridiculous and fun."

Anu chuckled softly. "I can almost hear her now. 'Stop being such a drama queen, Aksha. Life's too short to waste on tears when there's mischief to be made!'"

The two shared a laugh, their shared memory of Aahana bridging the gap between grief and joy.

As they stood to leave, the sound of laughter and voices from the farmhouse reached them, grounding them back in the present. The warm light spilling from the windows and the faint hum of music painted a scene of life and togetherness.

Aksha squeezed Anu's arm, her voice soft but filled with gratitude. "Thank you, Anu. You've no idea how much that means to me."

The night carried on, the farmhouse alive with stories, laughter, and the unspoken understanding that their bond, like the stars above, was constant and unbreakable.

Their conversation naturally shifted to Anu's life, and a spark of joy lit up her expression. "I'm waiting for that promotion, and you better believe I'm throwing the most epic celebration when it happens!" Anu shared, her smile wide with anticipation.

Aksha chuckled, appreciating Anu's infectious enthusiasm. "You're amazing, Anu. Thanks for being here, for understanding," she said, her voice full of warmth.

As they continued their walk, the night wrapped around them in a quiet serenity, offering solace in the shared moments of vulnerability and strength that only true friendship can bring.

"You know, Anu, living in the same city as Dev is like winning the friendship lottery. You get all the benefits without any shipping charges!" Aksha teased, winking playfully at Anu.

Anu burst into laughter, shaking her head. "Absolutely! It's like having Amazon Prime for friendships—fast delivery, exclusive content, and no extra cost!"

"Exactly! Friendship delivered at the speed of light. We should patent this idea!" Aksha joked, and they both continued their walk, creating imaginary ads for their "Friendship Prime" service, their laughter light and carefree.

"Anu, can I say something?" Aksha asked, her voice a little more serious now.

"Are you kidding me? Why are you asking? Just spill it," Anu encouraged, urging her friend to speak freely.

Aksha hesitated for a moment, weighing her words carefully. "No, I think I should not interfere in your life at all. Every decision should be yours, but... I think I can suggest something. I don't want to hurt you, but..."

"Go on, Aksha, speak up. What do you want to say? Don't overthink it," Anu stopped her, offering a reassuring smile.

Aksha took a deep breath and continued, "You and Dev are a good match. You should think about your future together."

Anu paused, her face lighting up with a playful grin. "Who?"

"You and Dev," Aksha repeated, her voice softer but still filled with hope.

"Hahaha, as a couple, we're like poles apart," Anu laughed, shaking her head.

"Opposites attract, Anu!" Aksha countered, her tone teasing yet gentle.

"I wish I could," Anu said quietly, her smile fading slightly as she thought for a moment. "But we're both broken-hearted. We're still hoping that the people who left us will come back one day. We don't want to lose hope, you know? We're friends, and we need each other's support to get through this. We are strength for each other, and we want to stay that way. I think we're a better match as friends than soulmates." She paused, wanting to say more but keeping her thoughts to herself. "I love him, he loves me. But as friends," she finished, her voice soft.

Aksha noticed the hesitation in Anu's eyes but chose not to press further. "Nothing like that. We are just friends," Anu said with a slight laugh, and Aksha joined in, their laughter filling the air with a bittersweet undertone.

The quiet night around them seemed to hold their unspoken thoughts, and for a brief moment, the weight of their conversation was palpable.

Aksha's voice grew quieter as she reflected on the deeper themes that lingered between them. "The pain of losing a loved one cuts so deeply, doesn't it? It feels like it erodes the very fabric of who we are. But even in that hurt, we learn so much about ourselves. Love and loss—it's all connected, intertwined. I wonder sometimes, is love just a fleeting feeling, or does it go beyond? Does it become part of us, even after someone is gone?"

Anu turned her head, the soft moonlight casting a gentle glow on her face as she listened, her heart understanding the complexity of Aksha's words. "It's a question we all ask ourselves, Aksha. Life is temporary, and relationships—no matter how deep—are fragile. We can't always hold onto them forever."

The conversation lingered in the cool night air, and Aksha continued, her voice almost a whisper, "But even in the sadness of loss, there's something greater. It's like Martin Heidegger's idea of 'being-towards-death.' The awareness that we won't live forever gives us meaning, urgency. And maybe that's where the healing begins—the recognition that love, even in loss, still shapes us."

Anu nodded slowly, feeling the weight of the truth in Aksha's words. "It's true. We may not always be able to move on, but we carry what we've loved with us. It stays in our hearts, long after it's gone. It's a reminder of how fragile and beautiful life really is."

There was a brief silence as they walked, both lost in their own thoughts. In the quiet of the night, they understood one another without words, knowing that the pain of losing someone teaches us how deeply we are capable of loving—and that love, in its purest form, remains with us, beyond time and space.

The air between Aksha and Anu grew lighter after their shared laughter, yet a faint undercurrent of introspection lingered. The night seemed to weave their words into a tapestry of vulnerability and strength, each moment deepening their connection.

"Aksha," Anu began, her voice softer now, "you're right about one thing—Dev and I have something special, even if it's not what people might think it should be. It's funny, isn't it? How friendships can sometimes mean more than the labels we try to give them."

Aksha tilted her head, considering Anu's words. "It's not about the labels, Anu. It's about the connection, the way someone can feel like home. And you both, well, you seem like home for each other. Even if it's just as friends, it's beautiful."

Anu smiled, her gaze fixed on the horizon as if searching for answers in the distant stars. "You know, Aksha, when you lose someone you love deeply, it leaves this... void. A place no one else can quite fill. Dev understands that void in a way no one else does. We're not trying to replace what we've lost, but we help each other carry the weight of it."

Aksha reached out and gently touched Anu's arm. "That's what matters, Anu. Having someone who understands, who doesn't try to fix you but just... walks beside you. It's rare, and it's precious."

Anu nodded, her voice carrying a mix of gratitude and melancholy. "Maybe that's why I can't think of us as anything more. We're both still holding onto something—or someone—that feels unfinished. It's like we're both waiting for a chapter to close before we can start a new one."

The philosophical undertone of their conversation resonated deeply with Aksha, stirring thoughts she hadn't dared to voice before. "You know, Anu," she said, her voice tinged with wonder, "love and loss—they're two sides of the same coin, aren't they? The deeper the love, the deeper the loss when it's gone. But maybe… maybe that's what makes it worth it. The depth of feeling, the way it shapes us, even in its absence."

Anu's eyes glistened as she turned to face Aksha. "You're right. Love does that—it leaves its mark, even when it's gone. And maybe it's not about moving on or letting go. Maybe it's about carrying that love forward, letting it guide us, even as we step into something new."

A comfortable silence settled between them, the kind that only exists between close friends. The soft hum of the night wrapped around them, and the world seemed to pause, as if giving them space to process the weight of their words.

Finally, Anu broke the silence with a chuckle, her tone playful again. "You've been reading too much philosophy, Aksha. You're starting to sound like an old sage."

Aksha laughed, the sound light and genuine. "Hey, don't blame me. The stars and the moon have a way of pulling out the deep thoughts. It's all their fault."

The two friends continued their walk, their laughter blending with the gentle rustle of leaves. The weight of their conversation lingered, but it no longer felt heavy—it felt like a shared understanding, a reminder that even in the face of loss, love and friendship had the power to heal.

ppp

"Excuse me! I have an important call to take," Roy said, his gaze fixed on his phone.

"Look at him! He's getting an important call," Dev teased, his voice dripping with mock seriousness. The lighthearted comment sent everyone into fits of laughter.

"Yes! I am a responsible person now. I have many works to complete. Many accounts to clear," Roy added with a grin, trying to play along. With that, he took a few steps ahead, finding a quiet spot to take his call without interruption.

As he spoke into the phone, his voice lowered, "Yes, everything is the same as you decided. But Anu is with her." Roy paused, glancing around, making sure no one was eavesdropping on his conversation. "Don't worry, we'll handle it." He ended the call quickly, his expression unreadable as he returned to the group, pretending like nothing had happened.

Dev raised an eyebrow, noticing the change in Roy's demeanor, but chose not to ask. The others continued to chat, unaware of the subtle tension that had crept in.

ppp

A Night of Unexpected Wonders

The lights flickered and then went off completely, just moments after Roy ended his call. The sudden darkness swept over the farmhouse, plunging everyone into an unexpected stillness, and leaving the air thick with uncertainty.

"Is it a power outage, or is something else going on?" Maher's voice, laced with confusion, broke the silence as he looked around in the growing darkness.

"Don't worry, it's probably just a small glitch," Momo said, trying to keep the mood light. She moved a few steps forward, her voice carrying reassurance. "Let me check it out. Stay where you are for now."

Anu and Aksha found a corner to settle into, the darkness wrapping around them like a cloak. Aksha was on the verge of asking Anu about her birthday, the question lingering at the tip of her tongue. But in the dim light and uncertain atmosphere, she hesitated, unsure if now was the right moment.

Suddenly, Anu's sharp eyes caught a glimpse of something unusual — a faint glow in the distance. It was a sign, marked with a glowing arrow, pointing toward the area beyond the farmhouse. She gently tapped Aksha's shoulder to get her attention. Aksha, assuming it might be part of a birthday surprise, stood up quickly, eager to follow the sign.

However, Anu's cautious nature led her to stop Aksha with a hand on her arm. "Wait," she advised softly. "We should wait for the others before we go any further."

"Are you both okay?" Aarush's voice broke through the darkness, his concern palpable as he approached.

"We're fine," Anu assured him quickly, smiling in the dark. Aarush, relieved, draped an arm over Aksha's shoulder, his presence offering comfort in the darkness. Aksha pointed toward the glowing sign. "I think we should follow it," she said quietly.

Maher, ever the pragmatic one, voiced his concerns. "I don't know... What if it's some kind of trap? We should wait until everyone's here before we do anything."

Dev, always the one to embrace adventure, let out a light chuckle. "We've been getting surprises all night, haven't we? Maybe the lights went off just for this one. What if the sign is leading us to the next surprise?"

Aarush, after a brief pause, nodded. "Maybe you're right. But let's stay smart about it."

"Alright then," Maher said with a sigh, giving in. "We'll wait for the others, and then we'll go together. No rushing into anything."

Dev immediately took out his phone to call Manan and Rishi, ensuring they would join the group before any decisions were made. The group settled into an expectant silence, the glow of the sign casting an eerie light across the room as they waited for the others to arrive.

As they waited, the air was thick with anticipation, the tension palpable. Whatever the night had in store, they were about to find out — but they would face it together.

Maher's voice broke the stillness again, his tone cautious but firm. "It's not about the surprise. It's about being safe. We don't know what's going on. We shouldn't rush into things."

Dev, ever the optimist, let out a short laugh, trying to lighten the mood. "Come on, Maher! What's the worst that could happen? It's just a sign. Besides, it's not like we're in a horror movie!" He grinned, but his eyes betrayed a hint of excitement.

Aarush, wrapping his arm more tightly around Aksha's shoulders, gave a gentle squeeze. "Let's not jump to conclusions. We'll wait for the others. But if it turns out to be some kind of birthday surprise for Aksha, I swear I'll be the first to thank whoever set this up."

Aksha, still uncertain, looked at the sign again, the glowing arrow beckoning them forward. "I don't know... it feels like it's guiding us somewhere. But I'm fine with waiting, if that's what you all think is best."

Anu, ever the voice of reason, nodded in agreement. "Better to be safe than sorry, right? Let's just stick together."

As Dev quickly called Manan and Rishi, the atmosphere remained tense. The flickering of the lights, the mysterious sign, and the soft rustling of leaves outside only heightened the feeling of suspense.

The farmhouse, normally a place of comfort and warmth, now seemed full of hidden secrets, and as the minutes passed, everyone waited, the air thick with anticipation. Whatever was ahead, they were about to find out together.

After a few minutes, Manan and Rishi finally joined them, their faces illuminated by the faint glow of their phone screens.

"What's going on?" Manan asked, looking around at the group. "Power outage?"

"We think it's a surprise," Dev said, his voice brimming with excitement. "There's a sign pointing outside. We're gonna check it out together. Ready for an adventure?"

Rishi looked at the sign, then at the group. "I'm all for surprises, but we're sticking together, right? No wandering off alone."

The group nodded in agreement, and with that, they took one last glance at each other, their hearts pounding with a mix of curiosity and caution. The adventure, whatever it was, was about to unfold.

ppp

The group stood in the shadow of the unknown, the weight of anticipation pressing down on them like a tangible force. The glow of the sign continued to beckon them, drawing their gaze and fueling their curiosity. The darkness around them seemed to pulse with an energy all its own, deepening the sense of mystery that hung in the air.

The promise of what lay ahead was clear — a revelation waiting to unfold, a journey that could transform an ordinary evening into something extraordinary.

Each member of the group felt the thrill of the unknown course through them. Aksha's heart raced, her mind alive with visions of the challenges they might face and the discoveries waiting to be made. The adrenaline surged through her veins as she imagined the possibilities, her pulse quickening with every beat.

Aanu's grin widened, his eyes glinting with a mixture of excitement and determination. He was ready — not just for the adventure, but for whatever came next. The thought of facing the unknown alongside his friends brought a sense of camaraderie that filled him with pride.

Roy's eyes sparkled with the thrill of the mystery ahead. His mind was already racing, envisioning the twists and turns they would encounter on their journey. He couldn't help but wonder what secrets would soon be uncovered, and how their bonds would grow stronger as a result.

Dev stood beside them, his fists clenched in anticipation. His eyes gleamed with a fierce resolve. Whatever obstacles lay in their path, he was ready to face them head-on. The fire of adventure was igniting within him, and there was no turning back.

As the group stood on the threshold of whatever awaited them, the excitement in the air was palpable. Each moment stretched on, every heartbeat a reminder of the thrilling journey they were about to embark on. The glow of the sign seemed to pulse with life, a beacon of adventure that would lead them into the unknown.

With every passing second, the promise of what was to come — the adventure, the challenges, and the rewards — grew stronger.

Group Nine was no longer just a team; they were a force ready to embrace whatever the night held in store. Their spirits burned brighter than ever, their bond unshakable, and the unknown was no longer something to fear — it was something to embrace.

❦❦❦

As they moved a few steps forward, Rishi spotted another glowing sign, this time pointing towards a tree. A large bin beneath the tree was also radiating an unusual glow.

"A bin in the jungle! That is not something you see every day," Manan exclaimed.

"Exactly, and the main point is, it's glowing," Roy added, supporting Manan's observation.

Anu, always ready with a witty remark, teased, "Is this your way of decorating bins for your guests, Momo?"

While the group engaged in light banter, Dev, standing by the glowing bin, suddenly shouted, "Hey, here's a note for us!"

Aksha, her fingers crossed with anticipation, whispered a hopeful wish, "Please, please, God! Let this note be for me."

Her imagination ran wild, convinced that this surprise plan was orchestrated by Aarush for her birthday. The atmosphere crackled with excitement and suspense as they waited to uncover the contents of the mysterious note. The glowing signs and unexpected notes added an air of intrigue to the night, leaving everyone on edge, eager to unravel the secrets hidden in the heart of the jungle.

"Aha, it's for you," Anu said with a grin as she handed Aksha the note that Dev had found.

"Honey, here's the first present for you. Not as pretty as you, but capable of bringing a big smile to your pretty face. Open the bin and have it," Aksha read the note aloud for everyone to hear.

"Be careful!" Aarush shouted with a mix of excitement and concern as Aksha dashed toward the bin. Aarush, cautious not to invite any unexpected problems, watched with bated breath.

"Oh my God! I can't believe this!" Aksha exclaimed as she opened the bin to reveal a large teddy bear neatly tucked inside. The teddy bear was positioned in such a way that when she opened the lid, it popped out, standing taller than her. The unexpected surprise added an element of joy to the mysterious night, and the sight of the oversized teddy bear brought a genuine, heartfelt smile to Aksha's face. The jungle, once filled with suspense, now echoed with laughter and the delight of unexpected surprises.

"Thank you, thank you, thank you so much, Aarush!" she exclaimed, hugging him tightly. In a single breath, she continued, "I thought you forgot my birthday, but how stupid I am. How could I even think like that? I should trust you. I should not doubt you." Aarush attempted to say something, but Aksha didn't let him speak; she kept talking. "This is such a big surprise for me. I love it, baby."

Aarush, torn between wanting to confess and not wanting to spoil Aksha's happiness, found himself battling an unease he couldn't shake. The sight of Aksha's glowing smile amidst the soft candlelight only deepened his guilt. How could he possibly tell her the truth—that he had forgotten her birthday entirely? A wave of guilt washed over him, heavy and suffocating.

"Surprise planning for the *wife's* birthday? Dude, it's an 'O' moment for sure," Dev teased, nudging Aarush with a mischievous grin.

Aarush's face fell, and he quickly pulled Dev aside, his voice low and tinged with worry. "No, yaar. I didn't do this. I didn't even remember her birthday... How stupid can I be?"

Dev's playful demeanor faded in an instant. "*What?* What the hell, man?" he whispered sharply, stealing a glance at Aksha to ensure she hadn't overheard. "You're telling me all *this* isn't your doing?"

Aarush shook his head, his unease growing. "Not even close. I didn't plan any of this. I've got no idea where it's coming from."

Dev frowned, the worry mirrored in his own expression. "Then who did? And why?" His voice dropped even lower, their conversation turning serious. "Man, this isn't funny. If you didn't set this up..."

"I know," Aarush muttered, running a hand through his hair, tension evident in his every move. "I'm just... hoping it's not anything dangerous. I don't want Aksha involved in something I can't explain."

"See?" Maher's voice broke into the hushed conversation, her eyes narrowed as she stood a little apart, observing. "There's something off about this. Look at that—another *sign.*" She gestured toward the path where another wooden creature had been left, its carved hand pointing into the shadows.

The group instinctively fell quiet, exchanging wary glances. The playful atmosphere of moments earlier now carried an undercurrent of suspicion.

"You're right," Dev murmured to Maher, keeping his voice steady. "This feels intentional. And if Aarush didn't plan it..." He trailed off, casting a sideways glance at Aarush, who stood stiff, his eyes darting between the shadows and Aksha's figure, still blissfully unaware of the growing tension.

"Guys, let's stay on high alert," Maher added, her tone firm yet calm. "Whatever this is, we don't take chances."

Meanwhile, Aksha, ahead of them all, noticed the faint glow from beneath a big tree bathed in a spotlight. Her eyes lit up with curiosity. "Look! There's another clue here," she called out, walking closer.

The group hesitated. Aarush stepped forward immediately, his protective instinct overriding his uncertainty. "Aksha, wait," he called, his voice slightly strained. She paused and turned toward him, her smile soft and unsuspecting.

"What's wrong?" she asked, tilting her head. "It's another gift—look how beautiful everything is."

Aarush forced a smile, though his heart hammered in his chest. "Nothing. Just... don't rush, okay? Let's enjoy this together." His voice softened as he approached her, his hand lightly brushing her arm—a subtle yet reassuring gesture.

Each sign Aksha followed seemed to lead to another thoughtful gift—delicate trinkets, hand-carved ornaments, and small, heartfelt messages. Yet, for Aarush, each step deepened the knot in his stomach. Someone else had orchestrated all of this, and though the gestures seemed harmless, a creeping unease told him not to lower his guard.

Dev moved closer to Aarush, his voice a tight whisper. "Are we sure this isn't someone playing games with you? Could this be a prank?"

"I don't know," Aarush muttered, his jaw tense as his eyes stayed on Aksha. "But whatever it is... I'm not letting anything happen to her."

The group trailed cautiously behind Aksha, the glow of the gifts softening the edges of their rising concern. The once light-hearted evening now carried a shadow of suspicion, leaving Aarush to silently promise himself that, no matter what, he wouldn't let anything—or anyone—hurt Aksha.

Suddenly, an unknown voice echoed through the cool night air, interrupting the celebration, "Hey buddy, welcome."

The cheerful chatter came to an abrupt halt, everyone freezing mid-motion. Their eyes darted toward one another, curiosity and suspicion flickering in equal measure. "Is this part of the surprise?" Roy muttered, his brows furrowing.

While others speculated and exchanged puzzled glances, **Aksha** felt her heart race. The voice, though unfamiliar to everyone else, struck a chord deep within her. It lingered, like a forgotten melody. For a fleeting moment, Aksha thought *it sounded like hers*—like the voice of someone she knew.

Her breath hitched as confusion clouded her thoughts. *Could it be?* The question gnawed at her, intertwining with the turmoil she had carried for so long. *Was it just a trick of the mind? Or was there a real chance...?*

Her thoughts spiraled. Aksha longed for answers. A part of her yearned to meet an old friend—someone who had once meant the world to her. Yet her pride, her ego, stood firm as a wall. Could she overcome the emotional scars of the past? Could she accept the olive branch that life seemed to be extending, or would she turn away and let the moment slip into oblivion?

The battle between her heart and mind was not an easy one. She felt the weight of indecision pulling her down, and she stood there, frozen at the crossroads between longing and self-preservation.

"Aksha?" Aarush's voice broke through her thoughts. His tone was soft but laced with concern. "You okay?"

Before she could answer, another voice note crackled to life. "Aksha, come forward and open the door."

Everyone turned their attention toward an old wooden door, bathed in the gentle glow of scattered fairy lights. Aksha's steps faltered for a second as Aarush walked beside her, his protective presence steadying her. His hand lightly grazed her shoulder in silent reassurance.

As they approached, a soft click echoed in the air. With a sudden whoosh, red rose petals began to cascade from above. They twirled through the breeze like whispered promises, gently landing on Aksha. The crimson petals framed her in a surreal, dreamlike moment, making her look almost ethereal beneath the starlit sky.

Gasps of awe escaped from the group behind them.

"Woah," Dev murmured, blinking. "This... this is something else."

Aarush, watching Aksha with a soft smile, whispered, "This might be the most beautiful surprise ever."

Aksha blinked against the petals, unable to hold back a small, grateful smile. It *was* remarkable—undeniably so. For all the confusion and tension brewing in her heart moments earlier, the sheer beauty of the gesture anchored her for now.

Still savoring the charm of the petal shower, Aarush gently tapped her shoulder. "Aksha," he said quietly, pointing toward another sign that had appeared beside the door. Her gaze followed his finger, and she spotted bold, gleaming letters:

"Press Me."

The sign sat atop a bright red button embedded into a carved wooden stand.

"What do you think, guys? Should she press it, or is this the 'danger' button?" Manan teased, trying to lighten the mood.

"Press it, Aksha! Come on, *we* need to know," Roy added with faux suspense, earning a chuckle from the group.

Aksha rolled her eyes with a smile. "Fine, fine, *I'll* press it. You guys are impossible."

With a breath of anticipation, she pressed the button.

Suddenly, soft golden light erupted, and twinkling fairy lights illuminated both sides of the narrow road ahead. The group gasped, their faces lighting up in unison as the magic unfolded. On either side of the path, strung delicately between trees, were rows of photographs—**her photographs.**

Aksha stepped forward in disbelief, her hand flying to her mouth. There they were—moments she had almost forgotten, captured and frozen in time. Photographs of her childhood, her college years, special family gatherings, and candid shots of her at her happiest. Some were newer, taken in the presence of her friends during their adventures. It was a heartfelt display that traced the journey of her life like a timeline made with love.

"I... I don't understand," she whispered, her voice quivering as she took it all in. "Who did this?"

Aarush stood a step behind her, watching her every reaction with a soft, unreadable expression. His worry, so present earlier, now lingered in the quiet depths of his eyes. Though the moment was breathtaking, the question still haunted him. *If I didn't plan this... then who did?*

But for now, he stayed silent, allowing Aksha to soak in the magic of a moment she would never forget.

"I wish my husband would do something like this for me," Anu whispered, a mix of nostalgia and yearning in her voice.

Dev, ever the joker, playfully vowed, "I wouldn't mind doing it for you," prompting a light-hearted giggle from Anu.

Amidst the banter and shared memories, Anu playfully exclaimed, "Stop it, chippo," lightening the mood.

Aksha, still caught in the whirlwind of surprises, found herself facing a round table in the middle of the open area. A beautiful cake adorned its surface, prompting Aksha to rush towards it.

Overwhelmed with emotions and gratitude, she hurried to Aarush, eager to express her feelings. However, Aarush, aware that the credit wasn't solely his, attempted to explain.

Dev, ever the mischievous friend, gently pressed Aksha's hand, silencing any protest. Instead, Aarush embraced her, his silent acknowledgment of the joy he felt in making her happy.

As the clock struck midnight, Aksha, radiating happiness, playfully suggested, "Come on, darling, let's cut the cake and see if Aarush can manage not to forget the candles this time."

Aarush, catching the teasing tone, responded with a grin, "Well, I can't promise anything, but I'll try my best."

The friends, always ready for a good laugh, gathered around, chanting, "Don't forget the candles!" and "Aarush, we believe in you!"

Amidst the birthday song, Roy couldn't resist adding, "Aarush, if you forget the candles, at least make sure you remember Aksha's age correctly."

Aksha, in good spirits, retorted, "Oh, please, Roy. We've been over this. A woman's age is like a software update – you never ask, and she never tells."

Laughter echoed in the night as Aarush prepared to cut the cake, surrounded by friends who found joy in every moment, even the mischievous ones.

Amidst the contagious laughter, Aarush and Aksha stood side by side, the glow of the cake's candles reflecting in their eyes. As they prepared to cut the cake, a subtle warmth lingered between them.

Aarush couldn't help but steal a glance at Aksha, her eyes sparkling with the flickering candlelight. With a mischievous smile, he whispered, "Ready for another year of adventures, surprises, and maybe a few forgotten candles?"

Aksha raised an eyebrow, suppressing a laugh. "Forgotten candles? Don't tell me you're still sulking about that time I forgot to bring the cake candles on your birthday."

Aarush clutched his chest dramatically. "*Forgot*? Aksha, that was a betrayal of the highest order! I blew out invisible candles that day."

Aksha rolled her eyes playfully, leaning closer. "And yet, you still made the *best* wish of your life, didn't you?"

Aarush paused, his mischievous smile softening. His voice dropped to a gentle murmur. "I did. And it came true."

Aksha blinked, her teasing tone faltering for just a second. "Oh really? What did you wish for?"

He tilted his head, studying her face, the flickering candlelight dancing in her wide, curious eyes. "You. Right here. Just like this."

Her breath caught in her throat, and for a moment, the playful banter fell away. She looked down, a faint blush creeping across her cheeks as she smiled. "You're ridiculous, Aarush."

Aarush grinned, reaching out to tuck a stray strand of hair behind her ear. "Only for you, Aksha. You're my favorite kind of ridiculous."

Aksha let out a soft laugh, shaking her head. "If this is how you plan to butter me up for another year, you're doing a pretty good job of it."

Aarush leaned back with a triumphant smile. "Then my work here is done... for today."

Aksha, unable to hide her smile, looked at him with mock warning. "Just don't expect me to remember candles *next* time either."

"Deal," Aarush said softly, his eyes holding hers. "As long as you're there, candles don't really matter."

The soft warmth between them lingered, unspoken words filling the air, as the candlelight flickered—marking not just another year of adventures, but another quiet moment of love.

Their friends, sensing the underlying romance, exchanged knowing glances and decided to add a touch of teasing to the moment.

Roy couldn't resist chiming in, "Aarush, don't forget to make it a *sweet* year for Aksha, too."

Aarush, with a twinkle in his eye and without missing a beat, replied, "Oh, Roy, sweetness is my *specialty*."

Manan smirked, leaning closer to the group. "Careful, Aksha. That sweetness might come with an overload of sugar and a sprinkle of drama."

Aksha shot Manan a mock glare, "You're just jealous, Manan, because Aarush remembers birthdays, unlike someone we all know."

Manan clutched his heart dramatically, mimicking a faint. "Ouch! Betrayed by my own people. Aksha, you wound me!"

Rishi, joining the fun, grinned at Aarush. "Bro, you've set the bar too high. Sweet talk, stolen glances, candlelight—this is dangerous. We single folks don't stand a chance!"

Aarush, grinning triumphantly, shrugged. "It's not my fault you guys are amateurs."

"Amateurs?" Anu interjected, raising an eyebrow. "Big words for someone who once tripped over his shoelaces while trying to impress Aksha. Shall I remind everyone of *that* romantic disaster?"

The group erupted into laughter as Aksha covered her mouth, trying not to giggle. Aarush shot Anu a playful glare. "That's ancient history, Anu! Why are we digging up fossils here?"

"Because it's too much fun!" Roy teased. "And Aksha, for the record, we're all taking bets on who's going to give up first—your patience or Aarush's smooth lines."

Aksha tilted her head, biting back a smile. "Don't bother betting. I've mastered the art of tolerating him. *Someone* has to."

"True love, guys!" Maher said dramatically, clasping her hands. "Two people putting up with each other's quirks. Aarush and Aksha are giving us all hope!"

The group burst out laughing again, the playful banter flowing effortlessly. Aarush threw his hands up in surrender. "Fine, fine! You guys win tonight. But mark my words, next year's birthday will be *perfect*. Candles, cake, and no shoelaces!"

Aksha leaned back with a smirk, raising her cup of tea. "I'll believe it when I see it."

The evening air filled with laughter and warmth as the group continued teasing and sharing lighthearted moments. These were the kind of memories that would stick with them—friendships overflowing with humor, love, and endless teasing.

9
The Treehouse of Secrets

As Aksha ascended the glowing steps of the treehouse, her heart swelled with awe and wonder, but amidst the overwhelming joy, a seed of doubt quietly took root in her mind. *This… this can't be Aarush,* she thought, her gaze drifting over the meticulous details—the twinkling lights, the perfectly arranged table, the delicate touches that spoke of someone who knew her heart inside out.

Her fingers trailed across the wooden railings, and a soft voice in her head whispered again. *Only Aahana knew… Only she knew about this dream.*

Aksha paused mid-step, her eyes darting to Aarush, who was smiling proudly as their friends teased him. A soft laugh escaped his lips as Roy hollered about how the bar for birthday surprises had been set impossibly high. Aarush looked so genuine, so content, but doubt lingered.

Did Aarush really plan all this? How could he? she wondered. Her childhood dream of celebrating her birthday in a treehouse was something she had shared only once, in the most unexpected of conversations—with Aahana, on the night of Aarush and Aksha's wedding.

She could still hear Aahana's words from that day, spoken softly yet so vividly etched in her mind. *"Aksha, you have a heart full of dreams. Someday, those dreams will find their way back to you, even if you don't believe it now."*

Aksha felt her chest tighten, a swirl of emotions rising—gratitude, confusion, and something else she couldn't quite name. *No... it can't be her,* she thought firmly, shaking her head. Her grip tightened on the railing as if to ground herself. She didn't want to face that possibility—not tonight, not after everything.

The thought of coming face-to-face with Aahana—of revisiting the echoes of their past—made her stomach churn. *Why would she do this? And even if she did... what does it mean?*

Aarush's voice cut through her thoughts as he called out softly, "Aksha, are you okay?"

She turned to him, startled, masking her doubt with a quick smile. "Yeah... just overwhelmed."

Aarush stepped closer, concern flickering in his eyes. "Is it too much? I just wanted you to have the perfect day."

Her heart softened as she looked at him—her ever-supportive Aarush, who would do anything to see her smile. *Maybe I'm overthinking this,* she scolded herself silently. *Maybe it really is him.*

But the whispers in her mind refused to fade. As she stepped into the softly lit treehouse, the joy mingled with an undercurrent of unease, a tug-of-war between her heart and her thoughts. Part of her wanted to believe that Aarush had done this all for her, but a small voice kept murmuring, *This has Aahana written all over it.*

Still, Aksha pushed the thoughts aside. Tonight was about joy, about the people who stood by her and celebrated her dreams. And if this was Aahana's silent way of reaching out, Aksha wasn't ready to face it—not yet.

For now, she let herself soak in the moment, a quiet smile on her lips as Aarush gently pulled her to sit beside him. The group erupted in laughter, already lost in their teasing banter, unaware of the storm of thoughts quietly brewing in Aksha's mind.

I'll figure it out later, she told herself, gazing out at the stars twinkling through the branches. For now, she would let the magic of the night envelop her, holding tightly to the warmth of the people who made her feel loved.

"Isn't Aksha just incredibly lucky?" Anu murmured, her fingers absentmindedly interlacing with Dev's. The two of them stood slightly apart from the group, Dev instinctively staying close to her, comforted by her presence in the dark surroundings. He had always shared his fear of darkness only with Anu—a small vulnerability he trusted her with completely.

"Why?" Dev asked softly, his voice barely above a whisper.

"To receive a surprise like that on your birthday is no small thing!" Anu said, her eyes lingering on the softly glowing treehouse where Aksha and Aarush sat amidst the flickering lights. "The main point is, it becomes even more special when it's done by your soulmate. Really, he worked so hard to organize all this perfectly. He deserves appreciation for that," she added with a smile.

Dev suddenly tensed, his gaze flicking toward her. "But it's not Aarush," he blurted out before he could stop himself.

"What?" Anu spun toward him, her voice just a tad louder than intended.

"Shhh! Keep it down, will you? We don't need to broadcast it to everyone," Dev whispered urgently, glancing over his shoulder to make sure no one else was listening.

"Okay, sorry!" Anu said, lowering her voice but leaning closer. "If not Aarush, then who? And how do you even know it's not him?"

Dev hesitated for a moment, then sighed. "Aarush himself told me," he revealed, watching her eyes widen with surprise.

Anu straightened up, her brows furrowed in confusion. "Wait... so if it wasn't Aarush, then who?" Her gaze darted toward the treehouse again, suddenly filled with suspicion. "Who would know about Aksha's childhood dream like that?"

Dev remained silent, clearly troubled.

"Dev," Anu said, her voice dropping even lower, "this doesn't feel right. Whoever planned this—what's their intention? Why would someone step in like that without letting Aarush take credit? I hope... I just hope it's not some kind of trap for us," she added, her worry bleeding through her words.

Dev looked at her, his expression grim but thoughtful. "I don't know, Anu. I really don't. But if someone's pulling strings here, we need to figure it out before it's too late."

Anu nodded, her playful demeanor replaced with seriousness as she cast another long glance at the glowing treehouse. For the first time that night, the enchanting lights and the magical atmosphere seemed to hold a shadow of something unknown—something yet to be unveiled.

ᗡᗡᗡ

As the door creaked open, Aksha stepped into the treehouse, her footsteps light but cautious. The moment she entered, an enveloping silence greeted her, followed by complete darkness that sent her senses on high alert. For a heartbeat, all she could hear was the faint rustling of leaves outside, mingling with her own racing pulse.

Then suddenly—**whoosh**—a bright flash of light beamed down on her, as if she had just stepped onto the center stage of a grand performance. The light created a gentle halo around her, making her the undeniable guest of honor for the evening. A startled gasp escaped her lips, but it was quickly replaced by a giddy smile. The thrill of anticipation coursed through her veins, her pulse quickening at the thought of what might come next.

Her eyes, slowly adjusting to the dim glow, swept across the cozy interior of the treehouse. The familiar warmth of wooden walls and faint twinkling lights played against the corners of the room. But what caught her attention was the pristine white screen hanging on the far wall, glowing faintly like a blank canvas waiting to tell a story.

A small table before the screen held a sleek black remote control. Aksha's heart skipped a beat. Her curiosity flared, and an irrepressible excitement surged through her like wildfire. She stepped forward, her fingers brushing over the remote as though it were a sacred artifact.

Without a moment's hesitation, she pressed the switch.

Instantly, the air seemed to crackle with energy, and a soft whirr filled the silence. Aksha stood motionless, her breath hitching, as a projection slowly lit up the screen. Her mind raced. **What could this be?** Her curiosity intensified as the screen flickered, a few words appearing in the faintest, most delicate script—like a whisper:

"Memories of You."

Aksha froze, her hands gripping the remote tighter. Her eyes widened, a mixture of wonder and emotion washing over her. The title alone was enough to send a rush of thoughts spiraling through her mind. This wasn't just a birthday surprise—it was something much more profound, something carefully crafted for her.

Her heart brimmed with anticipation, and her smile softened. "What is this...?" she whispered to herself, the question escaping her lips as if to the universe itself.

The air inside the treehouse felt sacred, like a moment suspended in time. And as the projection began to play, Aksha stood there, bathed in the glow of the screen, her curiosity, joy, and emotions intertwining into one overwhelming feeling—**this was a night she would never forget.**

As the slides began to play, Aksha's breath hitched, her eyes widening with each passing moment. The journey unfolding on the screen felt surreal, as if someone had carefully stitched together the pieces of her life she had forgotten to cherish. The very first frame took her back to the bustling corridors of their college—a time when life was simpler, laughter came easier, and bonds were formed without hesitation.

The screen flickered, and there she was—her younger self—standing beside Aahana, smiling brightly as if nothing could ever go wrong. The memories cascaded, showing snapshots of their late-night study sessions, shared lunches, endless giggles, and whispered secrets. **Aahana's voice**—soft, warm, and so unmistakably hers—narrated each moment, filling the room like a long-lost song.

Everyone froze. A collective silence washed over the group, the air thick with disbelief. Aahana's voice carried a weight that struck everyone in the heart. Her tone was steady yet full of love, a melody that once bound them all together. For a group that had always teased and laughed together, this moment left them utterly still—each word pulling at emotions they thought had been buried.

Aksha, clutching the remote, whispered to herself in disbelief, "This... can't be real. It's Aahana."

The others exchanged glances, unsure if they were hearing things. Anu, gripping Dev's hand tightly, muttered under her breath, "How... how is this even possible? Did Aahana plan this? Did she leave this for Aksha?" Her voice quivered, barely masking the emotional storm within her.

Dev remained quiet, his face unreadable, but his clenched jaw betrayed the memories resurfacing.

The slides moved on, frame by frame, showcasing Aahana's journey with Aksha—the bond they built over the years, the way Aahana was always Aksha's biggest cheerleader and confidant. Each image, each word in Aahana's voice, brought waves of emotions crashing down.

Aksha felt her knees weaken, as though the weight of nostalgia might crush her. Her trembling hands gripped Aarush's arm instinctively, and though her fingers dug into his skin, Aarush didn't flinch. He just placed his free hand over hers, steadying her, offering silent strength.

"I'm here for you, Aksha. Whatever you need," he whispered softly, his voice anchoring her amidst the torrent of emotions.

But the tears couldn't be stopped. Aksha's face was wet, the bittersweet joy of reliving those precious moments mingling with the gnawing ache of loss.

"This feels like a dream," she murmured, her gaze never leaving the screen, where Aahana's face now smiled back at her from a past frozen in time.

The rest of the ninjas stood as still as statues, absorbing the shocking revelation. Roy wiped a tear before anyone noticed, pretending to scratch his face, while Manan's usual witty retorts were nowhere to be found.

Anu's gaze flitted between the screen and Dev, her heart squeezing as she caught the shadows of grief on his face. Dev, who rarely showed his emotions, now looked as though he carried the weight of everyone's sorrow.

"This isn't just about Aksha," Anu realized, her voice barely audible. "Aahana left pieces of herself with all of us."

For a moment, the treehouse—once a haven of childlike wonder—felt like a time capsule, holding memories too precious to be forgotten but too painful to relive.

Aksha, now visibly overwhelmed, finally spoke through her tears. "Why, Aarush? Why does it feel like she's here? Like she planned this just for me?"

Aarush sighed deeply, brushing her tears away gently. "Maybe this... this is her way of reminding you. Of reminding us all. She hasn't really gone anywhere, Aksha. She's still with you—in every memory, every laugh, and every moment you hold on to her."

His words hung in the air, offering some comfort but not enough to quell the storm inside.

Anu, her voice trying to steady itself, finally added, "Aahana was always a step ahead, wasn't she? She knew exactly what we needed, even when we didn't."

Aksha nodded, her heart aching but full of gratitude. **Aahana's voice had become the echo of unsaid words**—the voice they all needed to hear to confront the past, to heal, and to remember.

The emotional turmoil gripped everyone. Yet, as the video reached its final frame—a photograph of the entire group, together, smiling under a setting sun—the heaviness began to lift, replaced by a quiet, collective resolve to hold on to what mattered most: their bond, their memories, and the enduring love they shared with Aahana.

For in that treehouse, amidst the flickering lights and overwhelming emotions, they all understood that *some people never truly leave—they just become a part of who you are.*

As the final moments of the video played out, the screen flickered one last time, and Aahana's voice—soft, familiar, and full of warmth—filled the room once again. It felt as though time had paused, holding everyone captive as they listened, their hearts bracing for what she had to say.

"If you're watching this, it means you've all come together... just as I hoped you would."

The room fell into complete silence. Aksha froze, her eyes locked on the screen, her tears momentarily forgotten as Aahana's voice carried her into a whirlwind of emotions. The others stood motionless, each word striking deeper than the last.

""Aksha... my Aksha." Aahana's voice lingered on her best friend's name with a tenderness that made Aksha's breath catch. "I always knew you would be the hardest to reach, the one whose walls are built the strongest. But I also know this: you are the strongest of us all, even when you refuse to believe it. I never wanted my absence to dim the light in your eyes or weigh you down with questions that don't have answers. This day—this moment—is for you, my dear friend. To remind you that you are loved, cherished, and celebrated. To remind you that life still has countless dreams waiting for you... even that silly treehouse birthday you always wanted.""

Aksha let out a choked sob, pressing her hand over her mouth. Aarush instinctively held her closer, his own expression torn between admiration and sorrow.

Aahana's narration continued, her voice filled with love and an undeniable sense of forethought.

""To all my ninjas, my second family, you've always been my greatest gift. Each one of you has a special place in my heart, and I wanted to make sure you knew that. Dev, with his quiet strength. Anu, the keeper of our sanity. Roy, the joker who carries more love than he lets on. Manan, whose loyalty knows no bounds. Maher, whose wisdom often surprises us all. And Aarush... Aarush, you've been my anchor when life

tossed me into storms. I entrusted this dream to you because I knew you'd protect Aksha when I couldn't."

The camera flickered to reveal handwritten notes and photos of Aahana's planning—details meticulously laid out. A small snippet of Roy's face appeared on the screen, grinning mischievously as he held up a sheet of paper.

"Oh, come on, Aksha! Give me some credit. Roy helped me pull this off, you know. He acted as my partner-in-crime when I wasn't around to tease you all myself. He's the silent executor of all the madness I left behind!"

Everyone turned to Roy, whose sheepish smile revealed his involvement. "You weren't supposed to find out like this," he muttered, trying to hide his tears behind a forced chuckle.

Aahana's voice returned, softening the room once more.

"I planned this reunion because I wanted you all to remember what truly matters—each other. Life gets busy. People move on. But love, friendship, and memories? They don't just fade. They become a part of us. So, I ask one thing of you—don't let the 'unsaid words' pile up. Don't let regret win. Cherish the moments, fight for the people you love, and when life tests you... come back to each other. Always."

The final slide appeared—a photo of all the ninjas together, including Aahana, her radiant smile lighting up the frame. Underneath it, her handwriting read:

*"This was never goodbye. I'm still here—in your laughter, in your love, and in all the **echoes of unsaid words.**"*

The room erupted into quiet sobs and shared glances of understanding. Aksha dropped to her knees, her hands pressed to her face, overwhelmed by love, grief, and gratitude all at once. Aarush knelt beside her, holding her tightly as tears ran down his own face.

Anu whispered softly, "She did this for us... for all of us."

Dev, his voice thick with emotion, finally spoke. "She knew exactly what we needed—even when we didn't."

The treehouse, which moments ago had felt like a mystery, now felt like a sacred space—Aahana's final gift to them all. The ninjas moved closer together, united not just by their loss but by the unshakable bond Aahana had left behind.

In that moment, they understood: *Some people never truly leave. They remain in every laugh, every tear, and in the quiet echoes of unsaid words.*

ᐅᐅᐅ

Aksha's heart was torn between the overwhelming desire to engulf Aahana in a tight embrace and the lingering hurt that gnawed at her soul, caused by her sudden departure. A part of her yearned to hold her best friend close, to talk for hours, to scold her for leaving when she needed her the most. Yet, another part of her—hardened by the pain of abandonment—refused to let go so easily.

Her breaths grew uneven as her mind spun in turmoil. *"Why now? Why come back when I finally learned to live without you? How could you think disappearing was better than staying and fighting with me?"*

A rational voice echoed in her mind, compelling her to turn away and let Aahana grapple with the weight of her guilt. Aksha blinked back her tears, steeling herself. Without a word, she turned around and began walking away, her footsteps resolute but heavy.

Aarush noticed her departure and immediately called out, his voice laced with concern, "Ashu... wait... Ashu!" He started after her, catching up quickly, followed closely by Maher, Manan, and Rishi, who were equally alarmed. The weight of unspoken words hung like a cloud over the reunion, turning the once joyful air into one of poignant ambiguity.

Back in the treehouse, Aahana crumbled completely, her usual confident demeanor nowhere to be seen. She sank to her knees, unable to bear the burden of being ignored by the people she loved most. Tears streamed uncontrollably down her face, her sobs breaking through the stillness.

"Please…" she whispered brokenly, her voice cracking under the weight of her emotions. "Please don't do this to me. I *need* you to understand me. I didn't have a choice—if I had, I would never have vanished like that. I've already suffered… more than I can say."

Her voice grew louder as desperation overtook her. "I miss you all. I miss *us*. Don't let me suffer more. Don't let me endure your silence and ignorance. If you want to scold me, scold. If you want to beat me, beat. Do whatever you want. Just… for God's sake… *talk to me*."

She broke down completely, burying her face in her trembling hands, sobbing as though years of bottled-up pain were now flooding out in torrents. "I need you all," she whispered through her tears. "I need your support. I need *you*, Aksha."

Hearing Aahana's raw, unguarded plea, Aksha stopped in her tracks. Her heart clenched, and her hands shook as the weight of her emotions threatened to shatter her composure. Aarush noticed her hesitation and softly placed his hand on her shoulder.

"She's suffering too, Ashu," he murmured gently. "You know it as much as I do."

Aksha bit her lip hard, as if trying to hold back a tidal wave of emotions. Maher spoke up softly behind her, his calm voice anchoring the tension in the air. "Aksha, I know she left, and I know she hurt you. But look at her now—she's not running away this time. She's here, asking for us."

Manan added quietly, his gaze somber, "We've waited so long for answers, Aksha. You've waited. Don't let this moment slip away."

Rishi, who'd remained silent until now, took a step forward and spoke with quiet sincerity, "Sometimes people leave not because they stop loving us, but because they're too broken to stay. Maybe Aahana wasn't as unshakable as we thought."

Aksha's eyes burned with tears she could no longer hold back. Her fingers curled into fists, and her voice trembled as she whispered, "She didn't trust me enough to stay. She knew *everything* about me—every dream, every fear—and still, she left."

Aarush tightened his grip on her shoulder, steadying her. "Then ask her why. Don't carry this silence anymore. You deserve to know the truth."

With a shaky breath, Aksha nodded. Slowly, she turned back toward the treehouse, her steps hesitant but determined. The others followed quietly, understanding that this was a moment they couldn't intrude upon.

When Aksha re-entered the treehouse, Aahana was still kneeling on the floor, her sobs softened but unrelenting. At the sound of approaching footsteps, Aahana lifted her tear-streaked face, her breath hitching when she saw Aksha standing before her.

For a moment, neither spoke. Aksha's gaze was steady, though her tears still glistened in the dim light. Finally, her voice broke the silence, soft but firm. "Why, Aahana?"

Aahana blinked, her lips parting in disbelief.

"Why did you leave me when I needed you the most? What was so unbearable that you thought I couldn't handle it with you?" Aksha's voice cracked, her anguish seeping through her words.

Aahana stood on shaky legs, wiping her tears but unable to hide the pain in her eyes. "I left because I thought I was protecting you," she whispered. "Because *I* wasn't strong enough to share my struggles with you. I didn't want to burden you with my pain when you were already going through so much. I thought... I thought leaving was the only way to keep you safe."

Aksha's tears fell freely now, her voice shaking with both anger and sorrow. "You weren't protecting me, Aahana. You were breaking me."

Aahana's face crumpled, and she took a trembling step closer. "I know... I know I hurt you, and I'll carry that regret for the rest of my life. But I came back because I couldn't stay away anymore. I couldn't let the silence between us win."

Her voice wavered as she continued, "This reunion... all of it... was my way of showing you how much you mean to me. I couldn't have done it alone. Roy helped me plan everything—every surprise, every detail—because he knew how much I needed to make things right."

Aksha's breath hitched at Aahana's words. The anger she held onto so tightly began to loosen its grip.

"You think a few surprises will fix everything?" Aksha asked, though her voice had softened.

"No," Aahana whispered. "But it's a start. I want to earn back your trust, Aksha. I'm here... and I'm not leaving again. That's my promise."

Aksha stood frozen as Aahana's voice filled the room, each word piercing her like a dagger. The memories—the good and the painful—came rushing back all at once, overwhelming her. But instead of softening, her expression hardened, her jaw tightening as she tried to keep her emotions in check.

Aahana, wiping the tears streaming down her face, looked at her with pleading eyes. "Aksha, please... just give me a chance to explain. I didn't mean to hurt you. I had no choice."

Aksha's gaze, sharp and cold, cut through Aahana. "No choice? *No choice?*" she repeated bitterly, her voice trembling with anger. "You *chose* to leave, Aahana. You *chose* to disappear when I needed you the most. Do you even realize what you did to me?"

Aahana opened her mouth to speak, but Aksha raised her hand, silencing her.

"You vanished on my wedding day," Aksha continued, her voice shaking with fury. "*My wedding day*, Aahana! The one day I wanted my best friend by my side. I kept looking for you. I thought something had happened. I was terrified. And then I realized... you weren't coming back."

The room was deathly silent. The rest of the group stood frozen, helpless witnesses to the emotional storm unfolding before them. Aarush, his face filled with worry, watched Aksha closely, wanting to step in but knowing she needed to let it out.

"You didn't just leave me," Aksha continued, her voice low but seething. "You abandoned *us*—the Ninjas, the people who loved you, trusted you. And now you're back with some grand surprise, acting like everything can just... go back to normal?" She let out a bitter laugh, shaking her head. "No, Aahana. It doesn't work that way."

Aahana's face crumbled. "Aksha, I know I hurt you. I regret it every single day. I—"

"Stop," Aksha cut her off coldly. Her hands clenched into fists at her sides as she fought back tears. "You don't get to explain it away. Not now. Not after everything."

She turned abruptly toward the door, her footsteps echoing against the wooden floor of the treehouse. Aarush, alarmed, called out, "Ashu... wait... please!"

Aksha didn't stop. She paused briefly at the doorway and looked back, her gaze landing on Roy. "And you," she said, her tone heavy with betrayal. "You knew. You *knew* she was in touch, and you said nothing. How could you keep this from me, Roy?"

Roy's face fell, guilt and shame written across it. "Aksha, I—"

"Save it," she snapped, shaking her head. "I trusted you, Roy. And you lied."

The weight of her words silenced him, and the guilt on his face deepened. Aksha took a deep breath, as though steadying herself, and turned back toward the door.

"I'm done with this," she muttered, more to herself than anyone else. Without looking back, she descended the steps of the treehouse and disappeared into the darkness of the night.

ᗺᗺᗺ

The remaining Ninjas stood in stunned silence. Aahana sank to her knees, her sobs breaking the stillness of the room. "I didn't mean for this to happen," she whispered brokenly, burying her face in her hands.

Roy stood motionless, his head hung low, unable to escape the weight of his own choices.

Aarush watched the doorway, his heart heavy as he thought of Aksha walking away into the night, alone and hurt. He ran his hands through his hair, exhaling sharply. "She needs time," he said softly, though his voice held no certainty.

Anu turned to Dev and whispered, "This is far from over."

Dev nodded grimly. "Yeah. But right now, it feels like we're more broken than ever."

The treehouse, once a symbol of joy and reunion, now felt empty—a silent witness to the cracks that time and secrets had created. Outside, the night stretched on, and the echoes of unsaid words lingered in the air.

Aahana sat curled up on the floor of the treehouse, her sobs echoing softly in the tense silence. The weight of everything—the years of absence, the misunderstanding, and Aksha's anger—crushed her spirit. Her body trembled, and her breath grew uneven as the overwhelming emotions pushed her to the brink of collapse.

Roy, watching helplessly, felt his heart ache at the sight of her. He crouched beside her, his hand gently resting on her shoulder in a steadying gesture. "Aahana… Aahana, listen to me," he urged softly, trying to steady her sobs. "You need to calm down. We'll figure this out. You're not alone, okay? We're all here for you."

But Aahana didn't respond. Her body shivered as tears streamed down her face uncontrollably. The guilt, the regret, and the pain of rejection swirled within her, growing heavier with every passing second.

"She's not okay," Roy muttered to himself, his voice laced with concern. Without wasting a moment, he pulled out his phone and dialed a number. "Heey bro… Aahana needs your help. Please come soon, dear," he said urgently.

The calm and reassuring voice of Nikhil, Aahana's psychiatrist, came through the line. "I'll be there in five minutes. Don't worry. Keep her stable till I arrive. She'll be fine, Roy. Just stay with her."

Roy exhaled sharply, reassured by Nikhil's confidence, and turned back to Aahana. Sitting beside her, he spoke softly yet firmly. "Easy, Aahana. Listen to me. I know it hurts. I know you feel broken right now, but this isn't the end. You've come so far, and you're stronger than you think. You can't let this moment undo everything you've fought for."

Aahana's sobs softened slightly, though her breaths still came in ragged gasps. Roy continued, his voice steady. "You're one tough girl. I've seen you face battles no one else could. This—this pain—it's not forever. Don't let it define you. Take a deep breath. Just one step at a time, okay?"

Aahana looked up at him through tear-streaked eyes, her face pale and exhausted. "I don't know, Roy... I feel like I've lost everything," she whispered weakly.

"You haven't," Roy replied firmly, holding her gaze. "You still have people who care about you. We'll fix this. But for now, you need to trust yourself—and trust us."

ᑭᑭᑭ

Just then, the sound of quick footsteps echoed from outside the treehouse. Moments later, Nikhil entered, his tall, lean figure exuding a calm, authoritative presence. His warm brown eyes scanned the room and settled on Aahana, immediately assessing the situation.

"Aahana," Nikhil said softly, kneeling beside her. The gentle cadence of his voice cut through the tension, a soothing balm to the chaos. "You're okay now. I'm here. Just breathe for me, all right?"

Aahana blinked, her trembling beginning to subside at the sound of his voice. Nikhil's reassuring smile, framed by his neatly trimmed beard and wire-rimmed glasses, felt like a lifeline in the moment.

Roy stepped back, giving Nikhil space. "She got overwhelmed. Aksha... she didn't take things well," Roy explained quietly.

Nikhil nodded in understanding, his demeanor remaining calm and composed. "That's okay. We'll get through this." He turned his attention back to Aahana. "I know this feels unbearable right now, but it's just one chapter. You're stronger than this moment, Aahana. And we'll work through it, together."

Aahana, her breathing slowing, nodded weakly. "I don't know how to fix this..." she murmured.

"You don't have to figure it out alone," Nikhil replied gently. "Right now, all you need to do is take care of yourself. Let's focus on calming down for now, all right? We'll take it one step at a time."

Aahana, though still fragile, seemed to draw strength from his words. Roy, watching from the side, felt a small wave of relief as Nikhil's presence worked its magic.

"Thank you," Aahana whispered faintly, glancing briefly at Roy before lowering her gaze.

Roy offered a small smile, stepping forward. "You don't need to thank me, Aahana. You've always been there for us. Now it's our turn to be there for you."

As Nikhil continued speaking softly to Aahana, helping her regain her composure, Roy walked to the window and gazed out into the night. His thoughts drifted to Aksha and the rest of the group. He knew the wounds weren't just Aahana's to carry. The fallout of tonight's events had left cracks in all of them—cracks that wouldn't be easy to mend.

For now, however, Aahana needed them the most. And Roy was determined to make sure she didn't face this alone.

ᐅᐅᐅ

10
The Weight of Regret

In the bustling corridors of college, where friendships were forged amidst shared laughter and the chaos of assignments, Dev's eyes always searched for *her*. Aahana—the enigma, the light, the heartbeat of the Ninjas. Her presence was magnetic, drawing everyone toward her with the effortless charm of someone who lived life with reckless joy. For Dev, she wasn't just a friend; she was a feeling.

Days turned into golden memories as Dev and Aahana spent endless hours together. Their conversations flowed like rivers—deep, comforting, and endlessly fascinating. They shared dreams of tomorrow, teased one another about silly habits, and revealed fragments of their souls that few were privileged to see. But while Aahana spoke freely of her world, Dev's heart guarded a secret—one that even he didn't know how to confront.

As his feelings for her deepened, Dev's smiles grew quieter. Every time she laughed, every time her eyes lit up in conversation, his heart whispered words he didn't dare say aloud: *"I love you."* The fear of losing their friendship became a chain that bound his confession. Instead of words, Dev turned to paper. His room, a small refuge of solitude, became the sanctuary where his unspoken emotions lived. Night after night, he poured his heart into letters—words filled with longing, admiration, and love he believed would never be returned.

"Aahana, if you only knew... You are the reason my world feels less empty. You've colored the silence of my life with laughter I never knew I needed. And yet, I can't tell you, because I'm afraid you'll walk away..."

Each letter held his truth—letters never meant to leave the confines of a secret box beneath his bed.

But life, as it often does, played a cruel hand. One day, without warning, Aahana disappeared. Her absence hit the Ninjas like a storm, but for Dev, it was shattering. She left no explanation, no goodbyes—only a void that consumed every unspoken word he'd hidden away. He searched for her, questioned their friends, even looked to the heavens for answers, but found nothing. She was gone, and with her, so was the chance to tell her what his heart had always known.

It was Anu who stumbled upon the letters. Being Dev's closest confidante, she'd always noticed the flicker of pain in his eyes whenever Aahana's name came up. One evening, curiosity guided her to the old, worn box hidden away in Dev's room. As she unfolded each letter, her heart ached for her friend. The ink, though dry, seemed to pulse with the weight of Dev's love.

By the time she finished reading, tears pricked her eyes. Anu became the silent keeper of a love story Dev never had the courage to live—a love story that deserved the world but was instead buried in the echoes of unspoken words. She confronted him once, asking, "Why didn't you tell her?" But Dev had no answer—only a faint, melancholic smile that spoke of regret too vast to articulate.

Years passed, and time carried the Ninjas forward. Aahana's absence became a ghost that lingered in quiet corners of their memories. Dev, ever the loyal friend, moved on with life, or so it seemed. Yet on certain nights, when the world was silent, he'd take out those letters, trace the words with his fingers, and allow himself to remember. For him, Aahana was no longer just a person—she was a memory frozen in time, a chapter of his life unfinished.

Meanwhile, joy found its way into the Ninjas' lives, despite everything. Manan, Maher, Rishi, and Roy celebrated the completion of their long-cherished dream: Ninja 9. Their laughter echoed through the room, vibrant and full of life. Manan, in particular, stood out—his elation was contagious, as though he were on top of the world.

But even amidst the joy, Dev felt something missing. The laughter was there, the friends were there, but *she* was not. Aahana's absence remained like an unplayed note in a melody—one that Dev, despite his best efforts, could still hear.

As the night wore on, Anu quietly watched Dev, a knowing sadness in her eyes. She knew his heart still carried the weight of unspoken love—a love that perhaps, someday, might find its voice. But for now, it remained hidden in the quiet between breaths, a story written in letters never sent, and in memories Dev was too afraid to forget.

ppp

The next morning, the room was quiet, except for the faint sounds of the world waking up outside. Dev sat there in the soft, dim light, looking tired and lost. It was clear he hadn't slept well, his eyes showing the weight of the emotions he had been struggling with all night.

Anu stepped into Dev's room, the comforting aroma of freshly brewed coffee and a warm cheese sandwich trailing behind her. Her eyes quickly took in the scene—a messy room marked by the signs of a troubled night. Burned-out cigarettes and a broken wine bottle silently told the story of Dev's inner turmoil.

When Anu walked in, she immediately felt the tension in the air. She looked at Dev, noticing the way he sat, silent but heavy with unspoken feelings. She could tell he was caught in a whirlwind of memories and emotions, reliving parts of his past he had tried so hard to bury.

Carrying the breakfast tray, Anu placed it gently on the table and pulled a chair closer to him. She gave his shoulder a soft tap. "Good morning, dear. Are you okay?"

Dev forced a small smile, his voice flat as he said, "First-class, as always."

116

"Dev," Anu said softly, breaking the silence. "You look like you've been carrying the world on your shoulders. What's going on?"

Dev sighed deeply, running a hand through his hair. "It's... complicated, Anu. The past has a way of sneaking up on you, you know? Some things just don't leave you alone, no matter how far you try to run."

"You don't have to go through this alone. Talk to me. I'm here, okay?"

Dev glanced at her, his walls slowly coming down. "Thanks, Anu. I just... I don't even know where to start."

"Start wherever you feel ready," she said gently. "Sometimes, just letting it out can make all the difference."

Dev's mind was a storm of emotions, where the echoes of unsaid words and feelings he had buried long ago clashed with each other. Aahana's sudden return had thrown him into a whirlwind of confusion. The pain of her leaving without a word years ago came rushing back, mixed with a flicker of hope her presence now ignited. His heart, still tied to the memories they had shared, longed for answers but was afraid of the vulnerability those answers might bring.

Questions raced through his mind. *Why did she leave? What made her come back now? Is this her way of healing old wounds, or just a cruel twist of fate?* His love for Aahana, hidden in the corners of his heart for so long, pushed against the walls he had built to protect himself.

Anu, always able to sense the emotions Dev tried to hide, approached him quietly. She could see the weight of what he was feeling, even though he kept it locked inside. She knew his emotions were deep, carefully hidden behind his calm exterior. Without pushing or questioning, Anu stayed close, offering silent support as Dev wrestled with the past and the mystery of Aahana's return. Her eyes filled with understanding. She knew better than to push him. His words didn't fool her, but she chose not to press further. She wanted to be his quiet anchor, not someone who added to his burden.

Choosing to listen rather than advise is a beautiful way to practice silent empathy. When we truly listen, we respect the importance of someone's personal story, understanding that their experiences hold their own wisdom. It shows humility, acknowledging how complex life can be and valuing shared emotions over quick solutions.

This approach embraces the power of simply being there for someone, building a connection through understanding rather than instruction. By being a listener, we move beyond the urge to fix things and instead join in a shared journey of growth and insight. In those quiet moments, we find the beauty of silent support and the deep bond it creates in human relationships.

After a moment, Dev broke the silence. "How's Aksha?"

"She's better now. Aarush messaged me," Anu replied.

No words were exchanged; she just wanted to stand by him, offering support.

"Hey!! Do you want to visit Subban Park with me today?" Dev suggested.

"Omg!! Seriously!! Are you asking for a day? My goodness!!" Anu teased.

"No, I am asking for a week, a month, a year, a life..." Dev replied playfully.

"I didn't mind going with you... On a date!" Anu said, saluting playfully, and left the room.

"Listen..." Dev called out. Anu turned. "You and me only," he emphasized.

"Ok boss! Finished your breakfast fast." Anu gestured a salute and left.

***

In the stillness of the morning, each ninja sat quietly, lost in their own tangle of emotions. They hoped that this reunion could untie the knots of their messy pasts and lead them toward a brighter, happier future.

In his dimly lit room, Dev faced a storm of feelings swirling inside him. Aahana's sudden return had brought back memories he thought he had buried long ago. Her unexpected presence filled him with a mix of hope and fear—hope for closure and fear of reopening old wounds. The pain of her leaving without an explanation years ago weighed heavily on his heart, clashing with the fragile hope sparked by her return.

Dev's thoughts were a jumble of unsaid words and unresolved feelings, echoing deep within him. As he tried to make sense of the past and navigate the uncertainty of the present, his emotions felt both overwhelming and impossible to ignore.

Anu, ever in tune with the quiet struggles of her friends, moved among them with a gentle understanding in her eyes. Each ninja carried their own story, filled with longing and unresolved feelings. The air was thick with the shared hope that this reunion would bring comfort and a sense of closure.

Maher, Manan, Roy, and Rishi, though laughing and joking on the outside, each bore the weight of their own hidden battles. Their smiles masked the storms within, as they tried to balance the joys of the present with the lingering shadows of the past. Every step toward happiness felt cautious, like walking a thin line between what was and what could be.

As the morning light streamed into the room, it became a place of raw emotions. Each of them faced their own maze of feelings, hoping that this moment together would spark healing and lead them toward the lasting happiness they all sought.

ppp

It had been four days since their group got back together, but Maher hadn't said anything about her husband. Not a single word. Every time someone asked, she would dodge the question—changing the topic, laughing it off, or just waving her hand like it didn't matter.

Rishi frowned, staring at the door. "Why won't you talk about it, Maher?" he muttered softly. It wasn't like her to keep secrets, especially about something as important as her marriage. Was she hiding something? Or was it just too hard for her to talk about?

Rishi's voice broke the silence. "Door's open! Come in!" he called out, not even looking up from his book. A knock at the door made him pause for a moment, but his thoughts weren't really on the story he was reading. His mind was stuck on Maher

The door creaked open, pulling him out of his thoughts. He looked up and sighed. "Come in already," he said, forcing a small smile. But even as he greeted the person walking in, his mind stayed stuck on the mystery of Maher and the questions she wouldn't answer.

Rishi couldn't shake the feeling that something was off about Maher. Over the past few days, he'd noticed her rejecting calls over and over, her face tightening with unease each time her phone buzzed. Once, she even switched her phone to airplane mode mid-conversation, almost as if shutting out the world was the only way to find peace. Whatever it was, she was clearly guarding it fiercely, and it only made Rishi's curiosity grow stronger.

He sat in his chair, staring at his book but not really reading. His thoughts kept circling back to Maher, the unanswered questions piling up in his mind. *Who keeps calling her? Why won't she talk about it?*

A sudden knock at the door snapped him out of his thoughts. He looked up to see Maher standing there, her expression calm but with a flicker of something—guilt? Apology? He couldn't quite place it.

"Sorry," she said, her voice soft. "I think you're busy. I'll come back later."

Rishi blinked, shaking his head as he stood up. "Wait... no, I'm not busy," he said quickly, pushing his book aside. "What's up?"

Maher hesitated, her hand resting lightly on the doorframe. "It's nothing urgent. I'll handle it. You carry on with your work."

"Maher," Rishi said, his tone firm but kind, "you've been acting... different. Is everything okay?"

She looked away for a moment, her fingers fidgeting with the hem of her kurta. "Everything's fine," she said, forcing a small smile. "Really. I just have a lot on my mind, that's all."

Rishi crossed his arms, his curiosity getting the better of him. "Fine doesn't usually involve avoiding calls and shutting your phone off. You know you can talk to me, right?"

Maher's smile faltered, and for a brief moment, Rishi thought she might actually say something. But instead, she shook her head, brushing past his words. "It's nothing, Rishi. Just leave it, okay?" she said, her voice firmer now.

Rishi sighed, watching her turn to leave. The air between them felt heavy, filled with tension and unspoken truths. He wanted to push, to demand answers, but he also didn't want to drive her further away. Instead, he called after her, "Maher... I'm here if you need me."

She paused at the door, glancing back with a faint smile. "Thanks, Rishi. That means a lot." And with that, she was gone, leaving Rishi with more questions than ever and the sense that whatever Maher was hiding, it wasn't something she could keep buried forever.

As Rishi turned back to his chair, another knock sounded at the door, but this time it opened almost instantly. Maher stood there, her expression more composed. "I was thinking of visiting the Balaji temple nearby," she said. "It feels better not to go alone, so I thought I'd ask if you'd like to join me."

"Oh, my pleasure!" Rishi responded, a small smile tugging at his lips. "Wait, let me guess—it's the same temple we used to visit after college hours?"

"Yeah, that's the one," Maher confirmed, her voice carrying a hint of nostalgia.

"Great! Give me five minutes to get ready," Rishi said, already moving toward his wardrobe.

"Okay, I'll wait downstairs," Maher replied before turning to leave the room.

As soon as she was gone, Rishi sat back down for a moment, murmuring to himself, "This might be the perfect chance to clear up all these questions."

By eleven in the morning, both of them were ready and heading toward the temple. The walk was quiet at first, with the warm sun filtering through the trees, but Rishi's mind was far from calm. He couldn't stop thinking about what had been bothering Maher and hoped this trip might give him the opportunity to finally get some answers.

ᐅᐅᐅ

"Don't you understand? Stop bothering me. I said, leave me!" Aksha shouted, her voice filled with frustration. But then, a voice from behind caught her attention.

She turned around, and her words stopped mid-sentence. It was Aahana.

"Hey... wait," Aahana said, her voice shaking. "Please don't go. Just talk to me."

Aksha's face hardened as she looked at her. "What's there to talk about now?" she asked, her voice calm but filled with pain.

"I'm sorry," Aahana said softly, taking a step closer. "I'm really, really sorry, Aksha. I hurt you so much. I know I did."

Her words were full of regret, and her eyes looked desperate for forgiveness. Aksha stood silently, torn between her anger and the small hope that maybe things could still be fixed.

"You better be," Aksha said, her voice heavy with disappointment. "But maybe it's my fault for trusting you." Her words stung with both hurt and self-blame, and her eyes glistened with the pain of betrayal.

"Please don't say that," Aahana pleaded, her voice trembling. "I need you, Aksha. I really do."

"Need me?" Aksha's voice rose slightly, her emotions surfacing. "Where were you when I needed you? When I was all alone?" Her question was filled with hurt, her eyes searching Aahana's face for answers.

"I didn't have a choice," Aahana whispered, her tone low and filled with helplessness. She looked down, the weight of her own regrets pressing heavily on her shoulders.

"Now you have a choice to hurt me again?" Aksha asked, her voice a mix of anger and vulnerability. Her eyes held a guarded look, as if bracing for more pain.

"I don't want to hurt you," Aahana replied softly. Her voice was gentle, almost pleading, and her eyes reflected nothing but sincerity.

"Then why did you come back?" Aksha's voice cracked slightly, revealing the effort it had taken to move on. "I was just starting to get better." Her words laid bare the struggle she had endured, the wounds that still lingered beneath the surface.

"I thought you'd be happy to see me again," Aahana said softly, her voice carrying a flicker of hope. Her eyes searched Aksha's face, longing for a positive reaction.

"Happy? Why should I be?" Aksha shot back, her voice sharp with pain. "Who even are you to me anymore?" Her question hung in the air, heavy with the confusion and hurt of a broken bond.

"You're hurting me, Aksha," Aahana said, her voice trembling as tears filled her eyes. Her emotions were raw, spilling out despite her attempts to stay composed.

"And you didn't hurt me?" Aksha replied, her tone laced with bitterness. Her gaze was steady, filled with the scars of the past that hadn't yet healed.

"Beat me, scold me, do whatever you want," Aahana pleaded, with cracking voice. "But please don't hate me. You have no idea what I've been through." Her words carried the weight of her struggles, and her eyes begging for a chance to be understood.

"And do you even realize what we went through?" Aksha's voice trembled, heavy with shared pain. "The Ninja was shattered. I was shattered. Completely broken. Do you have any idea what that felt like?" Her eyes burned with the weight of their collective suffering, frustration spilling over.

"I'm so sorry for that," Aahana said quietly, her voice tinged with guilt. She let out a deep sigh, her eyes full of regret. "I truly am."

"And you think one sorry is going to fix everything?" Aksha shot back, her words sharp and skeptical. Her eyes bore into Aahana's, searching for something beyond the surface apology. "Do you really think it's that easy?"

It wasn't just Aksha speaking—it was five years of bottled-up pain, anger, and heartbreak finally finding a voice.

"No, but…" Aahana began, her words faltering as she struggled to find the right thing to say. Her remorse was genuine, but she knew it wasn't enough to heal the wounds she had left behind.

"You know what, just leave it!" Aksha snapped, her voice trembling with anger and hurt. "There's no point talking to you. You can't understand anyone's emotions. And honestly, who even are you? I don't know you anymore." With those words, she turned and walked toward the house, her steps firm but heavy with pain.

"Aksha, wait… please!" Aahana called out, following closely behind. "Don't go. Just talk to me. Let it out—let all your bitterness out if you have to. Please!" Her voice was desperate, filled with an aching need to make things right.

But Aksha didn't stop. She kept walking, leaving Aahana standing there, her pleas hanging in the air like unfinished sentences, and the space between them filled with unresolved emotions.

Aahana dropped to the ground, her sobs filling the air. Her legs couldn't hold her anymore, and it felt like even breathing was too hard. The pain inside her was so heavy that it seemed to stop everything around her.

Time felt frozen as her tears fell, showing just how much she was hurting. Unable to handle the weight of her emotions, she fainted, a quiet sign of how deeply the past had hurt her.

ɔɔɔ

11
Broken Pieces

The peaceful garden suddenly turned chaotic as Aahana collapsed, unconscious. Dev, who was waiting there for Anu to join him for a trip to Subbon Park, saw the commotion from afar. Not knowing it was Aahana, he quickly rushed to the scene.

His steps faltered as shock gripped him—Aahana lay motionless on the ground.

"Oh my God... Help! Somebody help!" Dev's panicked voice echoed through the garden, breaking the stillness.

Hearing the urgency in Dev's cries, Roy, who was standing near the main door, immediately ran over, his concern evident as he approached.

"What happened?" Roy asked, his face filled with worry as he looked at Aahana.

Dev was too stunned to speak, but Roy quickly took charge. "Oh my God! This can't be happening," he muttered, seeing Aahana on the ground. He gently rubbed her palm and told Dev, "Rub her foot, quickly!"

Anu and Aarush arrived, clearly confused and concerned. "What's wrong?" Aarush asked, stepping forward.

"Come here, Aarush. Rub her palm," Roy instructed. "I need to inform Nikhil. Anu, check her bag for any medicine."

Anu nodded and began searching through the bag, her face tense. "Okay, I think we should call for medical help," she said, her voice steady but worried. As she continued searching, she noticed that Dev was shaking, his body trembling from the shock.

"Nikhil is her doctor. He knows better what to do," Roy said, focusing on Aahana and trying to keep calm.

Aarush looked confused. "How do you know that?"

"Stop it, guys! This isn't the time for questions," Dev snapped, his voice shaking. "Her health is the only thing that matters right now. Focus on her!"

Anu, still rummaging through the bag, looked up and said, "Look, Roy! Is this the one you need?" She handed him a packet of medicine.

"Yes, that's it! Thank God," Roy replied with a sigh of relief. He quickly took out a pill and gently placed it in Aahana's mouth, hoping it would help her.

"We need to take her to the city hospital. Nikhil will be there soon," Roy said firmly, his tone filled with urgency.

Dev, panicking, rushed toward the house. "Momo, mom... where is the key?" he shouted, his voice tight with stress.

Manan, hearing the chaos, came out and asked, "What's going on? You look really tense."

"There's no time! We need to get her to the hospital right now!" Dev explained quickly, barely able to catch his breath.

"Who?" Manan asked, confused.

"Aahana," Dev replied, his eyes wide with worry.

"What?!" Manan was shocked, clearly not expecting this.

"Yes! Please, hurry!" Dev pleaded.

"Okay, let's go!" Manan said, immediately understanding the urgency. He joined Dev, and they rushed out to help.

"I think we shouldn't wait for the ambulance. We can get to the hospital faster by car," Dev suggested, his voice full of urgency.

"Yes, you're right," Roy agreed quickly. The group, now fully focused on getting Aahana to safety, moved into action.

Manan, understanding the situation and sensing Dev's emotional state, took the driver's seat at Anu's request. Meanwhile, Aksha stood close by, torn between her anger and deep concern for

Aahana. Her heart ached as she hoped for her best friend's swift recovery, fighting the emotions swirling inside her.

At the city hospital, Nikhil was already waiting for Aahana's arrival. As Anu, Aarush, and Aksha pulled up in another car, Nikhil quickly took charge of the situation.

"How did this happen? Any idea?" Nikhil asked, his concern obvious as he approached Roy and Dev, who were carrying Aahana inside.

"No, she just collapsed when I saw her," Dev replied, his voice filled with worry.

"Alright, let me assess her. You stay here," Nikhil instructed, gently guiding Aahana into the assessment room.

In moments like these, no matter how angry or hurt we may feel toward someone, seeing them in pain—especially someone close to us—brings out a deeper sense of love and concern. Past grievances fade in the face of true care, reminding us of the strong bond that can exist despite everything else.

𑁍𑁍𑁍

Meanwhile, at the temple, Rishi noticed Maher lost in her rituals, but her phone kept buzzing, interrupting the peaceful moment. Deciding it was time to speak up, Rishi turned to her.

"Is this what you call harmony?" he asked, as they sat together, feeding the pigeons.

"Are you done with your rituals?" he asked, curious.

"Yup," Maher answered, offering him a smile. "Thanks for keeping me company."

"No problem. My pleasure, ma'am. Anything for you," Rishi replied with a playful tone, and they both laughed.

"Can we go now?" Rishi asked, ready to leave.

"If you don't mind, can we sit here a little longer? I'd like to enjoy this peaceful place for a while," Maher suggested, looking around at the serene surroundings.

Spending time at a temple surrounded by nature feels like a peaceful getaway, a perfect way to relax. The calm of the temple, mixed with the beauty of the outdoors, creates a soothing environment. It's not just about the rituals; it's about finding peace in the quiet moments, with the trees and the open sky around you. The combination of the spiritual atmosphere and the simplicity of nature works wonders, helping to ease stress. It's a time to pause, take a deep breath, and reconnect with a sense of calm. A visit to such a temple is like a therapy session for the mind and soul, leaving you feeling refreshed and peaceful.

"Sure, I don't mind," Manan agreed, settling in.

Maher's phone continued ringing, and she quickly disconnected the call and turned it off. Manan noticed and raised an eyebrow, curious about her actions.

"Do you still trust me?" Manan asked, his tone serious.

Maher blinked in surprise. "Uh, sorry, what?"

"Do you trust me or not? Simple. Yes or no," he repeated.

"Yes, of course, dear," Maher affirmed, though her voice had a hint of uncertainty.

"Then why are you acting so distant, like a stranger?" he pressed, his tone soft but direct.

"What? No, sit. You misunderstood me," she quickly said, trying to brush it off.

Manan shook his head, a playful smile on his face. "Stop acting. You know you're the worst actor," he teased.

Maher laughed. "Hahaha, good joke," she replied, trying to lighten the mood.

"Don't try to ignore my question. Tell me. What is bothering you?" Manan asked firmly, his eyes focused on her.

"No, nothing like that. Trust me," Maher reassured him, but she avoided making eye contact.

Manan leaned in slightly, his concern growing. "See, I hope you won't take it the wrong way, but is everything okay with your married life?" he asked, the weight of his words lingering.

Maher hesitated, her gaze drifting. "Uh, well... Yes, everything is fine. In fact, he's a great man. He takes good care of me," she replied, but there was an edge of uncertainty in her voice.

Manan wasn't satisfied. "Then why don't you wear the mangalsutra? You used to like wearing it, right?" he probed further, unable to let go of his suspicions.

Maher sighed, clearly frustrated. "Oh man! You and your overthinking! Nothing like that. I just don't feel like wearing it now, so I don't," she explained, dismissing his question with a wave of her hand.

Manan still wasn't convinced. "Uh, I can't believe it. I know you more than you think," he remarked, his tone soft but with a hint of disbelief.

Maher looked at him, her expression softening. "More than anyone else," she admitted, her words hanging in the air, full of unspoken thoughts and emotions.

Rishi, who had been silently observing, now felt the weight of her words. His eyes widened in astonishment. *Is Maher still in love with her ex-husband?* he wondered. Regardless, it was clear that her marital struggles were at the heart of her distress. Concerned, he reached for her hands, gently taking them in his, offering a silent show of support.

"Listen, whatever is troubling you, tell me everything. Don't worry; I will never judge you. You can trust me. You deserve to be happy, dear. Your face may be smiling, but you're not happy. I can feel that," Rishi comforted her, his voice soft but firm, as he gently held her hands.

Maher looked down, her struggle to hold back tears evident in the way her body trembled. The facade she had built was cracking, revealing the depth of her pain. After a long, shaky breath, she finally spoke, her voice barely above a whisper.

"Rishi," she began, her eyes glistening with unshed tears, "there's so much I've kept hidden. It's... it's been hard." She paused, her chest rising and falling with emotion. "I thought I could move on, pretend like everything was fine... but it's not."

Rishi stayed silent, waiting for her to continue, his gaze full of understanding."It's okay," he said gently. "You don't have to carry all of this alone."

""Listening is crucial for meaningful connections. It shows respect, builds trust, and fosters understanding. Being a good listener goes beyond giving advice; it's about creating a space for open expression, strengthening relationships through genuine connection.""

"Life has taken a dark turn," she confessed, her voice carrying the weight of her experiences. "My marriage, once the cornerstone of my happiness, is crumbling. Living with my husband has become a nightmare of abuse and torment. He's not just a partner; he's become a relentless source of pain."

Her eyes revealed a depth of suffering as she shared a revelation that left Rishi stunned. "The violence didn't spare even the innocence of my child. It's a heart-wrenching reality. But here's the twist – I didn't just leave. I decided to take control. I filed for divorce, not just for my sake, but to ensure my child's safety and a chance at a brighter future. Sometimes, the most unexpected turns lead to the most profound revelations." Maher split it out in a single go.

Rishi was speechless, his mind racing as Maher's words sank in. The weight of what she had just shared hung in the air, each sentence heavy with the pain she had endured. His heart ached for her, and for the child who had suffered in silence.

"I had no idea," he whispered, struggling to find the right words. "I... I can't believe you've been going through this all this time. You're incredibly strong, Maher."

She wiped away a tear, her eyes raw but filled with a quiet resilience. "I had to be. I couldn't just stand by and watch my life, and my child's life, fall apart. Leaving wasn't easy, but it was the only choice I had."

Rishi took a deep breath, trying to process everything. "You did the right thing. No one deserves to live in fear. And you've taken a huge step for both you and your child."

Maher nodded, her shoulders sagging slightly in relief. "It's been hard, but I'm trying to rebuild. It's not easy, but I'm finally taking control of my life, and I won't let anyone dictate my future anymore."

Rishi, still holding her hands, gave her a reassuring squeeze. "You're not alone in this. Whatever you need, I'm here for you. You're not just surviving, Maher. You're starting to thrive again."

She smiled weakly, the corners of her lips lifting just enough to show her gratitude. "Thank you, Rishi. I don't know what I would've done without you."

Rishi gave a gentle nod, his expression soft with understanding. "You're stronger than you think. You've already made the hardest choice. Now, the road ahead will get easier, step by step."

The exchange, simple yet profound, encapsulated the depth of Maher's journey. As she spoke about her daughter, her voice softened, revealing a tenderness that contrasted with the hardships she had faced. Her daughter, in many ways, was both a symbol of hope and a reminder of the strength it took to move forward. The love she had for her child was palpable, a protective force that kept her fighting through every storm.

Rishi, on the other hand, in his congratulatory words, wasn't just acknowledging the new life but recognizing the quiet courage in Maher's role as a mother. He understood that it wasn't just about celebrating a birth; it was about acknowledging the challenges of raising a child in the midst of personal turmoil. His congratulations held more weight than mere pleasantries—it was a recognition of Maher's resilience and a silent promise of support.

For Maher, hearing those words felt like a momentary relief, as if someone finally saw beyond her struggles to appreciate her strength. It wasn't about the circumstances or the hardship—it was about the love for her daughter that transcended it all.

In that brief interaction, the space between them filled with an unspoken understanding. It wasn't just about the present moment, but about the shared recognition of what it took to move forward, to rebuild, and to keep going. The small but meaningful exchange became a quiet acknowledgment of the path they both walked—one of healing, strength, and new beginnings.

In the midst of life's complexities, the presence of a daughter became a guiding light, a beacon of hope that illuminated the darkest corners of her world. And in his congratulatory words, he unwittingly became a witness to the strength and beauty that emanated from the simple but profound bond between a mother and her child.

"The best part is, You have a child?" he said.

"Yes, I have a three-year-old daughter," she shared. "but I don't know if I'm capable of providing her with a good future," she confessed.

"Means?" he asked.

"I filed for a divorce and applied for custody of her. To secure custody, I have to prove that I am capable of raising her in court," she explained.

"You don't need to prove that; you are already capable, dear," he reassured.

"The court doesn't believe in emotions; it demands practical evidence," she elaborated. "My husband claims that a single mother can't raise a child," she added.

"Useless fellow," he remarked. "So, what will you do now?"

"Don't know. Just pray and hope," she said.

Maher contemplated for a moment and then said, "Don't worry, I will testify in court for the custody of your daughter. I promise."

"What? How? You don't need to risk yourself. I don't want to involve you in a court matter," she protested.

"Don't worry, dear. It's on me. Just wait and watch," he reassured with a smile. "Your happy days are starting now. Enjoy."

ᐅᐅᐅ

Rishi's mobile vibrated, and he received a call. His expression turned grave as he tucked his phone back into his pocket. "Aahana is in a serious condition," he said, his voice tense with worry. "Everyone is at the civil hospital. We need to get there quickly."

Maher's eyes widened in concern. "Oh no! What happened? Is she going to be okay?"

"I'm not sure. They didn't give many details over the phone," Rishi replied, already reaching for his keys. "We need to hurry."

Maher nodded, a silent prayer forming on her lips. "I hope everything is alright," she murmured as they stepped out together, their pace quickening.

The drive to the hospital was quiet, the weight of uncertainty hanging between them. The city buzzed around them, oblivious to the storm of emotions building inside. Maher glanced at Rishi, his hands gripping the wheel tightly, his jaw clenched in focus.

"She'll be okay," Maher said softly, more to reassure herself than him.

Rishi gave a faint nod, his eyes fixed on the road. "I hope so."

ৡৡৡ

"Does anyone have any information about Aahana? What happened to her? Please, keep me in the loop—it will help me provide better care," Nikhil urged, his worry clearly etched on his face.

The ninjas, Aahana's close-knit group, were gathered in the hospital's visiting room. Yet, an uneasy silence blanketed the air. Aksha sat apart in a corner, shielding her face with her hands, her emotions hidden but palpable. Nikhil's gaze darted across the room, searching for someone who might speak up.

"Where's Dev?" he finally asked, noticing his absence.

The group exchanged glances, unsure. Anu, sensing the urgency and understanding the likely cause of Dev's absence, decided to look for him. Without hesitation, she made her way outside to the hospital garden, where she found him sitting on a bench under the shade of a large tree.

"Dev, are you okay?" Anu asked gently as she approached him.

Dev looked up at her, his face streaked with tears. The usually composed and cheerful young man was now a picture of heartbreak. Before Anu could say more, he stood and clung to her, his emotions spilling out in a torrent.

"I don't want to lose her again," he sobbed. "I can't afford that. I've waited for her for so long. I love her from the depth of my heart.

133

Why? Why does destiny always play with me? Why are we kept apart every time? I've missed her every day. I pray for her every day..."

Anu wrapped her arms around him, letting him release his pain. "Dev, calm down," she said softly. "Relax. I know everything. I know you love her—I read your undelivered letter to her."

Dev froze for a moment, his tear-filled eyes meeting hers. Anu smiled gently. "Be strong. Everything will be alright. Keep faith in the Lord. Aahana needs us right now, and she needs you to be strong for her."

Dev nodded, taking a deep breath to steady himself. Anu patted his shoulder. "Let's go inside. Everyone's searching for you."

Together, they made their way back to the visiting room, Dev mustering all his strength and hope for Aahana's recovery.

ᗡᗡᗡ

As the room's heavy silence persisted, Aksha, still sitting in the corner, struggled with her emotions. She clenched her fists, her mind racing with guilt and fear. Finally, she took a deep breath, gathered all her courage, and stood up. Her voice trembled, but determination laced her words.

"I need to say something," she began, her gaze avoiding the others but growing steadier as she spoke. "I can't keep it to myself anymore. You all need to know what happened before this... before Aahana collapsed."

The room fell silent, and all eyes turned to Aksha. Even Dev, who had just returned with Anu, froze mid-step.

Aksha continued, her voice faltering but resolute. "Earlier today, Aahana and I... we had an argument. A heated one. She came to me... to apologize, to talk... but I was so angry, so hurt from everything that happened in the past. I couldn't hold back. I said things I shouldn't have... terrible things." Her voice cracked, and tears began streaming down her face.

"I told her to leave... that I didn't want to see her anymore. I blamed her for everything—every ounce of pain I've carried for years. And she... she tried so hard to explain, to make me understand. But I didn't listen. I just pushed her away."

Aksha's shoulders shook as the weight of her confession settled over the room. "And then she... she collapsed. Right in front of me. I didn't know what to do. I didn't even call for help at first because I was in shock. I feel like this is all my fault."

The group remained quiet, processing Aksha's words. Dev's face was a mixture of anguish and anger, but he said nothing, his hands clenching into fists.

As Aksha stood amidst the heavy silence after her confession, the weight of her words settled over everyone. While the others processed her admission, Manan, who had been quietly observing from the side, finally stepped forward. His expression was stern, his brows furrowed with anger and disappointment.

"Aksha," he began, his voice firm but controlled, "do you even realize what you've done?"

Aksha flinched, her guilt deepening. "Manan, I—"

He held up his hand to stop her. "No, let me speak. You're not the only one who's been in pain. You're not the only one who's suffered because of what happened years ago. Do you think Aahana hasn't been hurting all this time? Do you think it was easy for her to face you today and try to fix things?"

His words were sharp, cutting through the tension in the room. "You let your anger blind you to her pain. Did you even try to see things from her side? Did you even think about how much courage it must have taken for her to come to you and apologize?"

Aksha's head dropped, unable to meet his piercing gaze.

Manan's voice softened slightly but still carried a firm edge. "I get it, Aksha. You're hurt. We all are in our own way. But that doesn't give you the right to push someone away when they're trying to make things right, especially when that someone is already struggling."

He paused, his emotions wavering between anger and sadness. "Aahana has always cared for you, despite everything. And instead of listening, you let your anger take over. Now look where we are.

She's fighting for her life, and you're drowning in guilt."

Aksha's tears flowed freely now, her hands trembling. "I... I didn't mean for this to happen. I was just so angry... I couldn't see clearly."

Manan sighed, running a hand through his hair in frustration. "We can't change what's already happened. But let this be a wake-up call, Aksha. Pain doesn't justify hurting others, especially the ones who care about us. Aahana didn't deserve this."

The room fell silent again as Manan stepped back, his anger giving way to quiet disappointment. Dev placed a calming hand on Manan's shoulder, silently urging him to ease up.

Anu, sensing the tension, spoke gently, "Aksha, take this as a lesson. You're not alone in this pain, and neither is Aahana. Let's focus on making things right and being there for her now."

Aksha nodded weakly, her guilt and regret evident. The group exchanged solemn looks, united in their shared hope for Aahana's recovery and a chance to heal the wounds between them all.

Nikhil stepped forward, his expression calm but firm. "Aksha, I understand how you're feeling, but this isn't the time for blame. What's important now is Aahana's recovery. We can sort everything else out once she's stable."

Anu placed a reassuring hand on Aksha's shoulder. "You did the right thing by telling us. We'll get through this together, for her."

Dev finally spoke, his voice tight with emotion. "Aksha, you might have said things in anger, but don't carry this guilt alone. Aahana is strong, and she'll get through this. Right now, we all need to focus on being there for her."

Aksha nodded, wiping her tears, as the group silently vowed to stand united for Aahana's recovery.

ᗧᗧᗧ

12

Echoes of Unsaid Words !!

The day of aarush and aksha's wedding ....

On the outskirts of Mumbai, where the busy city faded into peaceful greenery, Aarush and Aksha were ready to start a new chapter in their lives. Their destination wedding was a mix of traditions and simplicity, celebrated with their closest friends—Dev, Anu, Maher, Rishi, Roy, Manan, and the quiet but charming Aahana.

The venue was beautifully decorated with flowers and lights, creating a cozy and elegant atmosphere. Everyone felt at home, laughing, and chatting as they came together to celebrate.

The fun began with the Sangeet ceremony. Traditional songs and upbeat music filled the air as everyone joined in for the dances. Maher and Rishi's playful performance made everyone smile, while Roy and Manan's energetic moves had the group cheering loudly.

Dev and Anu surprised Aarush and Aksha with a special dance that showed how much they cared for them. Even Aahana, usually shy, joined in the fun with a gentle smile, adding to the joy of the evening.

The night was full of laughter, music, and heartfelt moments. It wasn't just about Aarush and Aksha's wedding; it was also about the strong friendship and love that held the group together.

The Sangeet was a beautiful start to the celebrations, leaving everyone with happy memories they would cherish forever.

As the stars twinkled above, the ninjas gathered in a cozy corner of the wedding venue, away from the bustling crowd and lively music. The calm night air was filled with warmth, a reflection of their deep bond and shared memories.

Roy, raising his glass, started a heartfelt toast. "To Aarush and Aksha—may your life together be full of joy, adventures, and unending love."

The soft clinking of glasses followed, accompanied by knowing smiles that needed no words. Aarush and Aksha glanced at their friends—their unwavering pillars of strength and love.

Maher, her eyes glistening, spoke with emotion, "You both are proof that love and friendship go hand in hand. Treasure every moment, just as we treasure having you in our lives."

Manan, ever the joker, chimed in, "Aarush, welcome to the official ninja family. And Aksha, congratulations on getting a lifelong partner to share the blame for all your mischief."

The group burst into laughter, the sound blending perfectly with the night's serenity. Holding Aarush's hand, Aksha looked around at her closest friends, her heart swelling with gratitude. In that moment, she realized their journey together—full of challenges and love—had brought them to this beautiful, unforgettable celebration.

Dev, typically the quiet observer, surprised everyone by speaking up. His voice was calm but full of emotion. "Aarush, take care of her. Aksha, take care of him. You both deserve all the happiness in the world."

The sincerity in his words touched everyone, making the moment even more special.

Anu, always the emotional anchor of the group, wiped away her tears as she added, "Seeing you two together brings back so many memories. Aarush, you've always been the glue for our ninja family. Now, make sure Aksha is just as happy as you've made all of us."

Their heartfelt words filled the air with love and warmth, leaving Aarush and Aksha deeply moved by the outpouring of affection from their closest friends.

In the midst of the joyful celebration, the ninjas felt the unbreakable bond that had carried them through life's ups and downs. This wedding wasn't just about Aarush and Aksha—it was a tribute to the enduring friendships and shared memories that made their group special.

Aahana, known for her elegance and grace, had planned a heartfelt performance for her dear childhood friend, Aksha. But as the festivities continued, Aksha noticed her absence. A sense of curiosity mixed with playful suspicion sparked in her mind.

"Where is she hiding now?" Aksha wondered, her mischievous smile betraying her thoughts.

Excusing herself from the lively crowd, Aksha embarked on a solo mission to uncover Aahana's whereabouts. She tiptoed past laughing guests and lively conversations, her excitement growing with each step. The search led her to the quieter corners of the venue, where she hoped to find her enigmatic friend preparing for her big moment.

Her steps were careful, weaving through the laughter and dancing, and she couldn't help but notice the glances exchanged among the ninjas. There was a shared secret, and Aksha was determined to unravel it.

Aksha caught sight of Dev and Anu, their smiles hinting at something more than the joyous occasion. She couldn't resist teasing them, "Alright, spill it. What's the secret? Where's Aahana?"

Dev, attempting an innocent look, replied, "Secret? What secret? We're just enjoying the wedding."

Aksha raised an eyebrow, her suspicion growing. "Oh, come on, Dev. I know that look. You're hiding something. Out with it!"

Anu chuckled, exchanging a glance with Dev. "Aksha, can't you just enjoy the moment? Why so curious?"

"Because I know my ninjas," Aksha said with a grin. "And you all are terrible at keeping secrets. Now, where's Aahana?"

Dev sighed dramatically, throwing up his hands. "Fine, fine. She's somewhere around. But if we tell you, it'll ruin the surprise."

"Surprise?" Aksha asked, her curiosity now fully piqued. "What surprise?"

Anu gently took Aksha's arm, guiding her toward a path leading away from the main venue. "You'll see soon enough. Just trust us. And remember, patience is a virtue."

With a mix of excitement and confusion, Aksha allowed herself to be led, her mind racing with possibilities. Whatever this surprise was, it seemed everyone was in on it. But one thing was certain—if Aahana was behind it, it was bound to be unforgettable.

Anu, not one to be outdone, added with a sly smile, "Yeah, Aksha, focus on your big day. Let the rest be a mystery."

But Aksha was not easily deterred. She continued her playful investigation, scanning the venue for any sign of the missing ninja. Her ninja senses tingled with anticipation.

As she approached Maher and Manan, they exchanged knowing glances. Manan, unable to contain himself, burst into laughter, "You're on a mission, Aksha! Good luck finding Aahana."

Maher chimed in, "Just follow the trail of mystery and twinkling lights."

Undeterred, Aksha continued her search, navigating through the sea of guests. The twinkling lights seemed to guide her, and she couldn't help but wonder if this was part of a larger conspiracy.

Finally, as if drawn by an invisible force, Aksha found herself in a secluded garden adorned with fairy lights. And there, under the softly glowing lights, was Aahana – a vision of elegance and mystery.

"Found you!" Aksha exclaimed, her eyes dancing with mischief.

As Aksha scanned the area, her eyes fell upon a delicate envelope placed discreetly on the table. The envelope bore no name, but its presence amidst the festive chaos intrigued her. With a mixture of curiosity and concern, she picked it up, her fingers trembling slightly as she broke the seal.

With a sense of anticipation, Aksha opened the envelope and discovered a handwritten letter:

"Dear Aksha and Aarush,

Firstly, congratulations on tying the knot! Your love is a beacon of joy, and I'm genuinely thrilled for both of you.

Now, about my sudden disappearance – ninja emergencies, you know how it goes. Duty calls at the most unexpected times. I've received a signal that needs my attention, and I can't ignore the ninja code.

Don't worry; it's nothing dire. Just a little mission that needs my touch. Besides, a ninja's work is never done, right?

I promise to make it up to you with tales of daring adventures and perhaps a surprise of my own. Until then, bask in the glow of your beautiful day. Cherish every moment, and know that I'm sending you both a shower of ninja blessings.

With all my love,
Aahana"

ᐅᐅᐅ

Aahana stood alone in the dim hallway, the sound of wedding music from Aarush and Aksha's celebration playing in the background. Laughter and happy voices filled the air, but it all felt far away to Aahana, who was lost in her own thoughts after hearing some bad news.

Her phone buzzed in her hand, and she saw an unknown number on the screen. A cold feeling ran down her spine as she answered the phone, the loud wedding music making everything feel even more confusing.

"Hello?" Aahana's voice shook, unsure of what to expect.

The voice on the other end sounded urgent. "Aahana, it's Aakash. You need to come to the city hospital. There's been an accident. It's Rajeev."

Aahana felt like the world had stopped. Rajeev? Her fiancé? She felt her heart race and her legs go weak.

"Rajeev?" she whispered, not sure if she heard correctly. Her mind was spinning, and the wedding sounds seemed to fade into the background as her focus shifted to the phone call.

"Yes, he's hurt badly. You need to come right away," Aakash said quickly.

Aahana hung up the phone, her hands trembling. She looked at the celebration happening around her, but it felt so far away now. She turned and started walking toward the exit, her thoughts focused on Rajeev and the hospital. The joyful noise around her no longer mattered—she needed to get to her fiancé.

Time seemed to freeze. Aahana's breath caught in her throat as Aakash's words sank in. Rajeev — her fiancé, her future — was in danger. The news hit her like a crashing wave, washing away the happiness she had just been feeling. The celebration that had been meant to mark the union of her closest friends now felt distant, overshadowed by the fear and worry gripping her heart.

She stumbled backward, seeking comfort in the quiet of the corridor, away from the noise of the wedding. The bright wedding decorations, once so vibrant, blurred together in her mind. It all seemed so surreal now. The laughter and music from the celebration felt strangely out of place as she struggled to take in what she had just heard.

Her heart was racing, torn between wanting to be there for her friends and needing to rush to Rajeev. The smell of flowers in the air mixed with the unease knotting in her stomach. A tear slid down her cheek as she tried to make sense of everything. The joy of the wedding felt so far away now, like a distant memory, while the fear for Rajeev's life took over every thought.

Aahana closed her eyes, trying to calm the whirlwind of thoughts racing through her mind. She could almost hear the thudding of her own heartbeat, the rapid, erratic rhythm echoing the turmoil within her. The wedding bells, which should have signified happiness, now rang with a somber note, the sound oddly matching the clash of emotions that churned inside her.

As the muffled cheers and laughter from the wedding guests filtered through the walls, Aahana made a quiet resolve. She wiped away the single tear that had fallen, and as her hand dropped to her side, her gaze grew steady with a sense of newfound determination. The celebration would continue without her, but her heart and mind were now with Rajeev, the man she loved. The corridor, stretching out before her, felt like a bridge between two worlds — one filled with joyous beginnings and another shrouded in the uncertainty of what lay ahead.

Taking a deep breath, Aahana straightened herself and stepped back into the vibrant chaos of the wedding. Each step felt heavy, burdened by the weight of her dilemma. Life's contrasting emotions — the joy of new beginnings and the dread of potential loss — intertwined in this single moment, shaping it into a chapter that would stay with her forever.

ppp

Inside the envelope was a letter, written in Aahana's graceful script. Aksha's heart raced as she read the words, her mind spinning with questions. The letter explained that Aahana had to leave unexpectedly due to an emergency, but it also conveyed her heartfelt congratulations for the newlyweds.

"Emergency?" Aksha whispered under her breath, her brow furrowing with worry. She looked around, scanning the room for any sign of what might have happened, but the lively celebration around her provided no answers. Instead, a sense of unease settled deep within her, an unsettling feeling she couldn't shake.

She turned back to the letter, reading Aahana's words again, trying to find any clue that might explain the situation. But there were no hidden meanings, only sincere apologies and warm wishes for Aksha and Aarush's happiness.

As the reality of Aahana's sudden departure began to sink in, Aksha's chest tightened with concern. Aahana was her closest friend — she wanted to reach out, to offer her support in whatever was going on, but with her whereabouts still unknown, all she could do was hope that everything would be alright.

With a soft sigh, Aksha carefully folded the letter and slipped it back into the envelope. She turned to Aarush, her eyes filled with a mix of worry and determination, silently promising herself that she would do whatever it took to find out what had happened to her friend.

"We need to find Aahana," Aksha said softly, her voice laced with urgency. "She wouldn't leave without a good reason. Something's wrong."

Aarush nodded, his expression mirroring the concern that had settled in Aksha's heart. The celebration they had been eagerly anticipating now felt distant, overshadowed by the sudden absence of their friend. Together, they made a quiet vow to uncover the truth behind Aahana's unexpected departure. They would do everything they could to bring her back safe and sound.

Aarush wrapped his arm around Aksha, offering a gentle squeeze as they stood amidst the twinkling lights of the garden. The night, which had been filled with laughter and joy, had taken an unexpected turn, leaving them both with a feeling of unease.

"I know it's unsettling, Aksha," Aarush murmured, his voice a soft, reassuring presence in the stillness of the night. "But knowing Aahana, there's a reason for everything. She's like a ninja — sometimes duty calls at the oddest hours."

Aksha nodded, her eyes reflecting a mixture of concern and determination. "You're right, Aarush. But Aahana wouldn't just leave without a word, especially not on our wedding day. It's not like her."

Aarush gently turned Aksha to face him, his gaze warm and understanding. "We'll find her, Aksha. Whatever it is, we'll face it together. Aahana's a tough ninja; she can handle herself. Let's trust that she'll be back soon."

Aksha managed a faint smile, grateful for Aarush's steady reassurance. "You're right. We'll get to the bottom of this. I just hope she's okay."

With a renewed sense of purpose, Aksha and Aarush made their way to the other ninjas, sharing the news of Aahana's sudden departure. The group, united by their concern for their missing friend, quickly gathered in a circle, brainstorming ways to track her down. Every ninja was on high alert, determined to uncover what had happened and where Aahana had gone.

As the night went on, the garden buzzed with conversation, theories, and memories of Aahana. Laughter and stories about her quirky moments filled the air, but beneath the surface, there was an underlying worry. Aksha, though still anxious, found comfort in the camaraderie of her friends. The unspoken promise between them — that they would stick together and find Aahana, no matter what — brought her a sense of peace amidst the uncertainty.

Though the wedding had taken an unexpected turn, Aksha knew that with the strength of her friends and Aarush by her side, they would navigate this challenge together.

ᚦᚦᚦ

Aksha struggled to make sense of Aahana's sudden departure on her wedding day. Frustration and confusion clouded her thoughts as she repeatedly tried calling her, but Aahana's phone went unanswered. The once joyful atmosphere of the wedding now felt heavy with worry, and Aksha couldn't shake the feeling that something was seriously wrong.

Determined to find answers, Aksha gathered her friends—Dev, Maher, Rishi, Roy, Manan, and Anu—and together they attempted to locate Aahana, but all their efforts were met with the same result: she was nowhere to be found. The group's concern grew, and the air was thick with uncertainty.

"Something isn't right," Dev said, his usual cheerfulness replaced with a serious tone. "Aahana wouldn't just disappear like this, especially not today." Maher, Rishi, and Anu all agreed, each expressing their worry that something was bothering Aahana that hadn't been shared.

Despite their best efforts, Aahana remained elusive, and the wedding continued with a sense of unease lingering in the background. Aarush, noticing Aksha's distress, approached her with a gentle touch. "We'll find Aahana," he said softly. "But today is about us. Let's focus on the joy we have right now."

Though still concerned, Aksha took comfort in Aarush's support, and together they returned to the celebrations, their friends working in the background to uncover the truth. The mystery of Aahana's disappearance remained unresolved, casting a shadow over the day, but Aksha knew they would face whatever came next together.

ᗡᗡᗡ

Aahana's mind was full of worry as she rushed to the hospital. Her heart was racing, and she couldn't shake the fear that something might happen to Rajeev. She gripped her phone tightly, hoping for some good news, but there was nothing yet.

"Please let him be okay," she whispered, her voice trembling. The thought of Rajeev, her fiancé, in pain made her feel like everything was spinning out of control.

The call had come out of nowhere, and it felt like her world had turned upside down. Rajeev, the person she was supposed to marry, had been in a terrible accident. She didn't know the details, but her stomach was tight with worry. She couldn't stop thinking about him.

As she walked quickly through the hospital halls, everything seemed blurry. Her mind was filled with memories of Rajeev — the way they laughed together, the plans they'd made, how he was always there for her. It hurt to think that something might happen to him.

The hospital felt cold, and the air was thick with worry. But Aahana didn't care about any of that. All she wanted was for Rajeev to be okay. She walked faster, hoping for news, praying that everything would turn out alright.

Aahana stepped into the cold, sterile hospital room, her heart racing in her chest. The medical staff looked at her with sympathetic, but sad eyes. The silence was thick, and she could feel the weight of the moment pressing down on her.

"Dr. Kapoor, please, just tell me he's going to be okay," Aahana pleaded, her voice trembling with desperation, almost pleading for a miracle.

Dr. Kapoor, who had always been calm and reassuring, now wore a sorrowful expression. With a gentle gesture, they motioned for Aahana to sit. "I wish I could give you better news, Aahana," the doctor began, their voice soft but firm. "Rajeev's injuries are severe, and I want to be completely honest with you about the situation."

Aahana's fingers gripped the edge of the chair tightly, her eyes locked on Dr. Kapoor's face, trying to read anything that might suggest hope. "Just... just tell me he's still alive. We can fight through this, right? He's strong. He'll pull through."

The doctor took a deep breath, their expression one of deep regret. "Aahana, I'm so sorry. Rajeev... he didn't make it. The injuries were too extensive. We did everything we could."

Aahana's body went cold. The words felt like they had shattered her world. "No, no, you must be mistaken! Rajeev can't be gone! He's strong! He'll pull through! Please... you have to do something!" Her voice broke, each word full of raw disbelief and heartbreak. She couldn't accept it. She couldn't fathom a world without him in it.

The doctor placed a gentle hand on Aahana's shoulder, offering what little comfort they could in the midst of the overwhelming pain. "I know this is incredibly difficult, and I wish there was something more we could have done. We're here to support you in any way we can."

Tears began to fall freely from Aahana's eyes, her chest tight with grief. Her breaths came in uneven gasps as the reality of the moment settled in. "This... this can't be happening. Rajeev and I had so many plans. We were supposed to face everything together," she whispered, the pain in her voice clear.

Dr. Kapoor nodded with deep empathy, their own heart aching for the young woman in front of them. "I can't imagine how hard this is for you. It's okay to take some time to process it. If you need someone to talk to, we have grief counselors available. They can help you through this."

Aahana nodded absently, but it was as if she couldn't hear the doctor's words. All she could think of was Rajeev, his smile, his touch, and the future they had dreamed of together. The hospital room, filled with quiet sympathy, felt distant and foreign to her now.

Aahana shook her head, unable to accept the devastating reality. "I just need Rajeev to walk through that door and tell me it's all a mistake. Please, there has to be something more you can do," she pleaded, her voice breaking as the tears streamed down her face.

But deep inside, she knew the truth. Rajeev was gone. The accident had stolen him from her, and she couldn't breathe with the weight of the loss pressing down on her chest. Her mind refused to believe it; it felt like a cruel nightmare she couldn't escape.

As the news settled in, a wave of despair crashed over Aahana, and she clung to the faintest hope that somehow, some miracle might bring Rajeev back. But the sterile hospital room, with its cold walls and indifferent silence, became the battleground between her desperate denial and the unrelenting truth she wasn't ready to face. She sank into a chair, her body heavy with grief, struggling to catch her breath as the world around her blurred.

In the days that followed, everything became a blur of funeral arrangements and tearful goodbyes. The house, once filled with Rajeev's laughter and the warmth of their shared moments, now felt empty and cold. The silence in every room was deafening. Alone with her thoughts, Aahana clung to the memories of their time together — their shared jokes, their dreams, the way he held her when everything felt right. She found comfort in the warmth of their love, but it wasn't enough to fill the aching emptiness in her heart.

Her heart ached, and in the quiet moments, she would whisper prayers — not for Rajeev's recovery, but for strength. Strength to endure, to carry on, and to help her family through the pain. The weight of grief was heavy, but Aahana knew she had to keep going, even if it felt like a long and lonely road ahead. The memories of Rajeev would always be with her, but the pain of losing him would never truly fade.

In the depths of her sorrow, Aahana found solace in the quiet, heartfelt conversations with her family. These moments became her lifeline, a fragile thread pulling her back from the overwhelming tide of grief. Together, they shared stories of Rajeev—his kind heart, his infectious laughter, and the way he had touched each of their lives. Each memory exchanged felt like a small beacon of light in the darkness, a way to honor the love they had all lost.

However, amidst the mourning, Aahana couldn't bring herself to reach out to Aksha or the group of close friends she affectionately called her "ninjas." Guilt weighed heavily on her, a painful reminder of how she had vanished from Aksha's wedding without a proper explanation. She replayed the moments in her mind, imagining their confusion and hurt at her abrupt departure on such an important day. The thought of facing them now, of explaining why she left, felt overwhelming.

"I failed them," Aahana whispered to herself, her voice trembling with regret. She wanted to call, to hear their voices, but her guilt held her back. How could she expect them to understand when she barely understood it herself? The pain of losing Rajeev had eclipsed everything, and in her anguish, she had let them down.

As Aahana faced the daunting task of moving forward without Rajeev, she vowed to keep his memory alive. Their conversations might have been silenced, but the echoes of their shared laughter and love would remain etched in her heart, a reminder of the precious time they had spent together. And though the guilt lingered, Aahana knew she couldn't avoid her friends forever. When the time was right, she would find the courage to face them, hoping they could forgive her for disappearing when they needed her, just as much as she needed them.

ppp

13

The Whispers of Hope

After six month....,

As the days passed, life seemed to regain its rhythm for everyone around Aahana. Friends returned to their routines, and laughter once again filled the spaces where sorrow had briefly lingered. Yet for Aahana, the world had stopped spinning. While everything around her seemed to move forward, she remained trapped in an unchanging moment, longing for the one thing she could never have again—Rajeev's comforting presence.

Despite the quiet persistence of time, Aahana clung stubbornly to the belief that Rajeev would walk through the door at any moment, his familiar smile dissolving the aching emptiness in her chest. She replayed the sound of his voice in her mind, hoping that this fragile tether to the past might bring him back. But reality stood as an impenetrable wall, and she refused to climb it, instead retreating deeper into the sanctuary of her denial.

Her world shrank to the four walls of her room, a quiet prison where she hoarded her grief like a fragile treasure. The vibrant energy of social gatherings, once a source of joy, now seemed unbearable. Invitations were left unanswered, her phone sat untouched, and even the thought of stepping outside felt like a betrayal of her sorrow.

Amid her isolation, the guilt of abandoning Aksha's wedding gnawed at her soul. She could still see the faces of her friends in her mind, their confusion and hurt as she vanished without explanation. Yet she couldn't bring herself to reach out. The weight of her grief was compounded by the guilt of her silence, a wall that seemed impossible to break down.

Aahana's world had become a muted echo of what it once was, defined by longing and loneliness. Every passing day brought her closer to the inevitable realization that she could not remain in this suspended state forever. But for now, she held on tightly to the memories of Rajeev, the only anchor in a sea of sorrow she wasn't yet ready to leave behind.

Day by day, the weight of negative thoughts pressed harder on Aahana's weary shoulders. Her mind became a battlefield, where sorrow and self-doubt relentlessly clashed with the bittersweet memories of her time with Rajeev. The comforting echoes of his laughter, once the soundtrack of her happiest moments, were replaced by an oppressive silence that amplified her loneliness.

Depression and stress crept into her life like unwelcome shadows, clouding every thought and moment. The isolation she had once embraced to protect herself now felt suffocating, trapping her in a prison of her own making. Despite their best efforts, friends and family couldn't reach her. Aahana had built walls so high and thick that their love and support seemed like faint whispers on the other side.

In the dim, quiet room where she sought refuge, Aahana replayed her memories of Rajeev over and over, as though clinging to the threads of a life that had unraveled too soon. His smile seemed almost close enough to touch; the echo of his laughter resonated faintly, teasing her with the illusion that he might still be near. His absence, however, was a chasm that no memory could fill, and each recollection was a painful reminder of all she had lost.

Aahana's world grew smaller with every passing day, her grief deepening the shadows of her thoughts. She found herself trapped in an endless cycle of longing, her mind clinging desperately to the past where Rajeev's presence had been her anchor. Each memory of him felt like a fleeting glimpse of light in a tunnel that seemed to stretch forever, yet it also tethered her to a reality she could no longer have.

Outside her window, life continued as if nothing had changed. The laughter of children, the distant hum of traffic, and the rhythm of daily routines carried on, indifferent to the storm raging within her. Time, often spoken of as a healer, felt more like a cruel tormentor, measuring out the days without Rajeev and reminding her of the void left in his absence.

Yet, deep in her heart, Aahana held onto a fragile hope — that one day, the dream of his return, the fantasy she replayed in her mind, would fade gently into acceptance. She yearned for the strength to let go, to embrace the possibility of healing. But for now, she remained caught in the web of her grief, unable to step beyond the walls she had built around herself, into the world that awaited her with open arms.

One morning, Aahana sat on her balcony. Beside her was an empty coffee cup, surrounded by books tossed around, food wrappers crumpled on the floor, and a thick layer of dust on everything. Her house was messy, just like how she felt inside—lost and broken.

She looked out at the sky, feeling heavy and tired. Sad thoughts filled her mind, and she couldn't stop thinking about Rajeev. She kept seeing the accident in her head, like a movie that wouldn't stop playing. It hurt so much, and no matter what she did, she couldn't make the pain go away.

The mess around her wasn't just in her house. It showed how she felt inside—everything was out of place. The books she once loved stayed closed, their stories too happy for her to handle. The food wrappers reminded her of all the times she tried to feel better, but nothing worked.

Sitting there in the quiet, Aahana felt like giving up. But deep down, just for a second, she thought about something else—what if one day things could get better? It was a small, tiny thought, like a spark in the dark. It didn't change anything yet, but it was there, waiting.

"I can't escape this nightmare," Aahana thought, her chest tightening as the memories overwhelmed her. She could hear the screech of tires, smell the sharp, bitter scent of burning rubber. It was like the accident was happening again and again, trapping her in a loop she couldn't break.

Her swollen face, marked with bruises from the crash, was a constant reminder of what she had been through. Every time she caught her reflection, the pain hit her all over again. "I'm broken," she whispered softly, her voice barely audible. "Not just outside, but inside too."

Aahana had locked herself away from the world, hoping to find peace in the silence, but the loneliness only made things worse. "I'm stuck in this darkness," she thought, tears spilling down her cheeks. "And there's no one who can pull me out." The walls of her room felt closer every day, closing in like a cage around her grief and pain.

The phone buzzed in the quiet room, the screen flashing with an unknown number. Aahana froze, her heart pounding. "What if it's bad news?" she thought, her chest tightening. "What if someone's calling to blame me for Rajeev's death?"

Her trembling hand hovered over the phone. She couldn't bring herself to answer, paralyzed by the fear of facing more pain. The ringing stopped, leaving behind an eerie silence that only deepened her anxiety.

The emotions she had bottled up finally spilled over. Tears streamed down her face as she broke into uncontrollable sobs. Each tear felt like a small release, but the weight in her heart remained. Her cries filled the room, echoing her pain, loneliness, and guilt.

Even as the tears slowed, Aahana knew this wasn't the end of her struggle. The haunting flashbacks and suffocating guilt still clung to her like shadows. Yet, deep within the darkness, a tiny spark of hope flickered. Maybe, one day, she could face her fears. Maybe, one day, she could find herself again.

᠅᠅᠅

One quiet afternoon, Aahana sat on her bed, mindlessly scrolling through her Instagram feed. It had become her daily escape, a way to drown out the pain and avoid the world that felt so overwhelming. She wasn't even on social media as herself anymore—she had created a profile under a pseudonym, a shield from the questions, judgments, and pity she feared would come her way.

As her thumb flicked up the screen, picture after picture passed by, each more meaningless than the last. But then, she stopped. A post stood out, different from anything she had seen.

It was an image of people sitting in a circle, blindfolded, hands clasped or resting gently on their laps. The caption read:

""Sometimes, the hardest thing is to speak your truth. Join us in a space where your voice matters, even if your face is unseen. No names, no judgment—just connection.""

The idea intrigued her: a gathering where people could talk openly, without revealing who they were. It felt strangely comforting, like a soft invitation to a world where she wouldn't have to explain herself or face the weight of her own identity.

Aahana stared at the screen, her heart pulling her in two directions. One part of her longed to stay hidden, cocooned in her sorrow. The other, curious and hesitant, felt drawn to the idea of stepping out—anonymously—to share the thoughts she had buried deep inside.

She saved the post, unsure of what she would do but knowing, for the first time in months, she had seen a glimmer of something that felt like hope.

Aahana sat back on her bed, her fingers still hovering over her phone screen as the decision weighed heavily on her. The idea of connecting with others without the usual pressures—no expectations, no need to put on a mask—felt like a rare opportunity to break free from the suffocating isolation she had built around herself.

She thought about how different it would be from the social media world she'd grown so accustomed to. On Instagram, she was just a quiet observer, hiding behind a fake identity. But this gathering, the blindfolded conversations, promised something more real, more raw. No one would know her name, her past, or any of the stories that had shaped her. For the first time in a long while, she wouldn't have to explain herself to anyone.

Her heart raced at the thought of revealing her true self—the version of her that was broken, lost, and searching for meaning. But then doubt crept in, just as it always did. *What if I'm not ready?* she thought. *What if my words aren't enough? What if I'm still too broken to talk to strangers?*

The idea of being vulnerable, of showing the parts of her she had kept locked away, felt like a step toward healing, but it also felt terrifying. She had spent so long shielding herself from the world that the thought of opening up—even anonymously—felt like standing on the edge of a cliff.

But, as she stared at the post again, something deep inside her whispered that maybe, just maybe, this was exactly what she needed. To speak to others who might understand her pain without judgment. To take that first, tentative step toward reconnecting with the world, even if it was just through a blindfold.

With a deep breath, Aahana clicked the link. The first step, she realized, was just to show up.

Aahana's heart raced as the phone rang, the weight of her decision pressing down on her chest. She had been avoiding moments like this—moments where she had to step out of her comfort zone, even if just a little. But today, something felt different. The anxiety gnawing at her insides was still there, but there was a flicker of hope that pushed her forward.

"Hello, this is Aahana," she said, her voice shaky but determined. "I'm interested in the blindfolded conversation campaign you're organizing. Could you tell me more about how it works?"

On the other end, the voice was warm and welcoming. The campaign manager explained the details clearly, reassuring Aahana that it was a safe, anonymous space where participants could share and listen without judgment. They emphasized that it was a space for emotional connection, without pressure to perform or meet any expectations.

Aahana listened intently, her grip tightening on the phone as she absorbed the information. Each word seemed to unlock a small door within her—a chance to step out of the darkness she had been trapped in for so long.

"Do you... do you think it's okay for someone like me to join? I mean, I'm not really... I don't know if I'm ready," she admitted, her vulnerability creeping through the phone line.

The campaign manager's voice softened. "Aahana, there's no rush. You can take your time. This is about connecting at your own pace. Whether you're ready to share everything or just listen, it's all okay. The most important thing is that you feel safe."

Aahana felt a tear slip down her cheek, the mixture of relief and uncertainty flooding her. "Thank you," she whispered, her voice barely audible. "I think... I think I want to try."

After a brief pause, the manager confirmed her participation in the next session and reassured her again that it would be a supportive, non-judgmental space.

As Aahana ended the call, she placed her phone gently on her lap and sat in the stillness of her room. For the first time in a long while, there was a sense of possibility, however small, stirring inside her. Perhaps this would be the beginning of finding her way back to herself.

Aahana sat quietly, the phone now resting in her lap, her thoughts swirling in a haze of uncertainty. The fear that had surfaced during the call clung to her like a shadow, but the small flicker of hope she'd felt lingered. It was as if she was standing at the edge of something new, but the weight of her past and the walls she had built around herself made it impossible to take that first step.

For now, she let the moment pass, the doubts quieting her resolve. She tucked the idea away, telling herself that maybe it wasn't the right time, maybe she wasn't ready. But deep inside, she could not help but wonder if the right time would ever come, or if she would always retreat, forever trapped in her isolation.

As she sat there, staring at the screen of her phone, Aahana realized that even though she had not joined the campaign yet, something had shifted within her. The seed of possibility had been planted, and no matter how much she tried to bury it, it would continue to grow, patiently waiting for her to acknowledge it.

Maybe tomorrow, or the day after, she would find the courage to act on it. But for now, she let herself sit with the uncertainty, knowing that just thinking about stepping forward was a small victory.

As Aahana stood in front of the mirror, her reflection seemed to echo her inner turmoil. Her face, usually calm and composed, now showed the uncertainty that gripped her. The decision to participate in the event felt like a leap into the unknown—a risk she hadn't been sure she was ready to take. Yet, the pull of something deeper than fear, something akin to hope, guided her hands as she finished getting ready.

Her heart raced as she picked up her phone, her fingers trembling slightly as she double-checked the details of the event. For a moment, she almost reconsidered—thought about turning back and staying hidden in her world of silence. But then she took a deep breath, feeling the weight of the last few days of internal struggle, and decided that today would be different.

ppp

"Maybe I don't have to face this alone," she whispered to herself.

With that quiet affirmation, she gathered her resolve. She had no idea what the future would hold or whether this decision would help her find the connection she so desperately needed. But for now, it was enough to take that first step.

Aahana grabbed her coat, took one last glance at her reflection—no longer just an image of hesitation—and stepped out into the day, knowing that whatever happened, she was finally doing something for herself. Even if it was just one small step toward healing.

As she made her way to the venue, Aahana's steps became slower with each passing moment. Doubt crept into her mind, making her question if she was doing the right thing. But with each small step forward, she reminded herself of the reason she came here—a deep need to connect with others, to share something real and feel understood.

When Aahana arrived at the venue, she was greeted by a crowd of strangers, all wearing blindfolds. The room buzzed with nervous energy, but there was something comforting about the anonymity. No one knew who she was, and she didn't know anyone either. She approached the registration desk, her hands a little shaky.

"Hi, excuse me, could you help me with the registration?" Aahana asked, her voice a little unsure.

The volunteer smiled at her, offering a calming presence. "Of course! Are you here for the blindfold conversation event?" they asked kindly.

Aahana nodded. "Yes, that's right. I saw it on Instagram, and I've been really curious about it."

The volunteer explained the registration process, and Aahana felt a wave of nervous energy rise inside her. "Thank you," she said quietly. "I'm nervous, to be honest."

The volunteer's smile grew. "Don't worry, a lot of people feel the same way at first. The blindfold helps everyone feel comfortable, like there's no judgment. It's a safe space."

Feeling reassured, Aahana took her welcome kit and moved towards the area where everyone was gathered. But as she stood there, watching the groups around her, the nerves returned. People were talking and laughing, but the blindfolds made it hard to see their faces. It was all so new and unfamiliar, and she wasn't sure if she was ready to join in.

"Hi there, mind if I join you?" Aahana asked, her voice soft and her heart racing with nervousness.

The group welcomed her warmly, their kindness easing her fears. "Of course, come sit," one of them said with a smile, making

Aahana feel a little less alone.

"It's my first time," Aahana confessed, her voice trembling slightly. "I'm feeling a bit nervous."

The others nodded in understanding, their quiet support giving her the confidence to settle into the circle. As the conversation began, she realized that she wasn't the only one feeling uncertain. Everyone was here to share and listen, to be heard without judgment.

As the conversation began, Aahana found herself opening up, sharing pieces of her story and listening to the others. It felt good to talk without fear of being misunderstood. She realized, in that moment, that this was the connection she had been looking for—a place where she could feel safe, understood, and, for the first time in a while, not alone.

Taking a deep breath, Aahana allowed herself to be enveloped by the blindfold, the darkness behind her eyes strangely comforting. It was as if she was shedding all the layers of fear, doubt, and identity she had carried for so long. In that moment, she felt free—free from expectations, free from the weight of her past.

As the conversations began, Aahana slowly found her voice. At first, her words were hesitant, unsure, but with each sentence, she felt a bit lighter. Each word seemed to lift a burden she hadn't fully realized she was carrying. The release felt like a quiet relief, a soothing wave that washed over her soul.

Amidst the voices of strangers, Aahana felt something unexpected—a bond. Despite not knowing who they were, there was a shared understanding between them. They spoke of pain, loss, dreams, and hopes, and in those words, Aahana found pieces of herself. It was as if their stories had mirrored her own in ways she couldn't explain. She wasn't alone. She wasn't invisible.

As the conversation continued, a calm and soothing voice emerged from the group. Aahana could tell immediately that the person speaking had a different kind of depth to their words. His tone was gentle but grounded, as if he had an understanding of pain without being overwhelmed by it. Intrigued, Aahana's attention shifted towards him.

He introduced himself as Nikhil, a clinical psychologist. His words were measured, empathetic, and filled with insight. Aahana was taken aback by the calmness in his voice—it felt like a lifeline thrown to someone drowning in a sea of emotions.

Nikhil spoke about how important it was to acknowledge the pain, to sit with it, rather than running away. His voice was soothing, and his words resonated with Aahana, like a beacon of clarity amidst the confusion of her thoughts.

As the conversation continued, Aahana realized that Nikhil's understanding wasn't just professional—it was deeply human. He wasn't there to fix anyone, but to listen, to allow space for others to explore their emotions without judgment. In that moment, Aahana found herself opening up more freely than she ever had before.

Nikhil listened without interruption, offering gentle words of reassurance. "It's okay to feel lost," he said. "Healing isn't linear, and there's no right way to grieve. What matters is that you're here, you're speaking, and you're allowing yourself to be heard."

For the first time in a long time, Aahana felt seen, not just as a person struggling with grief, but as someone worthy of being heard. As the blindfolded conversation drew to a close, she felt a quiet sense of peace settle in her heart. She may not have all the answers, but she now knew that there were people out there, like Nikhil, who truly understood.

The connection she felt that day, not just with Nikhil but with everyone in the room, became a pivotal moment in her journey. It was the first step towards opening herself up again, finding strength in vulnerability, and seeking the support she had long avoided.

In time, Aahana came to understand that healing wasn't about forgetting or erasing the past, but about learning to live with it, to find peace amidst the pain. Nikhil was there every step of the way, helping her find the strength she didn't know she had.

Through him, Aahana learned that healing wasn't just a journey through pain, but also a journey toward self-discovery and connection. And with Nikhil's support, she found a new sense of hope and the courage to step forward into a life she could rebuild, one small step at a time.

ᐳᐳᐳ

After the blindfolded conversation event, Aahana couldn't shake the feeling of something shifting within her. The rawness of the exchange, the vulnerability, and the understanding that had passed between strangers—it was unlike anything she had ever experienced before. In particular, Nikhil's calm demeanor and insightful words had stood out. He had spoken with such empathy, and his words about healing and moving forward had resonated deeply with her.

Aahana wasn't someone who usually sought help, let alone from a therapist. But something about the way Nikhil spoke—so understanding, so non-judgmental—had made her wonder if maybe, just maybe, talking to him again could help her work through the mess of emotions she'd been carrying for so long.

Her heart raced as she sat on her couch, staring at the contact information she had written down at the event. She had been holding onto it, unsure whether she should reach out. But after days of wrestling with herself, she finally picked up the phone and dialed the number, feeling a knot tighten in her stomach.

After dialing Nikhil's number, Aahana's heart raced with a mix of nerves and anticipation. As the phone rang, her mind raced with doubt, wondering if she was making the right decision. When he finally answered, his warm voice instantly calmed her.

"Yes, this is Nikhil. How can I help you?" His tone was welcoming, just like she remembered from the blindfolded event.

Aahana hesitated for a moment, then gathered the courage to speak. "Hi, Nikhil. This is Aahana. I attended the blindfolded conversation event, and... your words really stayed with me. I've been thinking about them, and I feel like I need help. I don't really know where to start, but I thought talking might be a good first step."

On the other end of the line, there was a brief pause, and then Nikhil responded in a reassuring, calm voice, "Aahana, I'm really glad you reached out. It's not always easy to take that first step, but I'm happy to be here. It sounds like you're ready to begin this journey. Would you like to meet in person? We can take things at your pace."

Aahana felt a rush of relief wash over her as she realized Nikhil wasn't judging her. His kind response gave her a newfound sense of hope. She didn't have to be perfect or have all the answers.

"Yes," she replied, her voice a little steadier now. "I'd like that. Tomorrow? I think I'm ready."

"Tomorrow sounds good," Nikhil agreed, his voice encouraging. "Take your time, Aahana. We'll talk when you're ready."

She thanked him and hung up, feeling a mixture of nervous excitement. She had taken the first step, and though she still wasn't sure what the journey ahead would look like, she knew she wasn't facing it alone.

The next day, as Aahana arrived at Nikhil's clinic, she felt a familiar knot tighten in her stomach. The waiting room was quiet, the atmosphere calming. Soft lighting, gentle music playing in the background, and the subtle scent of lavender gave the space a peaceful, almost serene quality. Aahana felt like she was entering a different world, far removed from the constant noise and pressures of her everyday life.

She approached the reception desk, and the kind receptionist greeted her with a smile. "Hi, Aahana. Nikhil is expecting you. He's just finishing up with a client, but he'll be with you shortly."

"Thank you," Aahana murmured, her voice still tinged with nerves. She sat down in one of the plush chairs, trying to steady her breathing, but the anxiety was still there. She couldn't help but feel exposed, unsure of what to say once she finally spoke to Nikhil.

She glanced around the room, taking in the warm, inviting décor, but her thoughts kept racing back to her emotions. Her grief, guilt, and feelings of being stuck overwhelmed her. She had tried to push through them, to move on, but it felt like she was carrying a heavy weight that wouldn't lift.

Before she could lose herself in her spiraling thoughts, the door to Nikhil's office opened, and he stepped out with a calm smile. Aahana immediately felt a sense of reassurance at his presence, his warmth making her feel just a little more grounded.

"Nikhil," she greeted softly, her voice a little uncertain. "I'm... nervous."

Nikhil's expression remained gentle, and he gave a small nod, understanding exactly what she was feeling. "That's completely okay, Aahana. I'm glad you're here. You're not alone in this. It's a big step, but you're in a safe space."

His words, simple yet sincere, helped calm her a little. Nikhil led her into his office, a cozy room filled with natural light and plants by the window. It felt inviting, not intimidating. As they sat down, Nikhil gave her a moment of silence, as if allowing her the space to settle.

When he finally spoke, his voice was patient and soft, "You don't have to share anything you're not ready to. We can take it one step at a time. What brings you here today?"

Aahana hesitated for a moment, her hands fidgeting with her bag strap. She had never been great at opening up, but she felt an overwhelming urge to say something. She took a deep breath, the words coming out more slowly than she'd expected.

"I've been carrying this weight inside me. Grief, guilt, just... this feeling that I can't move forward. I don't know how to let go of it. I try, but it feels like no matter what I do, it's always there, weighing me down." Her voice wavered slightly, and she glanced down, avoiding his gaze for a moment.

Nikhil listened intently, his eyes reflecting nothing but empathy. He nodded as she spoke, never interrupting, but his presence felt like an anchor, keeping her grounded. When she finished, he spoke softly.

"It's okay to feel that way, Aahana. Those emotions are powerful, and they often make us feel stuck. But the good news is, you don't have to carry them alone, and we don't have to figure everything out right now. We'll take this one step at a time, together."

Aahana felt something shift inside her. It was like she had finally been given permission to feel her emotions, to not rush through them or try to "fix" herself too quickly. She didn't have to have all the answers; it was okay to not be okay.

"I don't know where to begin," Aahana confessed, her voice quieter now, but there was a certain relief in her words. "I've been carrying this for so long that it's hard to even know what to say."

Nikhil gave her a reassuring smile. "You don't have to start with everything. We'll just talk, and when you're ready, we'll dig deeper. There's no rush. Right now, what matters is that you've taken the first step by being here."

As the session continued, Aahana began to feel the weight on her chest lighten, little by little. There was something comforting about Nikhil's steady presence—his understanding and patience. She wasn't being judged, and that was something she had feared for so long.

Over the course of their meetings, Aahana gradually opened up more, bit by bit. Nikhil didn't force her; he simply guided her, helping her understand her emotions without pressuring her to speed through the healing process. Every session brought her a little closer to understanding herself, to healing.

And by the time she reached a point where she felt ready to acknowledge the changes within her, she looked at Nikhil with gratitude in her eyes.

"I think I'm starting to see the light at the end of the tunnel," she said softly, her voice a little more steady than it had been before. "It's still far, but I think it's there. I couldn't imagine this before, but now... now I feel like I can keep going."

Nikhil smiled, his eyes proud. "You're doing great, Aahana. One step at a time. I'm proud of you."

And with that, Aahana knew she was on the right path. Slowly but surely, she was finding her way out of the darkness.

❧❧❧

14
Beyond the Shadows

Present day.......,

"Listen, everyone. Let me clarify one thing. I've been in contact with Aahana for the last year. She really misses us, especially you, Aksha. She's in big trouble and needs your support. Please be kind to her. She needs emotional support," Roy informed the group.

"What kind of trouble?" Aksha inquired.

"She's suffering from PTSD," Roy dropped the bombshell.

"What?" Dev exclaimed

"Yes, you heard right. Post-Traumatic Stress Disorder. She feared forgetting us, losing her memories, so she isolated herself," Roy explained.

"What PTSD is ?", Manan questioned.

Roy took a deep breath, his tone softening as he prepared to explain. "PTSD stands for Post-Traumatic Stress Disorder. It's a mental health condition triggered by a traumatic event. It could be anything—an accident, abuse, the loss of a loved one—anything that deeply impacts someone emotionally and mentally."

Manan furrowed his brows. "So, how does it affect someone?"

Roy continued, "It varies from person to person, but common symptoms include flashbacks of the traumatic event, nightmares, severe anxiety, and even physical reactions like a racing heart when reminded of the trauma. People with PTSD often struggle to connect with others and may isolate themselves, just like Aahana did."

Aksha, still processing the revelation, asked hesitantly, "So... she pushed us away because of this?"

Roy nodded. "Yes. She feared she might lose you all or hurt you in the process. Isolation was her way of coping, but it wasn't healthy. Instead of healing, it made things worse for her."

Dev interjected, his voice breaking, "Why didn't she tell us? We could've helped her."

Roy gave him a sad smile. "Dev, that's the thing with PTSD. It's not easy to open up about. The person often feels ashamed or fears being misunderstood. It takes immense courage to even acknowledge it, let alone seek help."

Manan rubbed his temples, frustration mingling with concern. "And now she's lying there because we couldn't see what she was going through."

Roy placed a reassuring hand on Manan's shoulder. "It's not your fault. PTSD isn't something that's obvious unless the person talks about it. But now that we know, we need to support her. She needs us more than ever."

Aksha, guilt etched across her face, whispered, "I didn't know she was suffering like this. I thought she had moved on."

"None of us knew," Roy said. "But what matters is that we're here now. Let's focus on helping her recover and making her feel that she's not alone anymore."

The group exchanged determined nods, their focus shifting to standing by Aahana and ensuring she felt the love and support she had been missing.

The room fell into a contemplative silence, the gravity of Roy's explanation sinking in. Each member of the group processed their emotions, ranging from guilt to resolve, as they came to terms with Aahana's condition.

"I've made a big mistake. I shouldn't have done that. I didn't understand her. I am at fault," Aksha admitted, feeling guilty.

"You're not, dear. Don't feel guilty. We all are at fault. We didn't understand the pain of our partner. What's done is not in our hands, but what we have to do is clear now. We will give her all the happiness. Let's pray for her speedy recovery," Anu reassured.

Aksha, tears welling in her eyes, finally spoke, her voice trembling, "You're right, Anu. What's done is done. But I won't let my misunderstanding ruin things further. I promise to be there for her from now on."

Roy nodded appreciatively, adding, "That's the spirit. Aahana needs us to be her support system. Recovery from PTSD isn't easy, but knowing she has people who genuinely care about her will make a big difference."

Dev, who had been silently staring at the floor, suddenly looked up, determination shining through his tear-streaked face. "I'll do whatever it takes to help her heal. She's not just a friend to me. She's... everything. I won't let her fight this battle alone."

Manan stepped forward, placing a reassuring hand on Dev's shoulder. "None of us will. This isn't just about her anymore; it's about all of us standing together as a family."

Rishi, who had been listening intently, chimed in, "And remember, it's not just about being there when things are hard. It's about helping her see the brighter side of life, one small moment of joy at a time."

Maher wiped away a tear and smiled softly. "Let's make her feel loved and valued. She deserves it after all she's been through."

Anu clasped her hands together, looking at everyone. "Then it's settled. From this moment on, we're all here for Aahana. No matter what."

The group exchanged nods of agreement; their unity stronger than ever. In that moment, they resolved to be the light that guided Aahana out of her darkness, knowing that together, they could help her find her way back to happiness.

ⵏⵏⵏ

"She is stable now. But..." Nikhil began.

"But what?" Dev asked, his voice trembling.

"But we're not sure when she will regain consciousness," Nikhil shared. "Don't worry; she is out of danger now."

"Thank God!" Maher exclaimed, her relief palpable.

A wave of relief washed over everyone, but the uncertainty loomed. The group exchanged hopeful but anxious glances.

"Can we see her?" Dev asked hesitantly.

"Yes, but only one or two of you at a time," Nikhil replied. "She needs rest above all."

"I'll go first," Dev volunteered without hesitation.

Aksha stepped forward, stopping him gently. "Dev, wait. Let me go with you. I need to... I need to apologize."

Dev hesitated but eventually nodded. "Alright, let's go together."

The pair walked toward Aahana's room, their steps slow and deliberate. The others stayed back, their expressions a blend of hope and lingering worry.

"She's going to pull through this," Roy said, breaking the silence. "She's stronger than any of us realize."

"She has to," Anu murmured, her fingers interlaced tightly in her lap.

Inside the room, Aahana lay motionless, her face pale but peaceful, illuminated by the soft glow of the monitors tracking her vitals. The steady beep of the heart monitor was a small comfort.

Aksha approached, tears filling her eyes as she reached for Aahana's hand. "I'm so sorry, Aahana," she whispered, her voice breaking. "I failed you as a friend. I should have been there for you, but I wasn't. I promise to make it right."

Dev knelt by the bed, brushing a strand of hair from Aahana's face. His voice was low, filled with emotion. "Come back to us, Aahana. Please. We're all here, waiting for you. I'm here for you."

The room was silent except for the hum of the machines, the air thick with unspoken words of love, regret, and hope.

Outside, the group waited, their hearts heavy but united. They resolved, without saying a word, to stand by Aahana through every step of her recovery. She wasn't just a friend; she was their family, and they wouldn't let her face this alone.

ᕤᕤᕤ

Two days had passed, and Aahana lay motionless on her bed, her body betraying the fight that raged within her mind. Her face was pale, her eyes shut, and her breathing steady but shallow. Anu, seated beside her, held a crumpled letter in her trembling hands—a letter from Dev, filled with words of hope, love, and strength. Anu's gaze flicked between the paper and Aahana's lifeless form, willing her sister to respond.

Suddenly, Aahana's fingers twitched. Anu gasped, her heart leaping. She gently touched Aahana's hand, tears of relief pooling in her eyes. "Aahana... Are you trying to say something?" she whispered, her voice trembling with hope.

Anu quickly grabbed her phone and dialed Nikhil, her voice urgent but controlled. "Dr. Nikhil, I think she's trying to move. She just... her hand, it moved. Please, can you come now?"

Nikhil's calm yet firm response immediately reassured her. "I'm on my way, Anu. Just stay with her for now. I'll be there shortly."

It wasn't long before Nikhil arrived, his presence bringing a calm authority to the room. He carried his bag, his expression serious but compassionate. Anu met him at the door, her face a mix of desperation and relief.

"She moved her hand. I'm sure she's trying to tell us something," Anu explained, her voice quivering.

Nikhil nodded and placed a reassuring hand on Anu's shoulder. "Let me see her. Sometimes the smallest movements are a way of signaling recovery. Please wait outside for a moment while I check on her."

Anu hesitated but complied, stepping out of the room and joining the others—friends and family who had been waiting in anxious silence. Among them were Dev's closest friends, who had promised to stay by Aahana's side. They exchanged nervous glances, their tension palpable.

Inside the room, Nikhil approached Aahana carefully, pulling up a chair to sit beside her bed. The air was heavy with quiet, broken only by the faint hum of the ceiling fan. He placed his bag on the floor and reached for her wrist, checking her pulse. It was weak but steady.

"Aahana," he called softly, leaning closer. "It's me, Nikhil. Can you hear me?"

Her eyelids fluttered slightly, a faint movement that filled him with cautious optimism. He gently placed his hand over hers. "If you can hear me, try moving your fingers again," he encouraged, his voice calm and steady.

After a few moments, Aahana's fingers curled ever so slightly. Nikhil's lips curved into a small, encouraging smile. "That's good, Aahana. You're doing great. Take your time. No rush."

He observed her carefully, noting the subtle tension in her brows, the faint struggle to communicate without words. Her body was exhausted, her mind overwhelmed, but the small movements told him she was fighting to come back to them.

Outside, Anu paced the hallway, wringing her hands. "Do you think she's okay? I hate not knowing what's happening," she murmured to Dev's friends, her voice filled with worry.

"She'll be fine, Anu," one of them reassured her, though his voice was as much for his own comfort as hers.

Back in the room, Nikhil decided to use a different approach. He spoke to her in a soft, soothing tone, recounting the blindfolded event where they first crossed paths. "You remember that evening, don't you? When you stepped out of your comfort zone and trusted a room full of strangers. You were so brave, Aahana. And I see that bravery now, even in these small movements. We're all here for you. Just take one step at a time."

A single tear escaped from the corner of Aahana's closed eye, trailing down her cheek. It was a response—a silent acknowledgment of his words. Nikhil gently wiped it away with a tissue, his expression full of empathy.

"You're not alone in this fight," he whispered.

As Nikhil emerged from the room, the crowd of worried faces turned to him, their anticipation nearly tangible.

"She's responding," he announced, his voice steady but cautious. "It's small progress, but it's progress nonetheless. Let's give her time and continue supporting her. She needs all of us to be patient."

Relief washed over the group, and Anu let out a shaky breath, her eyes welling with tears. "Thank you," she whispered, her gratitude directed at Nikhil.

The road ahead was still uncertain, but for the first time in days, there was a flicker of hope—a belief that Aahana's story was far from over.

After a few tense moments, Aahana's eyelids fluttered open. The ninjas, who had been anxiously waiting nearby, collectively exhaled in relief. Each face reflected a mix of worry, exhaustion, and hope as they gathered closer, hesitant but eager to ensure she was alright.

Aksha was the first to step forward, her voice trembling as she whispered, "Aahana, can you hear me?"

Aahana blinked slowly, her gaze sweeping across the room, taking in the concerned faces of her friends. Her voice, barely above a whisper, carried a note of confusion. "Where... am I?"

Manan, who had been leaning against the wall with his arms crossed, straightened up. "You're at the farmhouse. You fainted, Aahana. We've all been waiting for you to wake up," he explained, his usual aloof tone replaced with genuine care.

Anu moved closer to Aahana's side, tears brimming in her eyes. She gently touched Aahana's hand. "You scared us so much. I—I thought..." Her voice broke, and she took a deep breath to steady herself. "I thought we were going to lose you."

Aahana's brow furrowed, and she tried to piece together her fragmented memories. "I... I remember a treehouse," she murmured, her voice trailing off as she tried to recall more. "And then... darkness."

Aksha knelt beside the bed, guilt etched deeply into her expression. She reached for Aahana's hand, gripping it tightly. "Aahana, I'm so sorry. For everything I said... for not understanding your pain. I was wrong to judge you." Her voice cracked under the weight of her emotions.

Aahana's eyes softened as she looked at Aksha. For a moment, silence hung in the room, broken only by the faint rustle of the wind outside. Finally, she gave Aksha's hand a weak squeeze. "Aksha, it's okay. We all make mistakes. What matters is… you're here now."

Roy, who had been standing quietly at the back, cleared his throat. "Alright, everyone. Let's not overwhelm her. She just woke up." He glanced at Nikhil, who had been observing silently, and gestured for him to step in.

Nikhil approached the bed, his demeanor calm and reassuring. He checked Aahana's pulse, his practiced hands steady as he monitored her vitals. "Welcome back, Aahana," he said with a small, encouraging smile. "You gave us quite a scare, but you're going to be fine. You just need rest and no stress for now."

Rishi, always the jokester of the group, tried to lighten the mood. "See, Aahana? Even Nikhil agrees that you should stop stressing about us. We're perfectly capable of being disasters on our own," he said with a grin.

A faint smile tugged at Aahana's lips, the first sign of relief they had seen since she woke up.

Aarush, the quiet observer, stepped forward. "We'll be just outside if you need us," he said softly. His words carried an unspoken promise of support.

One by one, the ninjas left the room, casting glances over their shoulders to make sure Aahana was truly okay. Anu lingered for a moment longer, adjusting Aahana's blanket. "We'll take care of everything. You just focus on getting better," she said before stepping out.

In the hallway, the group gathered, their shared concern for Aahana binding them closer than ever.

"She's stronger than she looks," Nikhil said, addressing the group. His voice was calm yet firm. "But recovery isn't just about her physical health. She's going to need emotional support too. That means all of you have to be patient and understanding."

Dev, who had been silently watching from the corner, finally spoke. "She has us. Whatever she needs, we'll make sure she gets it." His words were resolute, carrying the weight of his loyalty to Aahana.

Manan clapped Dev on the back, nodding in agreement. "We've got this. She's not facing any of this alone."

As the farmhouse settled into a quieter rhythm, the ninjas dispersed, each carrying a renewed determination to support Aahana in her journey. Inside her room, Aahana drifted into a peaceful sleep, the faint sound of laughter and conversation from the hallway serving as a comforting reminder of the unwavering bond she shared with her chosen family.

ѢѢѢ

15
Unbreakable Bonds

The sun dipped below the horizon, painting the sky with hues of orange and pink. The group had set up a cozy gathering spot on the sprawling lawn of the farmhouse. Aahana was propped up on a lounge chair, a soft blanket draped over her legs, as the ninjas sat around her in a semi-circle. The soft glow of fairy lights strung across the trees cast a warm, magical ambiance over the scene.

"Okay, folks," Rishi declared, rubbing his hands together. "Operation Cheer Up Aahana is officially in session. Let's start with some fun—juicy gossip or embarrassing stories only. And no, Manan, your investment tips don't count!"

Manan adjusted his glasses, feigning indignation. "Excuse me, my advice is pure gold. Unlike your budget, which is... what's the word? Oh, non-existent."

"That's why Rishi keeps his savings in a cookie jar," Aarush teased, grinning. "You know, because banks are apparently too mainstream."

Rishi placed a hand over his heart, feigning hurt. "That cookie jar is an heirloom! It holds memories. You wouldn't understand."

Aahana giggled, her smile lighting up her face. "I missed this... you guys arguing over the most random things."

Roy leaned back, hands clasped behind his head. "It's not all arguments. Sometimes we tackle really important debates—like pineapple on pizza."

"That's not important!" Aksha interjected, groaning. "It's an insult to humanity, and you know it."

"Hold up," Anu raised her hand with mock seriousness. "Team pineapple here. Don't come for me."

"Traitor!" Dev gasped, clutching his chest as if struck by a mortal wound. "Anu, how could you betray us like this?"

The group laughed, and Aahana's laughter was the loudest, bringing a sense of relief to the ninjas.

"Alright, moving on," Maher interjected, his voice calm but laced with mischief. "Let's change gears. Rapid-fire round, anyone? Aahana, you're the queen tonight. You ask, we answer."

Aahana tilted her head, a playful glint in her eyes. "Alright. Rapid-fire it is. First question: What's the most embarrassing thing you've done recently?"

Roy groaned loudly, shaking his head. "Why do I feel like I'm always the sacrificial lamb in these games?"

"Because you are," Dev replied, earning laughter from the group.

Roy sighed in mock defeat. "Fine. Last week, I tripped over my shoelaces in front of my boss. Tried to play it cool, but instead, I knocked over her coffee. It was a disaster."

The group erupted into laughter, Aahana wiping tears from her eyes.

"Alright, my turn," Dev chimed in. "I accidentally sent a heart emoji to our plumber instead of a thumbs-up. Now he keeps calling me 'brother.'"

Aahana clutched her stomach, laughing harder. "Dev, only you could turn a plumbing problem into a bromance."

Aksha leaned in, a wicked smile on her face. "Maher, your turn. Spill it. What's your most embarrassing moment?"

Maher smirked, taking a sip of his cocoa. "Well, let's just say I found out the hard way that my 'mute' button wasn't working during a client call. The entire office now knows my opinion on pineapple pizza."

"That's karma for being Team No Pineapple," Anu teased, making Maher roll his eyes.

Manan jumped in. "Aarush, what about you? Any embarrassing adventures?"

Aarush chuckled, scratching his head. "Not embarrassing, but funny. I got locked out of my apartment last week—wearing mismatched socks and carrying a bag of groceries. My neighbors are still calling me 'Fashionista.'"

Aahana giggled, shaking her head. "You guys are impossible."

"That's why you love us," Rishi declared, pretending to bow dramatically.

"I really do," Aahana admitted, her voice soft but sincere.

The group fell into more playful banter, each ninja sharing stories, cracking jokes, and teasing one another. The air was filled with warmth, laughter, and the kind of comfort that only true friendship could provide. Aahana leaned back, soaking in the moment, grateful for the lightness her ninjas brought into her life.

ᑫᑫᑫ

"I am so sorry. Please forgive me," Aahana's words were barely above a whisper, but the sincerity in them was undeniable.

Aahana's voice trembled as she spoke, the weight of her words hanging heavily in the air. The silence in the room felt thick, each person processing her confession in their own way. Aksha's gaze softened, her heart aching for her friend as Aahana's vulnerability unfolded before them.

Aksha quickly placed a hand on Aahana's, her touch grounding and gentle. "Don't say anything. We came to know about your pain. I am sorry, dear. I didn't understand your pain before. We all are guilty. We should have noticed. I shouldn't have talked like that to you."

Aahana could see the sincerity in Aksha's eyes, but it didn't stop her from feeling the guilt gnawing at her. "No, let me have my confession today. Let me unload all the burdens I've been carrying. I owe it to you, to all of you," she urged, her voice breaking.

Aksha nodded, her own voice thick with emotion. "You don't need to say anything more, Aahana. We know what you've been through. Roy and Nikhil already told us... We understand now."

The weight of her words seemed to settle around them like a comforting embrace, and for a moment, Aahana was grateful for the understanding in her friends' eyes. She felt the room become quieter, more intimate, as each ninja processed her confession, their faces filled with empathy.

The air grew heavy as Aahana continued, finding her voice, slowly unravelling the complexities of her journey. "My disappearance wasn't meant to hurt you; it was my feeble attempt to shield you from the darkness that consumed me. I thought if I withdrew, if I disappeared, I could protect you from the mess I had become. But now, standing here, I realize the unintended consequences of my actions. I see the confusion, the pain I've caused."

Her gaze shifted to each of her friends—Aksha, Dev, Anu, Manan, Aarush, Roy, Rishi, and Maheer. Their faces reflected a mixture of sorrow and understanding, but also an unwavering support.

"You didn't need to carry that alone," Aksha said softly, her voice steady despite the tears glistening in her eyes. "We should've been there. We should've known. But you don't have to apologize, Aahana. We're here now, and that's all that matters."

Aahana's eyes welled with tears as she looked at Aksha, at all of them. "I thought I was alone in this... and that's what kept me in the darkness. But now, I see how wrong I was. I'm sorry for doubting you."

Roy, always the one to ease the tension, leaned forward, giving Aahana a small, teasing smile. "You're never alone, Aahana. Besides, with us around, you'd have to work pretty hard to be alone."

The group chuckled softly, and the tension in the room loosened, replaced by the familiar warmth of their camaraderie.

Nikhil, who had been silently observing, spoke up, his voice calm and reassuring. "The journey ahead isn't easy, Aahana. But with each step, you're not walking alone. We've got your back. And sometimes, it's okay to lean on us."

Aahana nodded, a quiet sense of peace settling over her. It wasn't all fixed, but this was a beginning. She didn't have to carry the weight of her past alone anymore.

And for the first time in what felt like ages, Aahana allowed herself to believe in the possibility of healing—not alone, but with her friends, her ninjas, by her side.

Aahana took a moment to collect herself before concluding, "My return is not just about the reunion of ninjas; it's about facing the consequences of choices made in the crucible of life. Together, let's find healing and understanding, transcending the barriers of time and circumstance."

The confession was not just about revealing hidden truths; it was an emotional catharsis, a journey through the labyrinth of Aksha's heart. Aarush felt a surge of empathy, realizing the depth of Aksha's struggles.

Dev's eyes, usually guarded, softened with understanding as he absorbed the weight of her words. Anu, Roy, Maher, and Manan formed a protective circle around Aksha, offering a silent promise of unwavering support.

As the night unfolded, the ninjas became witnesses to Aksha's vulnerability, each emotion etched on her face mirrored in the eyes of her friends. The air was charged with a mixture of sympathy, compassion, and an unspoken camaraderie that bound them together through the highs and lows of life.

After the last echo of Aksha's words faded, a heavy silence lingered. Aarush squeezed her hand gently, offering reassurance. Dev, usually the one with a witty remark, remained uncharacteristically quiet. Anu's eyes welled up with tears, reflecting the pain her friend had endured alone.

Roy, Maher, and Manan exchanged solemn glances, understanding the significance of the shared revelation. Their bond as ninjas had always been unbreakable, but this night unveiled a new layer of trust and vulnerability.

In that moment of shared vulnerability, Aarush broke the silence, his voice steady yet filled with emotion. "Aahana, we're all here for you, no matter what. Your pain is ours, and your journey is our journey. You don't have to carry it alone anymore."

His words resonated deeply, drawing nods and murmurs of agreement from the group. The weight of the evening transformed into something lighter, infused with a sense of unity and shared purpose. Each ninja silently renewed their unspoken pledge to stand by Aahana through it all.

For a moment, there was silence, not the heavy kind but one of understanding and connection.

Then Roy, ever the mood-lifter, leaned back and waved his hand dismissively. "Alright, stop it now. Enough of this emotional drama. All's well that ends well."

The room burst into laughter, the sound breaking through the emotional tension like sunshine through clouds. Aahana laughed too, the sound soft but genuine, a sign of the lightness she hadn't felt in a long time.

"Thank you so much, yaar," Aahana said, her voice filled with gratitude. "You've all helped me so much."

Roy raised an eyebrow and smirked, leaning toward her. "Hahahaha... Look at her now! This is the same Aahana who once called her friends 'kamini' without hesitation. And here she is, saying thanks? How times have changed!"

The group roared with laughter again, and Aahana blushed, shaking her head. "Oh, stop it, Roy! I didn't mean it like that!" she protested, though her smile betrayed her amusement.

Aksha joined in, teasing, "Yeah, Aahana. Don't go all soft on us now. We'll start thinking we've been replaced by someone else."

Manan added with a playful grin, "Let's make it official then. No 'thank yous' in this group. Only chai or treats will suffice as gratitude."

"Done!" Rishi chimed in. "But make mine with extra sugar."

Aahana laughed harder, her eyes sparkling with warmth as she looked around at her friends. "You guys are impossible," she said, her voice soft but filled with affection.

"And you love us for it," Aksha replied with a wink.

The evening continued with a lighter tone, the group swapping stories, cracking jokes, and enjoying the comforting presence of each other. For Aahana, it wasn't just a gathering of friends—it was a reminder of the unbreakable bond they shared, one that would see her through even the darkest days. In their laughter and love, she found a part of herself she thought she'd lost, and for the first time in a long while, she felt truly at home.

The backyard of the farmhouse was alive with a soft, magical glow. Fairy lights strung across the trees created an intimate cocoon for the group. The ninjas lounged around, sharing laughter and light-hearted banter, but Aahana's gaze frequently shifted toward the pathway leading to the backyard.

"Who are you waiting for, Aahana?" Aksha asked, catching the flicker of anticipation in her eyes.

"Nikhil," Aahana admitted softly, her fingers fidgeting with the edges of her shawl.

At the mention of Dr. Nikhil, Anu's face betrayed a faint, almost imperceptible glow, one that didn't go unnoticed by Rishi. He leaned closer to Aarush and whispered, "Did you see that? Anu's face lit up brighter than these fairy lights at the mention of Nikhil."

Aarush stifled a laugh and replied, "Looks like someone has a favorite doctor."

Anu shot them a warning glare, but her cheeks carried a telltale blush.

Moments later, the sound of footsteps broke the gentle hum of the evening. All heads turned toward the pathway as Nikhil appeared, a calm and reassuring presence as always.

"There he is!" Roy exclaimed dramatically. "The man, the myth, the healer of hearts—Dr. Nikhil!"

Anu rolled her eyes, though the slight upturn of her lips didn't escape anyone's notice.

"Sorry, everyone," Nikhil said, stepping into the circle of light. "Got caught up, but I'm here now." His gaze shifted to Aahana, his tone softening. "You called for me?"

Aahana nodded, her lips curving into a small smile. "I needed you here, Nikhil. This moment wouldn't feel complete without you."

Nikhil took a seat, instinctively settling next to Anu. A ripple of suppressed giggles passed through the group.

"Well, well," Rishi said, unable to contain himself, "someone seems to have found their permanent seat."

Aksha joined in with a sly grin. "Should we rearrange the seating chart to make it official?"

Maher smirked, adding, "Careful, Nikhil, or Anu might start billing you for occupying her personal space."

Anu, clearly flustered, shot a glare at all of them. "Can you all just stop being ridiculous?" she said, her voice betraying her embarrassment.

Roy leaned back, hands behind his head, and teased, "Ridiculous? We're just observing chemistry in action!"

Before Anu could retaliate, Nikhil chuckled, raising a hand to calm the group. "Alright, alright. Let's give Aahana her moment. She's been waiting patiently."

The group settled down, though sly smiles and knowing glances were exchanged.

Aahana looked around, her gaze lingering on each of her friends before landing on Dev. She took a deep breath, gathering her thoughts. "Before I say anything else, I want to thank you, Nikhil," she began, her voice trembling slightly. "Your words—they've stayed with me. You told me it's not selfish to think of our own happiness, and for the first time, I believe it."

The group fell silent, the playful mood giving way to an air of quiet anticipation.

"I've been carrying Rajeev in my heart for so long," Aahana continued, her voice steady but laced with emotion. "His place in my life is irreplaceable. Losing him broke something in me, and I thought moving forward would mean betraying his memory."

She paused, glancing at Nikhil, who gave her a reassuring nod. "But reading Dev's letter," Aahana said, her gaze shifting to Dev, "it made me realize something. It's not about replacing the past; it's about embracing the future."

Dev's eyes widened, a mix of surprise and curiosity reflecting in his expression.

"I found your letter, Dev," she said softly. "Anu gave it to me."

Dev's head whipped toward Anu, who offered him a sheepish smile and a shrug.

"That letter," Aahana continued, her voice breaking slightly, "made me see what I've been blind to all along. Your love, your patience... it's been my anchor, even when I didn't realize it. And now, I want to be yours."

She took Dev's hands in hers, looking straight into his eyes. "Dev, can you tolerate me for a lifetime? Will you be my anchor in this stormy sea of life?"

The ninjas collectively gasped, their eyes darting between Aahana and Dev.

Roy broke the silence with a loud, "Did that just happen?!"

"YES!" Aksha cheered, clapping her hands.

"Dev-haana! Dev-haana!" Rishi started chanting, prompting Aarush and Maher to join in.

Dev, clearly overwhelmed, blinked rapidly, trying to process the moment. He tightened his grip on Aahana's hands and finally smiled—a soft, heartfelt smile that spoke volumes. "Aahana," he said, his voice filled with emotion, "tolerating you for a lifetime? That's not a challenge. That's a privilege."

As Dev leaned forward to kiss her forehead, the ninjas erupted into cheers and teasing.

Roy pointed to Nikhil and Anu, smirking. "Looks like Aahana isn't the only one finding her anchor tonight."

"Stop it, Roy!" Anu exclaimed, though her flustered expression only fueled the laughter.

Under the blanket of stars, the ninjas shared this moment, knowing they had forged an unbreakable bond that would carry them through anything life threw their way.

ᐅᐅᐅ

The evening had settled into a comfortable, laid-back vibe as the ninjas gathered in the spacious backyard of the farmhouse. The cool night air carried the faint scent of freshly cut grass, and the soft glow of fairy lights twinkled above them, adding a touch of warmth to the night. A few blankets were spread out on the grass, and everyone had grabbed whatever snacks they could find—chips, fruit, some homemade sandwiches, and even a few drinks.

They were sitting in a loose circle, casually chatting and laughing, the comfort of being surrounded by close friends making everything feel easy. Manan, who had been in charge of organizing the snacks, was proudly leaning against a nearby tree, looking content as the others snacked.

"Manan, these sandwiches are legit. You're turning into a chef," Roy commented, munching on one.

"Oh please, this is nothing. You should've seen me back in the day—five-star chef in my own kitchen," Manan quipped, flashing a cheeky grin.

Rishi, who had been mostly quiet, suddenly stood up with a serious look on his face.

"Hey, guys, can I say something?" he asked, his tone unusually calm.

The group looked up, sensing the change in atmosphere. Anu raised an eyebrow, surprised. "What's up, Rishi?"

Rishi cleared his throat, his gaze flickering over to Maher, who was sitting nearby, chatting with Aksha. "Actually, it's something I've been meaning to say... Maher, can we talk for a sec?"

Maher froze mid-laugh, her eyes widening slightly. "Me? Right now?"

"Yeah," Rishi said, stepping closer to her, his voice low but steady. "I know we've all been through a lot lately, and I've been reflecting on everything. I see you. I see the strength it takes for you to keep going, and honestly, you deserve more than just good friends. You deserve someone who can be there for you. Someone who can love you the way you deserve to be loved. So..." He paused, taking a breath. "Will you marry me, Maher?"

The air in the backyard seemed to freeze for a split second. The ninjas, still snacking and chatting a moment ago, now stared at Rishi and Maher in stunned silence.

"What?!" Aksha blurted out, wide-eyed. "Rishi, are you serious?!"

Maher stood up quickly, a mix of shock and confusion on her face. "Rishi, what are you—"

"No," she cut herself off, shaking her head as she took a step back. "What are you doing? You don't just throw something like that out there."

Rishi, trying to remain calm, stood his ground. "I get that this is unexpected. But I needed to tell you. I care about you, Maher. I want to be there for you. More than just as a friend. I want to be with you."

Maher let out a sharp exhale, her hands clenched in frustration. "Rishi, you've completely misunderstood. I told you my story because I trusted you—*as a friend*—not so you could make some dramatic move like this."

The group exchanged glances, uncomfortable but curious. Roy, his mouth full of chips, looked around at the others, raising an eyebrow. "I... uh, I don't think this was the time, man. Maher's married."

Aarush, who had been quiet until now, stood up and crossed his arms, frowning. "Yeah, this... this isn't right, Rishi. You can't just—this is Maher's personal business. You can't just drop a bomb like that."

Anu looked over at Maher, then back at Rishi, her tone serious. "You know better than this, Rishi. This is crossing a line."

Rishi, though, didn't back down. He looked at Maher with sincerity. "I'm sorry. I just... I care about you, more than I let on. And I needed to let you know, no matter how awkward it makes things. I don't expect anything in return, but I wanted you to know how I feel."

The silence hung in the air for a moment before Maher spoke, her voice still shaking with a mix of disbelief and anger. "You can't take my trust and twist it into something like this. This is not the time or place. You had no right to do this, Rishi."

The group fell silent as Maher turned away from Rishi, her frustration clear.

A few moments passed before Rishi spoke again, his voice quieter. "I know I messed up. But I had to say it. And I'm sorry if it wasn't what you needed or wanted to hear. I never meant to hurt you."

Aahana, who had been quietly watching the exchange, broke the tension with a soft sigh. "Look, Rishi, we all know you're coming from a good place. But yeah... it could have been handled differently."

Roy, sensing the discomfort in the air, laughed awkwardly. "Man, you really know how to keep things interesting, Rishi. This is like a soap opera in real life."

The ninjas slowly relaxed, but there was still an uncomfortable edge to the evening. Maher, now calmer but still processing everything, looked at Rishi. "I just don't want things to change, alright? I don't need a romantic gesture right now."

Rishi nodded, his face serious but understanding. "I get it, Maher. I'm sorry if I made you uncomfortable."

Slowly, the group began to soften, some of the tension melting away. Aahana, sensing the mood shift, smiled warmly. "Well, this night sure turned into something we didn't expect. But Rishi, I've got to give you credit for going after what you want, even if it was a little bold."

Anu added, "Yeah, it might not have been the best timing, but honesty is important. I admire you for that."

Roy slapped Rishi on the back, grinning. "You're lucky you didn't get a bucket of water thrown at you, man."

As the night wore on, the group slowly returned to their lighthearted teasing, though everyone had a new level of respect for Rishi's honesty. Despite the awkwardness, the evening ended with laughter and playful banter, a reminder that in the world of ninjas, even the most unexpected moments could lead to growth and understanding.

The air around the ninjas had become thick with the tension of Rishi's persistence and Maher's emotional walls. Though Maher had tried to push Rishi's confession aside, he was unrelenting, determined to get through to her.

Maher took a deep breath, trying to steady herself. The others sat in silence, watching the back-and-forth between them, unsure of what was going to unfold next.

"I don't know how many times I have to say this, Rishi," Maher said, her voice quieter now but firm, "this is not the time. I'm not the person you think I am. I don't need a knight in shining armor."

Rishi shook his head stubbornly, his eyes locking with hers. "But I can't just walk away, Maher. I know what you're going through, and I know there's more to your story than you've let on. You don't have to carry all of this alone."

Maher's eyes softened for a brief moment, before she lowered her gaze to the ground, conflicted. "There's something you don't know," she said, her voice almost breaking. "You know, back in college, I had a soft spot for you. I always did. But now... with everything that's happened, it's not the right time for any of this. I'm not the same person anymore. I have responsibilities. I have a three-year-old daughter."

A collective gasp went through the group. No one had known about Maher's daughter. The ninjas exchanged looks of shock and curiosity, but they stayed quiet, giving her space to speak.

Rishi's expression softened, the stubbornness slowly fading. "I had no idea, Maher. But that doesn't change how I feel. I want to be there for you, for both of you."

Maher shook her head again, trying to hold back tears. "You don't understand, Rishi. You're right—I'm still carrying this burden. My marriage... it's been broken for a long time. I wanted out, but I couldn't leave. Not because I didn't try, but because I'm fighting for custody of my daughter. If I divorce him, I lose her. I can't live with that."

The room was utterly still now, the weight of Maher's words sinking in. Rishi, visibly shocked, took a step forward, his eyes soft with empathy. "I never knew," he whispered, his voice thick with emotion.

Dev, who had been standing off to the side, stepped forward at this point, his voice cutting through the quiet tension. "Rishi, you need to clear this up for us. What's going on here? What's Maher saying?"

Rishi turned to Dev, his eyes still on Maher. "Maher... She's trapped in a marriage that's been broken for years. But she stayed because she's fighting for her daughter's future. She's the one who's been holding everything together, no matter how much it tears her apart."

Maher didn't speak, but the way she looked down and pulled her legs closer to her chest spoke volumes. Rishi continued, his voice growing more certain. "I want to marry Maher. I'm not doing this out of pity. I'm doing this because she deserves a chance at happiness. And I want to be the one to give that to her, to help her get the custody she needs, so her daughter can have the life she deserves."

The group, stunned into silence, didn't know how to react at first. The emotional depth of the moment was overwhelming. The ninjas had never seen Rishi like this, vulnerable, yet so determined.

Maher's eyes filled with tears, but she wiped them quickly, trying to stay composed. "Rishi, you don't have to do this. I can't accept this from you. You're making things harder."

"I'm doing this because I want to," Rishi said, his voice unwavering. "You shouldn't have to carry this alone. You deserve so much more, Maher. And I will be by your side, no matter what it takes."

The group looked at each other, uncertain of how to process this new turn in their already emotional evening. Aahana, her hand resting on Dev's shoulder, whispered, "This is a lot... I don't know what to say."

Aksha, who had been quiet through most of the conversation, leaned forward and spoke softly. "Rishi, this is huge. But you're right, Maher does deserve more. You're giving her a chance she might never have had. You're taking a leap of faith."

Anu, her eyes wide with a mix of shock and admiration, added, "This is brave, Rishi. No one ever expects something like this. But... it could change everything."

Maher, though still conflicted, met Rishi's eyes. "But what about you? Are you sure this is what you want? It's not going to be easy. My life is complicated, and I don't want to drag you into it."

Rishi smiled gently, the warmth of his gaze unmistakable. "I'm not afraid of complications, Maher. I'm ready for this. For you. For your daughter."

The silence that followed felt heavy, but it was no longer awkward. The group, though surprised by the raw honesty, understood. Rishi had laid everything out, and now it was Maher's turn to make her choice.

Dev, after a pause, spoke up, his voice steady. "Rishi, I think you've made it clear what you want. I can't say I fully understand, but I know you're doing this out of love and respect for Maher. If you're sure about this, then we're all behind you."

The other ninjas nodded in agreement. Though it was a lot to process, they could see the depth of Rishi's feelings and the courage it took for him to put everything on the line for someone else.

Maher took a deep breath, her eyes flicking between the group and Rishi. "I don't know if I'm ready for this... But I know you mean what you're saying. And that means more than I can put into words."

The evening ended with a collective sigh, the air a little lighter now, but still full of the weight of what had been shared. Rishi had shown his heart, and though Maher wasn't fully ready to accept everything, she knew one thing for certain: Rishi had given her something to think about—something no one else had ever given her before.

The ninjas, who had witnessed so much raw emotion that night, knew that their bond had deepened once again. They might not have all the answers yet, but they had each other, and that was enough for now.

As the weight of Rishi's decision settled in the air, the ninjas remained quiet for a moment, allowing the gravity of the conversation to wash over them. The backyard, once full of light-hearted chatter and teasing, now felt like a space for deeper reflection.

It was Anu who spoke first, her voice filled with empathy. She turned to Maher, her eyes softening. "I never knew it was this difficult for you, Maher. I can't imagine the pain you've been carrying all this time. But I'm proud of you. You've been so strong, and now I see why you've kept your distance. It's not just about you—it's about your daughter, too. And I respect that."

Maher's eyes filled with tears again, but she quickly wiped them away. "It's been so hard, Anu. I've always tried to be strong, for my daughter... but sometimes, it felt like I was drowning."

"I know it's hard," Anu said, stepping forward and putting a comforting hand on her shoulder. "But you don't have to do this alone anymore. We're here for you. And Rishi's decision... that's a beautiful thing. I couldn't ask for a better man to stand by your side."

Roy, who had been observing the exchange with a deep sense of respect, nodded in agreement. "Yeah, man. What Rishi is doing takes a lot of guts. Most guys would run from a situation like this, but you're stepping up. That's not something you see every day. Maher, you're lucky to have someone like him in your corner."

Rishi smiled at Roy's words, feeling the weight of the support from his friends. He didn't know what the future held, but in that moment, he was certain of his decision.

Dev, who had remained silent for the most part, gave Rishi a firm, approving nod. "I don't know if this was the plan from the start, but it's a damn good one. You're showing Maher what it means to have someone truly in your corner. I respect that, Rishi."

Maher's heart swelled at the support she was receiving. The ninjas had always been a close-knit group, but the compassion they showed now, for both her and Rishi, made her feel like she wasn't just part of the group—but truly seen and cared for.

Aarush, who had been quietly listening, added with a grin, "You know, it's rare to see someone take such a big step for someone else. What Rishi is doing? That's love in its purest form. You've got my respect, man. And Maher, you've always been strong. Now, you've got a whole team behind you."

Maher looked around at her friends, each one offering words of encouragement and sympathy, and for the first time in a long while, she felt like maybe, just maybe, she wasn't as alone as she had thought.

Manan, who had been standing off to the side, finally spoke up, his voice thoughtful. "This is real. You're doing something incredibly noble, Rishi. Not everyone would go this far. And Maher, I just want you to know that I've always seen how strong you are. I can't imagine the pressure you've been under, but you've made it through with grace."

Aahana, who had been quietly reflecting, added with a small smile, "It's moments like this that make you believe in the power of friendship. Rishi, you're not just a friend right now. You're a protector. And Maher, you've got a lot of love surrounding you. I know you'll find the peace and happiness you deserve."

Rishi, overwhelmed by the sudden outpouring of love and support, glanced at Maher, who was still processing everything. She looked at him with a mix of surprise, gratitude, and a little bit of fear, but he could see the hesitation in her eyes slowly give way to something else—hope.

"Thank you, all of you," Maher finally said, her voice soft but steady. "I didn't expect this kind of support. And Rishi... I never expected you to be so selfless. But this... this feels right, even if I'm scared."

"You don't have to be scared anymore," Rishi said gently, his voice full of reassurance. "We're all in this together, Maher. And now, you have the freedom to live the life you deserve. No more holding back."

The group nodded in unison, their eyes filled with a shared understanding. It was clear that Rishi's decision had opened up a new chapter for all of them. One filled with growth, courage, and a stronger bond than ever before.

"Rishi's right," Anu said with a smile. "You deserve to be happy, Maher. And if you're ready, we're here for you every step of the way."

Everyone nodded, their faces filled with warmth and understanding. The support they gave Rishi and Maher wasn't just about helping with practical matters—it was about showing love, giving strength, and reminding each other that they didn't have to go through life's struggles alone.

And as the stars twinkled above, the ninjas knew that their bonds had only deepened, strengthened by the courage, love, and understanding that had been shared under the night sky.

As the warmth of the evening lingered in the air, and the support for Maher and Rishi flowed like a river, Nikhil, who had been standing quietly by the side, finally stepped forward. His calm demeanor and thoughtful expression drew everyone's attention.

"Rishi, Maher," Nikhil began, his voice steady and filled with understanding, "Sometimes, life throws us into situations we don't expect, but it's how we choose to navigate them that defines us. Rishi, what you've done isn't just an act of kindness—it's an act of love. You've chosen to step up when most would've stayed away, and that takes courage."

He turned to Maher, his gaze softening. "And Maher, I've seen the strength you carry, even when you've been struggling with so much. You've fought for your daughter, fought for your happiness, and now you don't have to fight alone anymore. You've got all of us—and Rishi—by your side."

There was a pause as Nikhil looked around at the group, his eyes meeting each of theirs. "Sometimes, we're afraid to reach out, to lean on others, because we think we have to do it all ourselves. But tonight, you all have shown what real friendship, real love, is about. It's about standing with each other, no matter the odds. It's about being there in the hardest moments, not just the easy ones."

He smiled softly at Rishi and Maher. "What's happening tonight isn't just a proposal or a confession—it's a reminder that we all deserve love, support, and happiness. And that we don't have to carry the weight of the world alone. I'm proud of all of you—for being brave enough to face your truths and to support each other in ways that truly matter."

The group stood in silence for a moment, taking in Nikhil's words. They knew they were not just friends—they were a family. And tonight, their bond had become something even stronger. Nikhil's quiet wisdom had added a meaningful note to the evening, a reminder that sometimes the greatest act of love is simply being there for each other.

As the night continued, the ninjas felt that the journey ahead would be challenging, but with each other, they could face anything. And with that, the evening of revelations, love, and friendship carried on under the starry sky, a testament to the power of standing together in the face of life's complexities.

ᗰᗰᗰ

The laughter around the backyard was still echoing, but Roy, ever the instigator, wasn't done yet. With a mischievous glint in his eyes, he leaned back and crossed his arms. "So, are we all done with the confessions, or is there anything left to be said?" He raised an eyebrow, making a sweeping motion toward Nikhil and Anu. "What about you two? Any confessions? Now's your chance, folks."

Anu shot him a look that was a perfect mix of amusement and annoyance. "Oh, please," she said, rolling her eyes, "I don't need to make confessions in front of all of you. You know, some of us prefer to keep a little mystery about ourselves."

Nikhil, feeling the heat of everyone's eyes on him, fidgeted in his seat, clearly uncomfortable. "I... I don't think there's anything left to say," he muttered, looking down at his hands. His shy demeanor only made the teasing worse, and the group couldn't help but laugh at how easily they had put him on the spot.

Manan, never one to miss a moment of fun, added, "Well, looks like the three ladies in the group are taken—Aarush has Aksha, Dev's got Aahana, and Rishi's got Maher. So, that leaves poor

Nikhil." He smirked, looking at Anu. "What about you, Anu? Got anyone special in your life?"

Anu turned her head slowly, her expression unreadable, and then replied with a smile that didn't quite reach her eyes. "I'm doing just fine, thank you. Some of us don't need anyone 'special' to be happy."

The group's teasing grew louder, with Roy chiming in, "Oh, come on, Anu! Nikhil's been staring at you for like, five minutes now. You can't hide it." He looked at Nikhil, who was now avoiding eye contact with anyone, clearly embarrassed. "Nikhil, do you have something to say to Anu? Or are we just playing the 'I'm shy' game here?"

Anu shot him a pointed look, then sighed dramatically. "You guys really love this, don't you?" She turned to Nikhil, her tone shifting to something more neutral. "You know, Nikhil," she said, her voice calm and diplomatic, "I appreciate everything you've done as a friend. But... I'm not looking for anything more than that right now. Life's complicated enough as it is." She gave him a small, reassuring smile. "You know where I stand."

Nikhil nodded, his face a mixture of relief and disappointment. "I understand, Anu," he said quietly, his voice soft but sincere. "I just... I wanted to make sure you knew how I felt."

The group, watching the exchange, didn't press further. Manan, sensing the tension, shifted the conversation in another direction, but not without one last playful jab. "Well, I guess that's settled then," he said with a grin. "Nikhil and Anu are definitely not 'a thing.'" He looked at Nikhil. "Don't worry, man, there's plenty of time. Just don't stare at her too much or you'll start making her uncomfortable."

Nikhil shot him an exasperated look. "Thanks, Manan," he said sarcastically, but the smile on his face showed he wasn't taking the teasing too seriously.

Meanwhile, Rishi, sensing the atmosphere lightening up again, leaned back and added, "Alright, alright, enough of this drama. We're all just a bunch of friends here. Anu, you're an independent woman, and we get that. Nikhil, you're just a little shy. No harm done."

Dev, always quick with a quip, jumped in, "Exactly. No one needs to 'confess' anything. We're all happy just being ourselves."

The conversation shifted once more, and the teasing turned into laughter as the group rallied around Nikhil and Anu, making light of the situation. It wasn't about love confessions anymore; it was about being together, laughing through the awkwardness, and enjoying the night as it came.

And so, the fun continued, with playful jabs, teasing remarks, and moments of true friendship that brought them even closer together. No matter how complicated things got, they knew they could always rely on each other to bring a little laughter into their lives.

As they laughed, each ninja carried a mix of emotions — relief, joy, and even a hint of apprehension about the unknown paths ahead. The camaraderie that held them together was now infused with a renewed sense of unity, making their journey through life's twists and turns all the more meaningful.

In the end, everyone was happy, and the air around them was filled with a sense of togetherness that had grown even stronger throughout the night. The laughter from earlier hadn't quite died down, but there was a shift in the atmosphere—a warm, comfortable feeling of old friends who had weathered the storms of life together.

Manan, with a mischievous grin on his face, couldn't resist teasing Aahana one last time. "So, tell me, Aahana Bhabhi, where did you find the love letter written by Dev Bhai?" he asked, his eyes twinkling with amusement.

Aahana, still enjoying the light-hearted mood, leaned back and smiled, her voice playful yet full of affection for her friends. "Oh, that letter," she said, her eyes glancing towards Dev, who had suddenly become very interested in his shoes. "I found it in Dev's cupboard while I was looking through some old photographs. Anu must have tucked it there. Quite the revelation, right?"

The room fell silent for a split second as everyone processed the news. Then, Dev's cheeks flushed a deep shade of red, realizing the mischief Anu had played on him by hiding the letter.

Manan, never one to let an opportunity slip by, added, "Well, well, looks like our Dev Bhai is a man of many talents—one of which is writing love letters! Who would've thought?"

The group erupted into laughter, and even Dev couldn't help but chuckle at himself, his embarrassment now mingled with a sense of light-heartedness.

"Well, if that wasn't enough of a surprise," Nikhil chimed in from the side, his arms crossed and an amused expression on his face, "you all look like stand-up comedians today. It's impossible to keep up with you guys!"

Aahana beamed at him, her tone playful as she responded, "Not stand-up, but definitely a reunion that needed some doctor-approved laughter, don't you think?"

Nikhil, with a sly grin, shot back, "Well, as the doctor on duty, it's my job to ensure you're all getting the right dosage of laughter. I'm just making sure you don't overdose."

He turned toward Anu, raising an eyebrow. "And you, Anu, seem to be the chief organizer of this laughter festival. Do you have a license for that?"

Anu's eyes sparkled with humor as she replied, "Well, Dr. Nikhil, if there's a license for spreading joy, then I'd be the first in line to get it. Maybe I should start charging you for my services!"

The banter flowed effortlessly as Nikhil let out a hearty laugh. "Alright, alright, I'll let it slide for now. But remember, too much laughter is not good for my business. We've got to keep it balanced, people!"

The entire group erupted into laughter once more, the warmth and genuine affection shared between them palpable. The backyard, which had started off with the surprises had now transformed into the lively setting of an impromptu reunion. The jokes, the teasing, the stories—they had all come together to make this moment unforgettable.

And as the laughter died down, a contented silence filled the space. For a moment, no one spoke; they just savoured the feeling of being with people who truly understood them, with no need for words, only the comfort of shared memories and experiences. It was a rare moment of peace, and for that, they were all grateful.

ᐃᐃᐃ

Epilogue

The soft glow of the early morning sun spilled across the terrace, painting the sky in hues of gold and lavender. A cool breeze fluttered gently, rustling the leaves and carrying the faint aroma of tea. Anu sat cross-legged on the low parapet wall, her hands wrapped around a warm cup of tea. Her gaze wandered into the vast morning sky as flashes of the reunion played in her mind—the laughter, the confessions, the tears, and the chaos.

"Everyone found their pieces," she murmured to herself, the edges of her smile fading.

The creak of the terrace door caught her attention. **Nikhil** stepped out, the breeze ruffling his neatly-pressed shirt. His soft, composed demeanor gave way to something more vulnerable as his eyes fell on her.

"Good morning," he said softly, approaching her with a half-smile.

Anu turned her head, smirking. "Morning, *Doctor*. Didn't expect to see you awake at sunrise. Shouldn't you be busy analyzing someone's dreams or solving their existential crises?"

Nikhil chuckled, taking a seat beside her. "Well, today's crisis brought me here—to you. My flight is tonight."

Anu blinked, surprised. "Flight? Where to?"

"London. I'm leaving for my fellowship," he said, the words landing heavier than they should have.

Anu's smile faltered briefly, but she quickly masked it behind a sip of tea. "Wow, big move. Congrats, *Doctor of the Year*."

Silence settled between them for a moment. Nikhil watched her carefully, sensing what she wasn't saying. Her usual wit was there, but beneath it, he could see the faint shadow of loneliness.

"You look unusually quiet this morning," he observed. "Not like you at all. What's going on in that head of yours?"

Anu snorted lightly, shaking her head. "Just thinking about life. Funny, isn't it? Everyone's running—towards something, away from something. Dev found Aahana, Rishi has taken responsibility for Maher... and me? I feel like I'm stuck in the same place."

Nikhil leaned forward slightly, his elbows resting on his knees. "You're not stuck, Anu. You're waiting. And sometimes waiting takes more strength than running."

Anu raised a brow, shooting him a teasing glance. "*Wow*, that's some textbook psychology right there. Nikhil, are you going to hand me a diagnosis now? 'Patient: Anu. Condition: Overthinking. Treatment: Long walk and tea?'"

Nikhil laughed, shaking his head. "You're impossible. I'm trying to be serious here."

"Oh, you're serious? Could've fooled me," Anu quipped, a playful glint in her eyes. "Imagine this—*a clinical psychologist* who doesn't have the courage to confess his own feelings? Nikhil, that's irony at its best!"

Nikhil groaned, rubbing his face with his palm as his cheeks flushed faintly. "You're not going to let me off easy, are you?"

"Not a chance." Anu leaned closer, her voice softening but still teasing. "You're a great listener, Nikhil, but sometimes you need to stop diagnosing people and start speaking for yourself. What is it they say? Oh yes—sometimes silence becomes the loudest sound. Or, as someone might call it..." She paused for effect, a mischievous smile tugging at her lips.

Nikhil looked up, locking eyes with her. "Go on."

"...'**Echoes of Unsaid Words**,'" she finished quietly, her tone laced with meaning.

Nikhil stilled for a moment, her words landing deeper than she realized. He looked away briefly, a small, self-conscious smile tugging at his lips. "That's not fair. You're better with words than I am."

"Or maybe I'm just provoking you into admitting something," she said slyly, tilting her head. "Come on, *Doctor*, it's not that hard. Say what you want to say."

Nikhil turned back to her, his face more serious now, the laughter replaced with an earnest softness. "Fine. You win."

Anu straightened up, mock-shocked. "The mighty Nikhil admits defeat? Go on. I'm listening."

Nikhil let out a deep breath, his voice softer. "Anu... I don't know when or how, but you've become someone I can't ignore. You challenge me, you frustrate me, but you... you also understand me. It's like you hear what I'm not saying. And honestly, I—"

He paused, his gaze holding hers, searching for the courage he'd been building up.

Anu blinked, waiting for him to continue, her heart racing a little too fast. "You what, Nikhil? Don't stop now. You're on a roll."

Nikhil groaned softly, laughing under his breath. "You're *so* difficult."

Anu shrugged, leaning back with a victorious grin. "And you love that, don't you?"

"I do," Nikhil replied quietly, surprising her with the sudden honesty.

Anu's smile faltered for just a moment before it returned, softer this time. She took a slow sip of tea, trying to steady her thoughts. "Well," she murmured after a pause, "it's about time you said it."

Nikhil smiled, shaking his head. "You knew, didn't you?"

"Of course I did," she teased, turning to him. "You think girls don't have a sixth sense? I've known for a while. I just wanted to hear you say it first."

"And what about you?" Nikhil asked, his tone cautious but hopeful.

Anu smirked, standing up with her empty cup. "Who said I'd make it that easy for you, *Doctor Nikhil?*"

Nikhil stood as well, stuffing his hands into his pockets as he watched her. "I'm leaving tonight, Anu. But I meant what I said."

She turned back to look at him, her face lit by the gentle morning sun. "Then don't keep me waiting too long. London isn't that far, *Doctor.*"

Nikhil smiled, feeling a sense of hope he hadn't carried before. As she walked away, her laughter lingering in the air, he whispered to himself, "*Echoes of unsaid words,* huh? Well, maybe some words are finally being said."

The sun rose higher, filling the terrace with warmth as the quiet between them gave way to something deeper. Somewhere, in the balance of unsaid words and unspoken feelings, they had found their answer.

ᔆᔆᔆ

Devanshi Kanani is a passionate writer and a dedicated mental health advocate, currently pursuing a Master of Science in Nursing with a specialization in Psychiatric (Mental Health) Nursing at the Gujarat Institute of Mental Health, Ahmedabad, Gujarat. Her academic journey began at Jawahar Navodaya Vidyalaya in Amreli, where she cultivated a deep love for learning and writing.

Devanshi made her debut in the literary world with her nonfiction book, *Failure: It Never Ends Unless...!!*, published in 2022, a powerful exploration of resilience and self-discovery. She has also contributed to the acclaimed *Community Health Nursing Volumes 1 and 2*, authored by Mukta Singh, and published by BookEra Publications. Her review chapter, *Empathy Unleashed: The Power of Emotional Intelligence in Nursing*, published in the IIPSeries, highlights her commitment to advancing nursing education and practice.

Inspired by the intricate emotions that define human connections, Devanshi penned her novel *Echoes of Unsaid Words*. Drawing from her experiences in the mental health field, she delves into the silences and unspoken emotions that often shape our mental well-being. She believes that mental health challenges frequently arise because there is no one to truly hear the "unsaid words," leaving only their echoes behind.

Deeply connected to the themes of friendship and understanding portrayed in her novel, Devanshi resonates with the idea that true support can bridge the gaps left by unspoken feelings. When she isn't writing, she enjoys reading, cooking, and traveling, finding inspiration in the simplicity of life and the beauty of her surroundings.

Born and raised in a small town in Amreli district, Gujarat, Devanshi now resides in Ahmedabad, where she continues to explore the intersections of mental health and storytelling, giving voice to emotions that often go unheard.

Contact information:

Email – *devanshikanani2802@yahoo.com*
Insta id - author_devanshi_
Linkedin - devanshi kanani